The Addict:

Carl Weber Presents

The Addict:

Carl Weber Presents

Lisa Lennox

www.urbanbooks.net

Urban Books, LLC
300 Farmingdale Road, NY-Route 109
Farmingdale, NY 11735

The Addict: Carl Weber Presents

ISBN 13: 978-1-64556-581-9

First Mass Market Printing April 2024
First Trade Paperback Printing September 2023
Printed in the United States of America

10 9 8 7 6 5 4 3 2 1

Distributed by Kensington Publishing Corp.
Submit Orders to:
Customer Service
400 Hahn Road
Westminster, MD 21157-4627
Phone: 1-800-733-3000
Fax: 1-800-659-2436

Dedication

This book is dedicated to all the readers who gave my voice a chance to be heard. I apologize if the use of the word *nigga*, the cursing, the explicit sex, and the violence offend anybody. Please don't get mad at me. This is just how the shit really goes down in the hood.

Lisa Lennox

Foreword

Studies show that animals addicted to cocaine preferred the drug to food even when it meant possible starvation, and many users of its second cousin, crack, report being hooked after only the first use. This horrible addiction is threefold: psychological, physical, and emotional.

The College of Communication, Boston University, September 1989

Prologue

Laci ran her hands down her body—first her chest; her flat, tight stomach; her curvy hips; and then her juicy thighs. "I don't remember feeling this way before," she said softly to herself. She had fought the pressure for long enough, and now she was allowing her body to give in to the seductive call for the very first time.

Heaven knows there ain't shit like the first time. Everybody remembers their first time for sure. Laci repeated herself, only this time there was no sound at all. *I don't remember feeling this way before*. The words played in her head. Her pouty lips, painted with a dark rose lip gloss, struggled to say them, but no sound came out. It was as if she was numb. It didn't matter. Laci was so far gone, anyway. She was too wrapped up in the way she was feeling at the moment to realize she was even holding a conversation with herself.

Her tongue rolled across her front teeth in slow motion. Hell, at this point, everything was in slow motion. Laci's life was idle, but yet the world continued going round and round . . . in slow motion. Who knew the first time would feel this way?

Laci moaned and threw her head back. She closed her eyes and took in the stimulating feeling. Caught up, the sensation of it all was fucking not only with her mind but with her body too.

This was an unfamiliar ecstasy for Laci, as her body had always been her temple. She had guarded it well up until now. But she had learned that life had a way of giving up that good-ass foreplay that got a muthafucka wet every time—the shit that would have a muthafucka's ass so wide open, not giving a fuck about a damn thing. Laci was proof of that as she sat there, soaking wet, longing for that orgasm, that point of no return that whispered to everybody. But only a few actually answered the call.

An unfamiliar feeling it was, but Laci wouldn't mind getting better acquainted. She could get used to this. As a matter of fact, this shit could become addictive.

Roll Call

The last few students rumbled into Mr. Giencanna's Introduction to Philosophy class like an angry mob. It was only first period—too goddamned early in the morning to be trying to philosophize over anything. No one felt like being there. Unfortunately, taking this class, not to mention dealing with Mr. Giencanna, was a necessary evil. Mr. Giencanna was one of those teachers who taught a little bit of everything, and no matter what, all students would cross his path sooner or later.

Standing at the front of the room, staring mercilessly at the students, Mr. Giencanna was in his usual hard-ass stance. He had been a counselor at a boys' home in New York City before becoming a teacher. The children there had been violent and hardened, so the staff had treated them as such. Now Mr. Giencanna displayed that same attitude with his current students.

Observing the angry youths, who seemed more pissed off about learning than grateful for the opportunity, Mr. Giencanna shook his head in dismay. "Look at y'all," he said with disgust. "Not one enthusiastic face in here eager to feed his or her mind. If you don't feed your mind, then how are you going to feed your belly when it comes time to survive on your own?"

The room was filled with blank faces. The response was silence.

"Mark my words," he continued, "without knowledge, you're all bound for the welfare line or the penitentiary."

Nobody was trying to hear him, so Mr. Giencanna proceeded with the daily roll call.

"Mr. Billy Jackson?" Mr. Giencanna called out, fixing his glasses on his hawklike nose.

"Here," said a young man in the rear.

"Bernard Wizner?"

"Right here," came another male voice.

"Miss Natalie Sethettini?" Mr. Giencanna said.

This time there was no reply.

"Natalie Sethettini?" he repeated.

A young man wearing a blue and gray varsity jacket nudged Natalie, who was sitting at her desk, dozing off.

"What?" she said sleepily and with an attitude to her classmate in the varsity jacket.

He nodded toward their instructor and replied, "That's what. Roll call."

"I'm here, Mr. Giencanna, sir," Natalie said, wiping around her mouth.

"Stay with us, please, Miss Sethettini," Mr. Giencanna said. Although he phrased it like a request, Natalie knew by his stern tone and the piercing look in his eyes that it was, without a doubt, an order.

Mr. Giencanna cleared his throat and continued. "Miss Julacia Casteneda?"

Once again, there was no reply. The classroom was silent as everyone looked around to see if there was another student dozing off somewhere. Everyone appeared to be wide awake.

"Perhaps we have another Sleeping Beauty among us," Mr. Giencanna said sarcastically. "Is there a Miss Julacia Casteneda present?"

Still there was no reply.

"Julacia Casteneda?" he repeated, very irritated this time.

The silence remained.

The welfare line or the penitentiary, he thought as he turned to write the topic of the day's lesson on the blackboard.

Chapter 1

I Wanna Be Down

"So, talk to me, Laci. We have a lot to discuss," Laci's mother, Margaret, said as she sat down Indian-style near the foot of Laci's bed. She looked more like one of Laci's peers than she did her mother.

Laci had always been closer to her mother than she had to her father. And it wasn't because her father wasn't a good one. It was because he was away from home more often than not. He was frequently out of town on work-related business and put in long hours at work when he was in town. But it was for the sole purpose of providing a better life for his wife and daughter. It was a life that Laci and Margaret never took for granted; therefore, there were no complaints from their end.

"What do you mean, a lot?" Laci said as she fumbled through articles of clothing in her oversize walk-in closet. She was in the process of throwing out old summer clothes that she hadn't worn in a while or that were worn out. She had to make room for the new ones she planned on purchasing during their annual mother-daughter shopping spree. The summer of 1989 was right around the corner, and she would need a new wardrobe to set things off.

"Just what I said. A lot," Margaret said, smiling. "I want to know everything."

"Everything like what?" Laci asked, intentionally stalling.

"Like whether you've chosen where you want to go on the trip your father plans to send you on as a graduation gift. Like if you have a boyfriend. "

"I knew there was something specific you were fishing for," Laci said as she flung a handful of clothes out of her closet and onto the bedroom floor.

"Well, you're only the most beautiful seventeen-year-old girl in the world," her mother said, gazing at Laci with genuine pride in her eyes.

Julacia, or Laci, as she was called, was indeed very attractive. She was small in stature and had a face like a porcelain doll's. Her long, shiny Shirley Temple curls fell slightly across the left side of her forehead, tickling her perfectly arched eyebrow. Her moody brown eyes complimented her butterscotch skin tone. Wearing a size six and standing five foot four, Laci was thick and curvy in all the right places. She was tight to def, with an apple-bottom ass; long, scar-free legs; and perfectly round titties. She had a bangin' body, and all her clothes were right. She owned a number of name-brand articles and a few choice pieces, but she would look good even if she were dressed in rags.

"Mom," Laci said wearily.

"Tell me, tell me, tell me," her mother said anxiously, bouncing on the bed like a gossiping teenager. "What's his name? What does he look like? Is he—"

"What are you talking about?" Laci asked, then sucked her teeth. "There is no he. And you know you'd be the first to know if there was."

"So you say," Margaret said, giving Laci a doubtful look.

"Mom, I'm not seeing anybody," Laci said in a definitive tone.

"Come on, baby." Margaret winked. "I'm not only your mother but your friend too. I won't tell your father. I promise. Have I ever told him any of our secrets? Nooo . . . so come on. Get to talkin', girlfriend. Is he tall, short, thin, buff, or what?"

"Mom," Laci said, stepping out of the closet in a pouty manner, with an old sundress in her hand. "You are relentless." Laci shook her head, rolled her eyes, and let out a soft laugh. "I don't have a boyfriend. I promise." She threw the sundress in the pile she had started on the floor, then walked over to her bed and sat in the middle of it. "But when I do get one, you'll be the first to know. Okay?"

Margaret let out a sigh of defeat. "Okay, if you say you're not seeing anybody, then I'll have to believe you." She grabbed ahold of Laci's favorite teddy bear, which was lying on the bed. "So where are you going on your vacation? Have you thought of someplace nice?"

Laci got excited and was delighted about the change of subject. "I was thinking of Puerto Rico," she said excitedly.

"Ooh, that sounds nice," her mother replied with awe. "Whom are you going with? Your boyfriend?" she added with a wink.

Laci laughed and playfully threw a pillow at her mother.

"Oh, boy, you shouldn't have done that." Margaret prided herself on being one of the best pillow fighters in the business. "You don't want to tell me who your boyfriend is, huh? Then take that!" She pounded Laci with the pillow and began to laugh hysterically.

"Mom, please," Laci pleaded. "Stop! You're messing up my hair!"

"If you didn't have a boyfriend, then you wouldn't care how your hair looked. Now, what's his name?" Margaret asked, out of breath, getting in another hit.

"Wait, wait," Laci said as the phone began ringing on the night table next to her bed. Out of breath, she picked up the receiver. "Hello?" she said in a raspy tone. She held her hand up to her mother, who was still poised to get one last lick in with the pillow she held tightly.

"Hey, Laci?" said the voice on the other end.

"Yes, this is she," Laci replied, not recognizing the voice. "Who is this?" She slowly lowered her hand and gave the caller on the other end her full attention.

"Girl, it's Monique," the caller said in a pleasant tone. "What you doin'?"

"Laci," her mother whispered behind her, "you wanna do the 'girls' night out' thing? Ya know, celebrate the approaching end of the school year and you going off to college?"

"Hold on, Monique," Laci said before covering the phone. She turned her attention back to Margaret. "What'd you say, Mom?"

"I said, Do you wanna go out and celebrate tonight? With graduation right around the corner and you going off to college, I figure that is cause enough for us to get out of this house and go do something."

Whenever Margaret wasn't volunteering as a nurse at the hospital, she enjoyed spending time with Laci. She had been a full-time head nurse until after Laci's birth. And before Laci started preschool, she'd been a full-time stay-at-home mom. But with Laci out of the house for those few hours, Margaret had thought she'd go stir crazy. She'd sat at home, worrying about Laci and what was going on with her at school. And when she hadn't worried about Laci, she'd worried about her husband.

She loved and trusted him with every ounce of her being, but with him being away from home so much, her insecurities sometimes got the best of her. One time, she'd even gone as far as hiring a private investigator to follow him. She'd spent a whopping twenty thousand dollars, not including the flight and hotel fees she had to pay, for a private eye to travel across the country to follow her husband. She'd probably spent a total of thirty thousand dollars to find out that her husband was doing exactly what he was supposed to be doing. But for her piece of mind, she'd felt it was worth every penny. However, not wanting to splurge in such a way again, she had later decided to do volunteer work at the hospital to occupy some of her time.

"Okay, Mom. After I get off the phone, let's decide where we want to go," Laci responded before directing her attention back to her phone conversation. "Monique, you still there?"

Laci's mother hit her again with the pillow and threw it on the bed. Laci tried to hurry up and grab the pillow to get the last lick, but her mother was too quick in exiting the room.

"Yeah, I'm here," Monique answered.

"Okay, girl," Laci said, chuckling and breathing hard.

"Why you breathing so hard?"

"Fooling around with my crazy mother. She and I were having a pillow fight," Laci giggled. "She wants to take me out to celebrate my upcoming graduation."

As usual, Monique tried to make Laci's words into something they weren't. "Why you tryin' to throw shit up in my face?" Monique snapped.

Laci should have seen it coming. Of all the girls in their little clique, which included Shaunna, Nay-Nay, and Lisa, Monique seemed to be the most envious of Laci's relationship with her parents, especially the one she had with her mother.

Monique had lived with her grandmother for the past few years. Her mother had died of AIDS when she was just a freshman in high school. She hadn't been an addict herself, but she had made the mistake of sleeping with a dope fiend who was infected with the HIV virus.

"What are you talking about?" Laci asked, getting sick of Monique's attitude.

"What are you talking about?" Monique replied, mimicking Laci's speech. "You sound like a White girl."

Laci shook her head, exasperated. If one more person said she sounded White—even though with her Black mother and Black father, she was clearly Black, she would lose her mind. What did White people sound like compared to Black people, anyway? Laci would often think. And how did one go about *sounding* Black?

"Look," Laci huffed, "was there a reason for this call, or did you just feel like picking an argument?"

"Never mind," Monique said after sucking her teeth. "You ain't gon' wanna go. Forget it. I didn't mean to interrupt your pillow fight. Go hang out with your mommy. I need to call the rest of my girls to make sure they're wit it. Peace out."

Before Laci knew it, the dial tone was buzzing in her ear from Monique hanging up on her.

Laci replaced the phone on the receiver, confused. Her face revealed the frustration she endured on a daily basis as a result of interacting with her girlfriends. It was safe to say that Laci was the prima donna of the pack. She definitely had the most going for her. And she was sweet and very low key, not loudmouthed and boisterous like her counterparts. Even though her parents were very well off and showered her with both love and material things, she didn't floss it at all— not on purpose, anyway. But all that she had was quite visible, and it stood out all the more among a group of chicks who didn't have shit. And during her earlier years, Laci had attended private school, while some of the other girls had attended public school or had just said the hell with school altogether.

It would probably be in her best interest to not associate with a flock of have-nots. And being connected with a popular clique of females, it was also probably in her best interest to be seen and not heard. No matter what came out of Laci's mouth, it was always viewed as bragging, although she would never brag intentionally. Wanting so badly to be a part of something had blinded her to the point where she couldn't see that not everybody was down for her. Some of those broads wanted to be her, and it was only a matter of time before jealousy would rear its ugly face to the point of no return.

Laci was so taken aback by Monique's negative attitude that she didn't even notice that her mother was standing at her bedroom door.

"Laci, what's the matter?" Margaret asked, noticing the sudden change in Laci's disposition.

"Uh, nothing," Laci lied.

"Laci . . . ," her mother said, giving her the "Don't lie to me" look.

Laci sighed. "It's just that the girls are always so confrontational with me. Everything I say is bad. Like when they ask me questions, it's almost like they do it just to argue with me," Laci said in frustration.

"I don't understand," her mother said, leaning in the doorway, with her arms folded. "Give me an example of what you're talking about?"

"Like you and Dad." Laci sighed again as she plopped down on the bed.

"What about us?" Margaret asked, confused.

"When I talk about you guys, they get all uptight. Most of them have only one parent or none at all. I'm tired of being sorry for having two parents who love me."

"Really?" Margaret asked in a concerned voice as she walked over to the bed and sat down next to Laci. "I didn't know this about your new friends. None of them live in a two-parent home?"

Laci nodded. "And I don't care about that, Mom. I just want to hang with them, you know? When's the last time you've known me to have a group of friends?"

Margaret remained silent.

"Exactly." Laci's shoulders fell, as did her head.

"And why is it that you want to hang out with them? I'm sure there's plenty of nice kids at your school."

Laci was silent for a moment. "Because . . . I don't know. The other kids at school are blah. I just like having more down-to-earth friends—people I can relate and talk to. I love talking to you, but I don't have sisters or brothers or anyone my age to kick it with."

"I know you're more intelligent than that," Margaret said, hating that her daughter was so desperate to associate with the in-crowd. "I've never picked your friends for you."

"That's because the pickings have been slim to none," Laci said.

"Maybe so, but with this group of so-called friends, the writing is on the wall, Laci. If a group or a person isn't good for you, then you don't need to be around them. Are you telling me that you don't care how they treat you, that you're willing to accept whatever to be a part of a clique?"

Laci let out a deep sigh. "Mom, please don't lecture me . . . not today." Laci fell back on the bed from emotional exhaustion.

"Okay, okay," Margaret said, holding her hands up in surrender as she got up from the bed and walked over to the door. "You're old enough to handle yourself. I'm not gonna tell you what to do, but I will tell you to be careful. You're my daughter, and I love you. You know I'm here for you if you need me, Julacia."

"Yeah, I know," Laci said, turning over onto her stomach and resting her chin on her hands.

"I'll always be here for you . . . no matter what."

After ending her call with Laci, Monique phoned Lisa to hate on Laci with someone who shared in her envy. In their clique, misery always had company.

"What up, Lisa?" Monique asked through the phone receiver.

"Shit. Trying to get everything ready for y'all bitches. My house looks like shit," Lisa said, lighting her loosey. She had just finished making a pitcher of red Kool-Aid. "What time y'all shooting through? Did you talk to everybody?"

"In about an hour," Monique said. "I tried to be nice and called Laci to tell her to come through, but you know how that stuck-up bitch is."

"What did she say?" Lisa asked curiously.

"Pretty much nothing, "Monique said after smacking her lips. "I hung up on that bitch."

"What? Why?" Lisa asked as she sat down at her kitchen table, dying to hear the 411.

"'Cause before I could even say anything, she started up on that Mommy tip, what her and her *Mommy* were doing and what her and her *Mommy* were about to do," Monique whined. "I didn't want to hear all that bullshit."

"Child, you got issues," Lisa said, shaking her head and taking a puff at the same time. She exhaled smoke rings.

"She's the one with issues. Miss damn Goody Two-shoes. I don't drink. I don't smoke," Monique said, imitating Laci's voice.

"You stupid." Lisa laughed. "I feel you, though. If that bitch knew what our world tasted like, she'd stay buzzed trying to forget about the reality of it," she said, then sucked her slightly crooked teeth. Crooked teeth or not, Lisa was still easy on the eyes. Her complexion was the color of a coconut's shell. She wasn't dark skinned or light skinned, just a perfect in-between. Her skin was smooth, but sometimes when she raised her eyebrows a certain way, the skin on her forehead folded over on itself like that of a pug. Lisa always wore her burgundy-dyed hair in some updo with pin curls. For Lisa, the weave was the best invention since the wheel. Her petite frame didn't match her big, fly-ass mouth by far.

"Yeah, well, that bitch would need something a little stronger than a drink and a joint to bring her into our world," Monique said, rolling her eyes, as if Lisa could see her through the phone.

Lisa gazed at nothing particular, squinting her eyes from the smoke that was curving toward her face. Suddenly, a slight grin showed up on her face. "Yeah. I can see her prissy ass now, all fucked up. But you're right."

"Right about what?" Monique asked curiously.

"She'd need something much stronger. Yeah, much, much stronger." Lisa smiled. "Do me a favor, Mo. Call her back."

"Why the fuck I gotta call her back?" Monique huffed.

"To make sure she comes through," Lisa answered.

"I don't give a fuck whether that bitch comes through or not, and you shouldn't either," Monique said. "You supposed to feel me on this one fo' sho'."

"Stop huffin' and puffin' and just get her on the phone and make sure she come through tonight," Lisa said in a commanding tone. "It ain't even that serious."

"A'ight, fuck it," Monique muttered. "I'll call her back. But it ain't like she's ever the life of the party. All she ever does is sit back, turn her nose up, and watch us like we're an experiment or something. I can only imagine the shit that be running through her head."

"Don't worry about it," Lisa assured her. "I'm about to make sure she has a good time this time around. As a matter of fact, I'm going to see to it that, that bitch is on cloud nine."

Lisa giggled, and Monique just sat there on the phone, puzzled by Lisa's sudden interest in Laci hookin' up with them.

"Was Nay-Nay home?" Lisa asked Monique.

"Yeah," Monique replied. "She was chillin' with her dude."

"Dame?"

"Who else?"

"Kool with a *K*," Lisa said. "Anyway, you get Laci on the horn. I need to holler at Nay-Nay for a minute."

"Peace," Monique said before hanging up the phone.

Lisa hung up the phone and quickly called up Nay-Nay.

"Yo, Ne, this is Lisa," she said.

"What's good, peoples?" Nay-Nay asked.

"Nothing much," Lisa replied. "Just hung up with Monique."

"Yeah, I just talked to her. I'm sitting here getting dressed now, fixin' to head your way. What time everybody else supposed to be shootin' through?"

"In a bit," Lisa said. "Everybody but Laci, anyway. Monique called her up, but she be always letting her personal feelings get in the way of business."

"What business?" Nay-Nay said as she held the phone between her ear and her shoulder while she pulled on her sock.

"Hey, is Dame around?" Lisa asked quickly, changing the volume of her voice to almost a whisper.

"Yeah, he's in the shower."

"Perfect!" Lisa said enthusiastically.

"Damn, girl. What's up with you?" Nay-Nay asked. She wasn't used to not knowing what was going on with her girls. Nay-Nay was kind of like the leader of their little clique, or more like the nucleus. Everyone was associated through her. Every one of the girls who were friends now had been Nay-Nay's friend first.

Nay-Nay had a small build and a toffee-colored complexion. She could be a straight up bitch, the devil's liveliest advocate, when she wanted to, but she had the soft, winning smile of an angel. Her bright white teeth sparkled like her light gray eyes. She looked a little like Vanessa Williams, wearing her shoulder-length hair relaxed straight, with a part down the middle. Nay-Nay had a rough edge about her. She always wore pants and sneaks with either a wife beater in warm weather or a T-shirt in the cold. Although she seemed a little tomboyish, her femininity stood out. She had her smile to thank for that.

"Well, while Monique and I were talking, something came to mind," Lisa said, like she was some mad scientist. "Let me run it by you real quick. I think I'm going to need you to solicit Dame's help. Unknowingly, of course."

After hearing exactly what Lisa had in mind and ending her call, Nay-Nay sat on the bed for a moment and thought about how to execute the plan. Dame was still in the shower. He was worse than some woman with those long-ass showers. This was the perfect time to do what she needed to do without him knowing. Nay-Nay was a bad bitch, but Dame was a beast. She knew that if he caught her snooping through his shit, he'd beat her ass like she was some nigga.

Nay-Nay wasn't totally comfortable with Lisa's plan, but she, too, at times felt that the only reason Laci hung around them was to make herself feel important, like she was just sitting back and laughing at them, using them as a reminder of how good she had it in life. Well, it was about time somebody had a laugh at her expense.

Nay-Nay tiptoed over to the bathroom door and put her ear against it. She could hear the shower water still running, and Dame was singing the hook to one of the songs from the soundtrack to the movie *Color*.

"Ah, Dame," Nay-Nay called out.

"What?" he grumbled. "You know I'm in the shower."

"I was just going to ask you if you wanted me to roll a blunt," she lied. "But never mind."

No one was as suspicious as Dame. He didn't trust anyone, especially not no bitch. His antennae were always going up, alerting him to something shady. There was something in Nay-Nay's voice that made him cut his shower short.

Nay-Nay didn't know where Dame kept his stash, because he was always moving it from spot to spot. She had to search several different spots before he got out of the shower. She searched his jacket pockets as well as under his mattress and bed frame. Nothing. She went through his closet and VHS rack and still couldn't find it. It was then that she looked over at his television and noticed an abnormality.

The back of the television was crooked. The only reason Nay-Nay noticed it was that she stood eye level to the TV. She walked over to the television set and wiggled the back of it and sure enough it popped off.

"Jackpot!" she said in a soft whisper.

She removed the ziplock bag from the exposed slot in the back of the TV and took two capsules from it. Then suddenly she heard Dame creeping, so she quickly placed the baggie back in its place and sealed the television back up. It was just in the nick of time, too, because Dame opened the bathroom door.

Acting like she was slingin' on the corner and the po po had just rolled up on her, Nay-Nay placed the capsules in her mouth, one in each cheek. That was a trick she had learned from her days working for Dame on the block.

"What the fuck you doin'?" Dame asked as he strode into the room, nude and wet. Dame was a short man who was built like a stone gargoyle. He had thick arms and legs, with a barrel chest. His beady eyes bore into Nay-Nay as he waited for an answer.

"Oh, you scared me," she gasped. "I didn't hear you get out of the shower."

Dame stood there, piercing her with his eyes, waiting on a response.

"I was trying to see if I left my purple thong over here. You seen it? Maybe it's at the other apartment."

Dame was really suspicious now. Nay-Nay knew damn well that the other apartment was off limits to her. That was where he kept his shit, his quantity, his real weight. She had been there a time or two, the occasions when he had had to stop and take care of some business and she had just happened to be rolling with him. But it was the last place she'd find any of her shit.

"I've looked everywhere and can't find it," Nay-Nay continued. "I can't wear this purple bra without the matching thong. You sure you ain't seen it?"

Dame's answer was to grab Nay-Nay and squeeze her, then run his hands over her body, feeling for something that she wasn't supposed to have. When he came up empty, he kissed her and flipped his tongue around her mouth. Nay-Nay hadn't expected him to go that far, but she'd been ready for it, nonetheless. Her tongue skills were superior, so she had led the dance and Dame had never felt the capsules.

Nay-Nay wasn't going to get away that easy, though. All the touching made Dame horny. He began to rub on Nay-Nay, letting her know he wanted sex and she would have to give it to him. Capsules in her mouth or not, Dame had to get broke off. She cocked over and let Dame handle his business.

Grudgingly, Monique called Laci back. Laci's mother answered the phone, then went into Laci's room to tell her that the phone call was for her.

"Laci?" Monique asked timidly.

"Yeah," Laci said, then confirmed that it was Monique. "Monique?"

Laci's mother stood in the doorway . . . just in case. If it was one of those ghetto bitches trying to fuck with her daughter again, she was gonna snatch the phone and give that girl a piece of her mind.

"Yeah . . ." Monique hesitated. "It's me. Listen, about earlier . . . I'm sorry. I had some shit on my mind, and I didn't mean to take it out on you."

A smile came across Laci's face. "Don't worry about it. We all have our days," Laci said, glad that Monique's actions earlier weren't personal.

"Yeah. Listen, Laci. What I had called you for earlier was to tell you that all the girls are gonna get together at Lisa's house in a few. We wanted you to come through. You know, we just gonna do a girls' night thing."

Laci looked down at her watch. It was a nice little Movado with a single diamond in the face that her father had gotten her from Macy's for her sixteenth birthday. It was engraved with the words *It's time to let you fly*, which was a reference to Laci's flight toward adulthood. It was one of the most expensive gifts he had ever gotten her. It was the most symbolic also. Laci treasured it.

"I don't know," Laci sighed. She wanted to say that she and her mother were about to go out, but she didn't want to hit a nerve again with Monique. "Well, what time?"

"We all just getting dressed and heading over to Lisa's," Monique said.

Laci looked at her mother, who was still standing in the doorway.

"Okay," Laci said hesitantly. "I'll be there."

Her mother could tell what was up by the look on Laci's face. She didn't beef. She just walked over to Laci, kissed her on the forehead, and exited the room. All she could do was sit back and try not to run her daughter's life. Laci would make mistakes in order to grow. Margaret only hoped that Laci could bounce back and recover from any mistakes that she made. Little did Laci's mother know that some mistakes didn't come equipped with a bungee cord to allow a muthafucka to bounce right back. Some came with nothing but an old-fashioned rope, which simply left a muthafucka hangin'.

Chapter 2

Born Killa

Wayne had seen his mother, Gloria, bring home replacement fathers one after another. By the time he was fifteen, thirteen of his years had been spent watching men come and go. Early on, he had paid no mind to their comings and goings, but as his teenage years rolled around, he began to recognize and accept what his mother's intentions were for the men in her life.

Financially challenged, Wayne's mother did the best she could to support them with no help from friends or family. All she had was Uncle Sam's handout to work with. Women in her position were known, and sometimes expected, to swallow their pride and go from man to man until they found one who was willing to take on some of their burdens. Men, on the other hand, knew that a single mother was an easy picking. She'd put up with anything if she felt it would benefit her situation, which in the end it usually didn't.

The men Wayne's mother brought into their environment found it difficult to be the father or man of the house, especially since it was clear that the responsibility wasn't theirs. In Gloria's case, as in most cases, the man would hang around until the sex got stale and then would move on to the next victim. And sometimes things could even get violent.

A couple of years earlier, Wayne's mother had brought a man named Buck into their home. He was the man of the hour. He was about six foot one, sloppy, overweight, and had a lazy left eye. The only reason he was able to even get at Gloria in the first place was that his money put meat in the freezer. Gloria was numb to the physical appearance of men when they proved useful to her. It didn't matter what they looked like or how much they weighed. The only thing Gloria saw was dollar signs, and as far as she was concerned, all money looked alike and spent the same—quick and easy, which were the very words that could be used to describe her. She was quick to find a man and easy enough for him to have his way with her. Buck was no exception.

Although Wayne was only fifteen years old at the time, he had already seen more than enough of his share of these types of cats. Buck was just another number, and like some of the other men, he probably wouldn't even stay in the picture long enough for Wayne to learn his last name.

"Hey, li'l man. What's happening?" Buck asked Wayne as Gloria introduced the two of them. "What kind of candy you like?"

Wayne just stood there in the doorway next to his mother. He'd heard that question plenty of times. It was always the same words, different nigga. Wayne almost answered Buck before he even asked the question. The words seemed to fall out of his mouth in a robotic fashion.

"Any kind," Wayne replied, putting his head down, his mother smiling and patting him on the head like he was a six-year-old child.

"Ain't he so cute?" Gloria said, as if she was trying to convince someone in the pet store to buy the runt of the litter. "He's quiet, but he's a good boy. He ain't like all them other little nappy-headed niggas you see running around here, not going to school and thangs. My boy goes to school. He's gonna be a doctor someday."

Where in the fuck did she get that idea? Wayne thought.

Buck was staring down at Gloria, but he didn't hear a word she was saying. All he saw was her lips moving and a pair of nice round titties. And all he cared about was sending li'l man to the store to buy candy to suck on while he sucked on Gloria's titties. Wayne had seen the look Buck was giving his mother several times before. Same look, different nigga.

"Too much candy will make your teeth fall out," Buck said, addressing his comment to Wayne but continuing to eye Gloria while licking his lips. "But sometimes it tastes so sweet it's worth the sacrifice, wouldn't you say, son?"

From that point on, Buck never looked at Wayne again, even when he was addressing him. All he did was stare at Gloria, with lust in his eyes. And Buck and Wayne never would see eye to eye. To Buck, the kid would probably end up being more of a burden than anything, always in the way.

Gloria seemed to like Buck, as she was all smiles with him. Wayne had already decided from the beginning that he wasn't going to say too much to the man. After all, why should he start up a relationship with someone who would soon be replaced by the next man, anyhow?

Buck loved running up in Gloria in the back seat of his truck. That was usually what their dates

consisted of, if they could be called that. Gloria
would usually meet him at the construction site he
was working at over on Wall Street. She would be
his lunch. And the sex never cost him much, either,
just a few dollars here and there. Gloria would
usually get a bag of groceries or two out of the deal.
Since she wasn't a begging, greedy broad, acting
like her pussy was lined in gold, Buck decided that
perhaps seeing her on a regular and tolerating her
kid would be worth it. He reasoned that if the li'l
nigga was going to be around, they should at least
have some type of understanding. And Buck was
well aware that the best way to get on a kid's good
side was to bribe him with money or candy. Since
he wasn't trying to pay into the situation any more
than he had to, he went with the candy.

So when they first met, Wayne didn't respond
to Buck's comment about candy making your teeth
fall out. He just stared at him, sizing up the man
who wasn't going to stick around until Wayne's
next birthday. He was young, but he wasn't young
enough to be bought off with any goddamned
candy. Buck would do better using cash as an
icebreaker.

Wayne knew the rules to the game his mother
played with these men, but Buck was the worst
physical specimen of a man he'd seen his mother

date. He felt that if his mother was going to take part in the game, she should at least play in her league.

Buck stood there, still staring at Gloria, as he reached into his pocket for his wallet. He pulled out a dollar. "Run on down to the store and get you some candy, son. Eat it out there on the stoop." Buck held the money out to Wayne, but he didn't take it. What the fuck did he think Wayne was supposed to do with a lousy dollar?

"What's wrong, homeboy? You don't like candy, after all?" Buck asked.

Wayne was silent. He hated what he was being exposed to. Gloria was protective of her son, but when it came to appeasing men, Wayne took a back seat. His mother giving all her attention to the man of the hour was a typical practice that he had become accustomed to.

"Of course he does," Gloria said, answering for Wayne, whacking him on the back of the head. "Boy, you answer people when they talk to you." Gloria turned her attention back to Buck. "He knows better than to ignore people. He just gets a little shy sometimes. He's a good boy, though."

"That's all right, Gloria," Buck said, running his fingers down her cheek. "If the li'l nigga don't want to talk, forget it." Buck realized right then and there that Wayne peeped and understood the game. That shit was going to be a problem, and he didn't like it one bit. "I just guess you one of the few kids who don't like candy, huh, son? If you did, you'd be takin' this here dollar and going to get you some."

Wayne remained silent.

"Boy, you open your mouth and answer Buck, or I'm gonna whip yo' ass!" Gloria warned.

Wayne's young body shook with rage. At that moment, he could've killed both Buck *and* his mother. She was forcing him to humble himself for the love of a man and his pockets. Wayne felt as if his dignity was being stripped away from him, right along with his mother's.

"Yes, sir, Mr. Buck," Wayne growled underneath his breath, trying to hold back the well of tears. "I like Kit Kats."

"Whatcha say, li'l man?" Buck asked triumphantly.

"Kit Kats," Wayne said, tightening his lips and wiping his eye with the tail of his shirt.

"Now, was that so hard?" Buck laughed mockingly. "Here ya go, li'l nigga. Take it." Buck handed Wayne the dollar. "Now go on down to the store and get you a Kit Kat. And take yo' time, 'cause me and ya mama here got some business to discuss." He winked at Gloria.

Buck had one hell of an itch going on and wanted Wayne out of his hair so that he could scratch it. After giving Wayne the dollar, Buck opened the door, hinting that Wayne should get to steppin'.

Wayne grabbed his skully from the television, positioned it on his head, and got on his way.

Buck immediately locked the door behind him, figuring that if Wayne couldn't get back in, he couldn't interrupt the freaked-out sex he had in mind for himself and Gloria. With Gloria's ripe body clouding Buck's brain, it never dawned on him to make sure the back door was locked also.

Gloria looked at Buck as he smiled menacingly at her. She didn't really like the way he had brushed Wayne off, but she figured it was better for him to be the bad guy rather than her. But Wayne was a smart kid. He could plainly see that Gloria was an accomplice to the bad guy.

Wayne was no exception to other youngsters in similar surroundings. Like most kids in the hood, he had no childhood. He was wise enough to know that it wasn't what Buck said that made him the bad guy, but that it was what his mother didn't say. She kept her mouth shut out of fear of saying something that could make Buck leave. The fear of him leaving and taking his wallet with him was what forced her to go along with whatever he put down.

Once the youngster was gone, Buck wasted no time in jumping on Gloria. He pushed her up against the door and lifted her rainbow-colored striped shirt over her head. He then tore off her dingy off-white bra and began to suck viciously on her huge brown nipples.

"Slow down, baby," Gloria said, trying to dodge the hot, wet kisses Buck began burning her neck with. "We got plenty of time."

"Uh-uh," he said as he continued to grope her body. Buck was far too anxious to get it poppin'. He didn't even bother to remove her panties. He just pulled them to the side and rammed his crooked dick into her.

Gloria attempted to scream out in pain from the sudden penetration. Buck hadn't even gotten her wet yet. He managed to cover her mouth with his hand as he pressed his body up against hers to balance himself. He humped her and began growling like a bear. Slobber running down the sides of his bulbous lips, he tried to swallow her tongue. Gloria thought she was going to throw up from the taste of his stale breath.

She just held her breath and let Buck continue fucking her. It was evident he was about to cum by the way his growl was getting louder and louder. She looked at his face and saw that it had become grossly twisted. He was cumming inside her.

Gloria relaxed her body and let out a sigh. She was relieved that he had climaxed so soon and that it was over with so quickly. But Buck was no one-minute man. Gloria soon found this out when he viciously turned her around, pushed her against the door, and entered her from behind. He began to hammer away, never even noticing that his roughness had made her start to bleed a little. He kept grunting and pumping away like a wild animal. Tears ran down Gloria's face as she prayed for him to finish fucking her and just to get the hell out, but not without leaving a few ends first.

Meanwhile, Wayne walked down the block, letting tears flow freely down his chocolate face. He tried to hold them in, but as he walked to the candy store, he just couldn't. He didn't mind crying, but he didn't want that fat bastard to know he had gotten to him. On top of that, he was sick of the abuse his mother brought on herself and forced him to put up with.

Wayne scoped out his neighborhood as he walked. Across the street was some dude parked in a shiny cream-colored Cadillac. He was puffing on a cigarette, and a couple of nice-looking broads were leaning inside the driver's window, hollering at him. He looked like a slick muthafucka. About a block farther down the street were about four cats who appeared to be just hanging out, dressed in bomb-ass Nike jogging suits and sporting the latest Air Jordans.

If only I was old enough, I could get out on my own and make a life for myself, Wayne thought. *I could have a nice ride and clothes too.* And with any luck, Wayne thought he could do something for his mother. He could give her all the money she needed to take care of herself so that she didn't have to trick for it.

Wayne approached the store and saw a drunk man wearing dirty, funky clothes begging for money. Everybody was walking by, trying not to look at him. He was only a reminder of where they were. All Wayne's hopes that he had thought about on the way to the store vanished. He felt stuck, and he felt no love.

Upon walking past the drunken bum, Wayne nodded to a few of the neighborhood boys he knew who were standing across the street. He then ducked into the corner bodega. He grabbed a Kit Kat. While the clerk retrieved his change from the cash register, Wayne snatched up two loose cigarettes from a box on the counter and cupped them in his hand.

"Have nice day," the clerk, who barely spoke English, said to Wayne. Wayne slipped out of the store with his Kit Kat in hand, two stolen cigarettes, and his change.

He looked up at the sun shining brightly in the sky. He blocked his eyes with his hand and thought about the power of the sun. Up until that point, he had never even noticed it. As far as he was concerned, the sun didn't shine in the ghetto. But today he did notice it, and it seemed happy. It appeared to be smiling at him, as if it knew something he didn't. Wayne suddenly felt a sense of hope. He looked over at the bum whom everybody pretended not to notice. He jingled the change from the Kit Kat in his hand, handed it to the bum, and walked away.

After approaching the group of boys he had nodded to on his way into the store, Wayne managed to cop a book of matches from one of them. Niggas in the hood could always be counted on to have at least one of three things—a knife, just in case they had to cut a nigga's shit up; a gun, just in case they had to shoot a nigga's shit up; and a light, just in case they had to burn a nigga's shit up.

Wayne decided to take the back streets to his house so that he could smoke one of his cigarettes without some nosy-ass neighbor running back and telling his moms. That would just give her something else to knock him upside the head for.

Wayne's mother had been whipping his ass ever since the first man who tried to take on the role of his father had come into the picture. Wayne was too young to remember more than just flashes of what the man had looked like. All he could remember was his fists. And instead of doing anything about the beatings, his mother had kept quiet. She had eventually started hitting on Wayne too. Gloria had always had a tough time raising Wayne, and she wanted to make sure he knew how vicious it was out in the streets. That was what she had tried to convince Wayne and herself of, anyway.

The kids on the block would sometimes give Wayne hell about his mother's sexual habits, and he had always found himself having to go head up with one of them. Wayne's size had always put him at a hell of a disadvantage. Even at the age of fifteen, he didn't look like the average fifteen-year-old boy in the neighborhood. He looked about twelve years old compared to the boys his age. Nonetheless, he never backed away from a confrontation.

Once Wayne could see his apartment building from the back alley, he took a few last puffs and stomped out the cigarette with his foot. He approached the back door and didn't think twice about knocking. He figured he'd been gone long enough for Buck to have finished tagging his mother and to be on his merry way.

Wayne walked in the door and closed it behind him. He didn't see or hear anyone, so he figured that his mother and her company had left. Wayne breathed a sigh of relief at the idea of being alone. He figured he would watch some television and figure out what to do with the rest of his Saturday.

He plopped down on the old plaid couch in the living room and scrambled for the remote to turn on the old floor-model television. Just then, Wayne remembered that the TV had gone out a few weeks earlier. Since the broken television just sat there, it was by force of habit that Wayne would sit down in front of it and attempt to turn it on. Sometimes his mother would allow him to carry the little thirteen-inch set out of her room upstairs and set it on top of the broken TV so that he could watch something. But Wayne wasn't in the mood to lug that thing all the way downstairs, so he decided he would chill up in his mother's room, eat his Kit Kat, and watch television there. Wayne took his Kit Kat out of his back pocket and headed upstairs. When he got to her closed bedroom door, he stopped and opened his Kit Kat. He broke off a piece, took a bite, and proceeded into his mother's room.

As soon as Wayne opened the door, the Kit Kat fell to the floor. All he saw was his mother on the bed on all fours and Buck's big, fat, naked ass behind her, slamming into her as she held her ass high. Wayne's eyes welled up with tears at the sight of a man hitting his mother doggy-style, as if she was a dog . . . a female dog . . . a bitch. Then the scene got worse. Wayne watched in shock as Buck pulled his penis from out of Gloria's beat-up pussy, yanked her over onto her back, and exploded all over her, including her face.

"Ma," Wayne said in a nervous whisper.

Gloria jumped up and tried to cover herself. She tried hopelessly to wipe the semen off her face. She thought she'd die of shame as Buck grabbed one end of the sheet and began to wipe his dick off with it, as if it wasn't nothing but a thang.

"Wayne!" Gloria said, wrapping the sheet around her. "Wayne, baby, I know what it looks like, but Mama was just—"

"No sense in sugarcoating it," Buck said, getting up off the bed and putting on his pants. "The boy's got eyes. He might be young, but he ain't blind, or all the way dumb, for that matter. He knows what his mama's up to. Probably got him a li'l tender of his own, with all these fast-ass little girls running around here. Don't ya, boy?" He looked over at Wayne and waited on a response.

Wayne gritted his teeth and remained silent.

"You probably be doing to those little girls just what I was doing to your mama here, huh? 'Cept y'all probably keep y'all's clothes on, huh?" Buck laughed as he buckled his belt and pulled his wallet out of his pants pocket.

"Be quiet, Buck!" Gloria snapped. "This is between me and my son. Just get the hell out and I'll call you later."

"So it's like that?" Buck asked, getting angry, as he snatched up his shirt from the floor. "Ain't I the one that gave you grocery money the other day? You couldn't wait to get me up in this piss hole, and now, just because this muthafucka sees his cunt of a mother for what she really is, I gotta go? You know what? Fuck you and this li'l nappy-headed nigga."

"What?" Gloria asked as her eyes squinted. "Fuck my son? No, you fat, nasty fucker, fuck you! Get the hell out of my house, you fat bastard!"

Buck didn't take well to women ordering him around and calling him out of his name. He had to show Gloria what happened to women who disrespected him, especially cheap-ass tricks like herself.

Buck nodded his head back and forth, as if he was plotting. He looked inside his wallet and pulled out a wad of money, just to tease Gloria with it. "Fuck me?" He laughed. "Naw, fuck you, you broke-ass bitch. Let's see how fat I am when you and ya little bastard's ribs start rubbing together. I'm getting the hell out of here, all right." Buck pulled his shirt down over his head and slipped on his shoes. "I might be fat, but so is my wallet." Buck stuffed the wad of money back in his wallet, closed it up, and put it back in his pocket, letting Gloria know that he wasn't giving her a god-damned dime. He then walked out of the room, knocking Wayne to the floor on his way out.

"You son of a bitch," Gloria yelled as she followed behind Wayne. "You get back here. You know I need some money."

"You gonna have to learn not to disrespect me," Buck said, making his way to the bottom of the stairs and heading toward the door. "Now, if you stop while you're ahead, I just might come back and let you try to earn your keep again. But this time, you done gone and let your mouth fuck it up for you."

"Fuck you!" Gloria screamed as she ran down the steps, the sheet still covering her. She tripped over the sheet when she was midway down the steps, and fell. She landed at the bottom of the stairs, buck naked.

As Buck unlocked the front door, Gloria ran and threw her naked body in front of it.

"Don't you leave without giving me some fucking dough," she screamed. Tears of anger flowed down her face. She had allowed this man to fuck her and nut up inside her and all over her, all in the name of the almighty dollar. And now here he was trying to eat and run.

Buck grabbed Gloria by the arm, flung her away from the door, and slammed her against a bookshelf, knocking it down. The splintered wood and falling books scraped Gloria's arms and face.

By now, Wayne had managed to pick himself up off the floor and make his way down the steps in an attempt to rescue his mother. Wayne tripped over the sheet that was on the steps, and he fell down the stairs too. When he reached the bottom of the staircase, he looked up and saw his mother on the floor, hurt by the fallen bookshelf and books. Wayne picked up his basketball, which was the nearest thing to him, and hurled it at Buck as hard as he could. The ball hit Buck square in the face.

Buck grabbed for his face as blood squirted from his nose. "You little muthafucka," he said, wiping his bloody nose with his shirt.

Buck took off toward Wayne, expecting him to try to run from him. To Buck's surprise, Wayne held his ground. Though it was a noble effort, Wayne was no match for the grown, fat-ass man. Buck hit Wayne in the chest, folding him.

Gloria managed to make her way to the kitchen and pulled out the entire silverware drawer as she was going for a knife. She had to do something, or Buck would kill Wayne. She darted from the kitchen and ran toward Buck, who was now on top of Wayne, choking the life out of him. "I'm gonna kill you, muthafucka!" Gloria yelled. "Get away from my son."

Buck stood up and was able to restrain Gloria by her wrists, forcing her to drop the knife. He let go of Gloria and hauled off and slapped the holy shit out of her, leaving his handprints on her face.

Wayne, still gasping for air, watched helplessly as his mother was brutally beaten. He'd been bullied his entire life, and now he lay there, watching his mother be bullied too. He wished he had a gun. That would even the playing field for sure. He hated the fact that he couldn't protect his mother or himself. At that very moment, he promised himself that once he got a piece, he'd never be caught without it. He would fear no man.

Buck stood over Gloria and laughed. "Like I said, fuck you, bitch." Buck sniffed back the blood and mucus in his nose, bringing it to his throat. He hacked it up and spat in Gloria's face. "Punk muthafucka," he mumbled as he looked over at Wayne before heading out the door.

Naked, bruised, and swollen beyond recognition, Gloria crawled over to her son and tried to comfort him. "I'm so sorry," she cried. "Oh, my baby, I'm so sorry."

Gloria tried to put her arms around Wayne, but he pushed her away. The damage had already been done, and Wayne began to rot from the inside. Hate consumed his being, and it was quickly growing like a cancer. He had no intentions on going out like that.

Wayne got up and walked out the door, leaving his sobbing mother behind. He had to start putting together a plan. Fuck waiting until he got older. Shit was broke now and needed fixin'.

As Wayne huffed and puffed down the street, he decided that the first thing he would need was a gun, and he knew of only one place where he might be able to cop one. He was in hot pursuit. Something in him had snapped, and he was now swiftly moving toward becoming a killer. He had never felt this way before. He felt as though he'd received a calling, and it was as loud as thunder.

After four hours Wayne spotted the cat he'd been scouring the streets for. He was sitting outside, on an apartment stoop, talking to some kid. He was a slightly older dealer whom Wayne had heard people refer to only by some nickname, which seemed to have slipped his mind at the moment. Wayne had seen him around the way plenty of times but had never held a conversation with him. Wayne had simply always given him a "What up?" nod or some dap whenever he crossed his path. Wayne didn't know much about the dealer, but he was the only person who had come to mind as Wayne had pondered the person to turn to for what he needed at the moment. As Wayne neared the stoop, he saw the dealer hand the kid a few dollars and give him some dap, and then the kid walked away. Wayne recognized the kid as Rich, some punk-ass, "I wanna be a gangsta when I grow up" loser.

Wayne took a deep breath and mustered up some courage before approaching the dealer and speaking.

"Sup, yo?" Wayne asked.

"Chilling, li'l man," the dealer responded. He expected Wayne to move on, like he usually did, but instead, Wayne stayed put. The dealer noticed the hunger in Wayne's eyes, and he could tell that he wanted something. He knew the look well, but it was usually from one of the fiends trying to score. "What you doing sniffing round these streets all by yaself? It ain't no joke out here, kid."

"I'm trying to cop something," Wayne said.

"Word?" he asked, in shock. "I would have never pegged you. You're too young to have a habit. What are you? Eleven, twelve, or something?"

"Naw. I'm older than that," Wayne said, sticking his chest out.

"Oh, then you just a grown-ass man, huh?" the dealer said sarcastically and began to chuckle.

Wayne stood there, with hunger still burning in his eyes. The dealer could easily see that Wayne wasn't in a joking mood.

"So what can I do for you, li'l man? What you need? Some coke, rock—"

"It's personal," Wayne said in a hushed tone, cutting him off.

"Shit, it can't be that damn personal if you're running up on a nigga you don't really know. You must want to share it with somebody?" he replied. "For real, though. Talk to me, li'l man."

Wayne looked into his eyes and saw genuine concern. Usually, dealers played twenty-one questions with a cat they weren't cool with, but this one didn't appear to be nosy. He just wanted to know what had Wayne combing the tough streets with a mean look in his eyes.

Wayne took a deep breath and told him an edited version of what had just gone down between Buck, his mother, and him. He told him how Buck had tried to leave them for dead. The fact that he had caught his mom turning a trick and not getting paid was something he didn't feel the need to share.

The dealer listened attentively. He was drawn in by the intensity with which Wayne told his story. Like a rapper sharing his tale on wax, he could feel what Wayne was saying, even though he hadn't experienced it firsthand.

"That's some heavy shit, li'l man." The dealer sighed, sliding his hand down his face. "Now I can see why you're out here stressin'. So what now?"

"I need a gat," Wayne said without hesitating.

The dealer laughed. "What you gon' do with a gun?" he asked, not reading between the lines.

"What you think?" Wayne said, sounding a little harsher than he intended to. "I need to be able to protect myself and my moms. A nigga never gonna run up in my crib again. Ya heard?"

The dealer took a deep breath and then let out a sigh. "That's a tall order, li'l man," he said, rubbing his hands together. "All kinds of fucked-up shit happens with guns. A little dude like yaself might get hurt or hurt somebody and bring a lot of heat down on the niggas out here serving. The first thing they'll be wanting to know is where you got the piece from."

Wayne wasn't up for reasoning. He could see now that he needed to move on. "Yo, if you don't wanna hook me up, then I'm out!" Wayne held his hand out to give him some dap. He wanted him to know that even though he wasn't going to help him out, they were still cool.

"Hold on, hold on. I didn't say that I didn't want to help you out," the dealer said, grinning. "But this is business." All of a sudden, he started sounding like the alter ego, devil voice that rappers used in their songs. "How you going to pay for what you need, homeboy?"

In Wayne's haste, he had never thought about that little obstacle. In his quest for revenge, he had forgotten the most common law of the streets: nothing came without a price. Though this was something that hadn't crossed his mind, he wouldn't be swayed.

"I ain't got no money," Wayne confessed.

"Then you're shit out of luck," the dealer said, turning his back to Wayne.

This was typical. One minute a muthafucka was up in your corner, and as soon as he found out your pockets were full of lint, he turned his back on you.

"Hold on, man," Wayne said, tapping him on the shoulder. "Maybe I can work it off?"

"I feel for you and all, but damn, li'l man. This ain't Burger King," he snarled over his shoulder. "I deal in cash, baby. Besides, what the hell can you do? You ain't no drug dealer. You ain't even no mule. You ain't got no street savvy, or you wouldn't have ever stepped to me like you did in the first place. I can see your ass fuckin' up the game for everybody, so why should I put you on?"

Wayne thought on it for a minute before speaking. "I can do other things for you. Whatever you need done, if you know what I mean," Wayne said, throwing his hands up humbly. "No need frontin' me a gat if it's no use to you. Point a nigga out, and he's a memory."

The dealer laughed. "That's big talk for a li'l man. But if your heart is as big as your mouth, then we just might be able to work some shit out. But peep this." He leaned down to speak with Wayne. "You don't just wake up one morning and decide that you want to be a killer. It don't work like that. Besides, that don't even seem like ya style. You need to have yo' li'l ass in school or something."

"It's my fuckin' style, and fuck school. School might allow for a nigga to survive on Wall Street, but it don't teach nothin' about surviving in these streets. I'm tired of getting stepped on. A mutha-fucka ain't gon' never catch me without something no more." Wayne spoke angrily, spitting his words.

The vision of his mother crying as Buck spit on her would be locked in his memory forever. He went on. "I'ma eat, sleep, fuck, and take a bath wit my shit. It's nineteen eighty-seven, and I ain't takin' no shorts."

"I don't know, homeboy," the dealer said to Wayne. "Killing somebody ain't easy. You gotta have that shit in your heart. Pulling that trigger is a mafuck. The power behind it . . . the pull, the smoke, and the heat. A lot of niggas are carrying guns, but everybody ain't busting them, know what I mean? Some of these cats wear their shit around their waist, like they makin' a fashion statement. You might just be talking out ya ass because you all pissed off right now."

"I'll tell you what," Wayne said, getting angry. "Hook me up wit a piece, and you can watch me put a nigga's head to bed."

Just then, some girl came heading their way. She was a hottie for sure. She had light skin and baby hair around her forehead, which she probably molded every morning with a toothbrush. The little bit of makeup she was wearing was just enough, as her skin was as smooth as the leather interior of a Caddy. She was wearing the cutest little dress, with high-heeled shoes that showed off her slender legs.

"Hey, Daddy," she said, approaching the dealer.

"Hey now, baby girl," the dealer replied as he stood up from the stoop and met her a few steps down. "What can I do you for?"

"I know what you like." She winked. "And you know what I like."

"I'm straight on that stuff," the dealer said, turning away from her. "My old lady took care of that for me before I left the crib, so no bartering tonight, baby girl. No cash, no stash."

"I got money," she said, copping that light-skinned girl attitude.

"Then we straight," the dealer said, looking around. He then pulled a condom out of his pocket. She held out her hand, and he emptied a crack rock into it from the condom. Her eyes lit up. She slowly pulled her sundress up and stuck her hand down her panties.

"Here you go, Daddy," she said, handing him some money. "Take a whiff of that to remind you of me. What I got is better than money, and you should never forget it."

"Later," the dealer said, unimpressed.

She was a bum, but not like the man outside of the bodega. She was a bum to all the dudes in the neighborhood. That was how they referred to old pussy. And there was certainly something better than old pussy—new pussy. Her shit was done.

The girl blew the dealer a kiss, then looked over at Wayne. "Breaking them in younger and younger every day, huh?" she said to the dealer. "He's a little cutie too. Maybe one day you might wanna do something nice for your little worker bee. You know I'm always willing to work for mine. Later, fellas." She strutted away.

"Sorry about that," the dealer said, stuffing the condom back down in his pocket. "That was just Angel, some trickin'-ass geeker. Ho will do anything for a rock."

Wayne stood there in awe, watching her walk away. She didn't look anything like the neighborhood crackheads he had seen before. She seemed so sweet and innocent—not to mention that she was fine. No way was she copping that shit for herself.

The dealer observed Wayne staring at the girl until she was out of sight. "Well, looky here," he said, laughing. "Li'l man diggin' on Angel. Man, she's gotta be twice your age. How old did you say you were again?"

"Why?" Wayne snapped, not appreciating being laughed at. "Is that gon' make a difference in whether you let me hold something?"

The dealer looked at Wayne and shook his head as he smiled. "You really is a hard li'l nigga, huh? I see the potential. I like your heart, and I just may have some work for you. But I don't even know your name, homeboy."

"It's Wayne."

"Wayne? Wayne what?"

"Just Wayne," he said, figuring that was all dude needed to know for now, unless he decided to help him out for certain.

"Okay, tough guy," the dealer teased. "You sure don't look like no Wayne. With that skully sitting on top of ya head like that, you look like a black-ass Smurf. And you kinda act like the little angry one. Matter of fact, fuck that *Wayne* shit. I'm gonna call you Smurf. That's yo' new name, li'l nigga. Get used to it."

"Whatever," Wayne said, waving him off. "So can I get that piece now or what?"

"What's the hurry, Smurf?"

"I need to take care of some important business. I've already wasted enough time."

"What exactly *is* your business?" the dealer asked, searching Wayne's face.

"What kind of business you think?"

"There you go again with that shit. If you gonna be down wit a nigga, you gotta keep it real. You gotta lay your shit out flat."

"First off," Wayne said, obliging, "I need to take care of some shit. I don't want to get all the way into the future and have to backtrack on some shit. I want to go ahead and knock down the first domino."

The dealer nodded and smiled. Wayne wasn't the street-breed type of cat, but he could tell that he'd seen a lot. And his street fineness seemed to flow naturally. It needed some polishing, but the kid had potential.

"Second off, do you really want me to make you an accessory before the fact?" Wayne said, using the language he had learned from prime-time law shows.

"Okay, Smurf," the dealer said with a chuckle. "Follow me."

He led Wayne over to his parked car, which was a Honda Accord. He ordered him to get in on the passenger side as he seated himself in the driver's seat. He opened the glove box and pulled out a brown paper bag. He handed it to Wayne.

Wayne opened the bag and saw a shiny .32. He stroked the pistol inside the bag. He didn't dare pull it out on the Ave, also known as the Avenue, like that. He could feel the hammer singing to him as his finger stroked the metal. He sat there like a deer caught in headlights, admiring the pistol.

"Think you can work with that?" the dealer asked.

"Hell yeah," Wayne said, snapping out of his daze. "I'll bring it right back when I'm done."

"Nah, it's yours now. You keep it. And just remember, if anything happens, forget where you got it from."

"Word?" Wayne said, smiling and rocking his head. "Thanks, man. I owe you for real."

"Hell yeah, you owe me, and I plan to collect," he said. "Where you live, yo?"

"I'll connect with you right back here in a couple of days," Wayne said, ignoring the question.

"That's cool. I feel that," the dealer said, smiling at Wayne, who was acting like Santa had just brought him exactly what he'd asked for on his Christmas list. "Damn, you do look just like a Smurf."

"I'll be that," Wayne said. "I'll be a Smurf all day long, just as long as I got the heat."

The dealer reached into the back seat and grabbed a book. He began to flip through the pages. "You read, Smurf?"

"Nah," Wayne said, tucking the bag under his shirt.

"You ever heard of the Dutchman?"

"Who?"

"The Dutchman. Lucio Dutch."

"Nah. Who is that?"

"Damn, Smurf. You got a lot to learn." The dealer loved to read, and he passed books on to people he knew didn't but needed to. "Here. Read this," he said, handing Wayne the book. "I want you to read a few pages and tell me what you think the next time I see you."

"I don't want to read no book," Wayne protested. "Ain't nobody got time for all that."

"You ain't got no money for that burner, either," the dealer reminded him.

Wayne had no response.

"All right, then," the dealer continued. "Read a couple of pages and catch up with me."

"Cool," Wayne said, giving him a handshake and some dap. Wayne opened the car door to exit, but then he paused and looked at the dealer. "In case I don't see you around and I need to ask if anyone's seen you, who do I say I'm looking for?"

"The name is Dink. Just mention your name, and they'll know to hit me up. And remember, from this point on, you're Smurf. But don't worry. I'll be here. You just show up and tell me about what you read."

"I got it. Don't you worry. Smurf will be here," Wayne said, getting out of the car. He leaned in. "Oh yeah, by the way, I didn't just wake up one day and decide that I wanted to be a killer." After a quick pause Smurf added, "I was born one." Then he closed the door behind him.

Dink nodded with respect as Smurf walked away.

After copping the piece, Smurf went straight home to check on his mother and prepare for what he planned on doing with his new gat.

As soon as Smurf walked through the door, Gloria threw her arms around him. "Damn it, boy! Where have you been? I been worried sick. I thought you done ran out here and done something stupid," she said frantically.

"I'm all right, Mom. I didn't do nothin' stupid."

His mother sat him down on the living room couch and continued quizzing him about his whereabouts, but he fed her only lies. Finally, she gave up. Smurf sat there and watched her down a bottle of rum. She eventually fell over onto him in a drunken sleep.

As she snoozed on the living room couch, Smurf felt a pain in his heart. He hated to be hard on his mother, but she didn't seem to want it any other way. He had promised himself that he'd help her get out of her rut. He wanted to help her more than anything, but he had to help himself first. After staring at her for a few more moments, Smurf slid out from underneath her and headed up to bed.

Smurf couldn't think straight. He sat up all night in bed, holding the gun, staring at it, and aiming it. All day Sunday he damn near did the same thing. The gun was like a new puppy.

On Monday he couldn't wait to get out of school that afternoon, go home, and let his new puppy out to piss. He daydreamed all day long in school, thinking about putting one through Buck's head.

After school he did his homework, ate dinner, and prepared to skip out of the house without his mother noticing. Time was of the essence. He went up to his bedroom and dressed in a black sweatshirt and black jeans. And, of course, he wore his skully, the inspiration for his new street name. And with it came a new attitude, one that bred confidence.

But what the fuck did he know about the streets? He knew what went down, but he didn't have firsthand knowledge of it. He had no idea how the streets operated, but he did know one thing, and that was that he had business to settle with Buck.

When Smurf's mother had prepped him for Buck's very first visit to their home, she had tried to make Buck sound like a dream. She had bragged about how he had a good job working as a night watchman at a construction site on Wall Street. This was where Smurf would run up on him.

Smurf had itched to get at the nigga all weekend, but he had decided to wait until Monday, when he thought Buck would more likely be working. He tucked his pistol deep into his pocket and dug into his top dresser drawer for some loose change before heading downstairs. He looked at his mother lying on the couch in the same drunken position she had been in the past couple of days. Smurf walked over to her, kissed her on the forehead, and dipped.

He boarded the Number 2 train and rode it south to the Wall Street station. He had the jitters the entire ride to Manhattan. He thought about turning back, but his conscience wouldn't let him. Buck had violated his home and family. The laws of the jungle had determined that he be handled.

After the train ride, Smurf jogged up the subway stairs toward the exit. Once he was on the street, the evening air greeted him. The cool wind against his face was just what he needed. It didn't take him long to locate the construction site. It was the only one on the block. Smurf walked past it, but he made sure to stay on the opposite side of the street. As far as he could see, there was one entrance in the front and another one, where deliveries were made, on the side. He decided that the latter would be his point of entry.

Smurf crept to a side window and tried to get a good look into the structure. Through the dirty glass he could see Buck sitting behind a desk, watching a small television. As far as Smurf could tell, he was alone. He could climb right through the window and blow Buck's fuckin' brains out without worrying about witnesses.

Smurf crept to the side door and sighed. There was an alarm attached to the door. This was something he hadn't counted on, but he thought of a way to use it to his advantage. He pushed against the door, setting the alarm off, and then waited.

After a few moments, Buck poked his fat head out the door to investigate. His skin turned stark white at the sight of the youngster pointing a pistol at his dome. Smurf smiled at the big man, who looked as if he was about to pass out.

"Back yo' fat ass up," Smurf ordered.

Buck nodded and did as he was told.

Smurf followed him through the door and secured it behind them. "Guess the tables have turned, huh?"

Buck tried to keep a straight face, along with his composure, as he nodded, but his knees wouldn't stop shaking. He'd gotten a thrill out of savagely fucking Gloria and kicking the shit out of her kid, but it didn't seem worth it at that moment.

"Listen, boy," Buck pleaded. "I know you're angry, but—"

"Shut the fuck up!" Smurf ordered. "You don't know how I feel, so don't say another fuckin' word."

The more Smurf talked, the more unsteady his hand became. He had never held a gun up to somebody before, let alone used one. He was just as scared as he was angry. Smurf looked at Buck and saw that Buck was even more frightened than he was. The sniveling coward before him wasn't the same beast who had beaten a woman and her son.

"You ain't so muthafuckin' tough now, is you?" Smurf asked with an insane-looking grin. "You felt like a big man when you was hittin' on a woman and a kid, but now you ain't shit . . . fuckin' coward. Why you ain't popping that shit now?"

"I didn't mean it," Buck said, crying freely. "Shit just got out of hand. I was angry, man. I didn't mean to hurt you and your moms. I swear to God."

"You lyin' muthafucka!" Smurf screamed, slapping Buck with the gun. Buck crumpled to the ground, holding the side of his head as blood poured from the wound. Karma was a bitch.

Seeing Buck humbled in such a way sent a rush through Smurf. He was the only thing that stood between Buck living and dying. He felt godlike in a sense. He felt a surge go from the back of his head and through his arm, before it eventually moved to his hand, which began to stiffen. Finally, the powerful sensation spread to his finger.

The first shot hit Buck in his chest. Smurf tried to gain control of his hand, but he couldn't. Whatever evil lurked within the firearm possessed him. His arm jerked over and over, filling Buck's body with lead. Buck's screams mingled with the sound of the barking gun, threatening to drive Smurf mad. When it was all said and done, the only thing that could be heard was the squeaking spring in the gun's hammer.

Smurf stared at Buck's bullet-riddled body and nearly threw up. He forced his dinner to stay down long enough to admire his handiwork. Buck was hit up real ugly, but it was a suitable death for a man who'd done such ugly things. Smurf took a moment to spit on Buck's corpse before disappearing.

Tomorrow would be a new day, and he was anxious to see what kind of work his new employer had lined up for him. But little did he know then that more than two years later, he'd still be putting in work for Dink.

Tomorrow would be a new day, and he was anxious to see what kind of work his new employer had lined up for him. But little did he know then that more than two years later, he'd still be putting in work for Dink.

the evening air greeted him. The cool wind against his face was just what he needed. It didn't take him long to locate the construction site. It was the only one on the block. Smurf walked past it, but he made sure to stay on the opposite side of the street. As far as he could see, there was one entrance in the front and another one, where deliveries were made, on the side. He decided that the latter would be his point of entry.

Smurf crept to a side window and tried to get a good look into the structure. Through the dirty glass he could see Buck sitting behind a desk, watching a small television. As far as Smurf could tell, he was alone. He could climb right through the window and blow Buck's fuckin' brains out without worrying about witnesses.

Smurf crept to the side door and sighed. There was an alarm attached to the door. This was something he hadn't counted on, but he thought of a way to use it to his advantage. He pushed against the door, setting the alarm off, and then waited.

After a few moments, Buck poked his fat head out the door to investigate. His skin turned stark white at the sight of the youngster pointing a pistol at his dome. Smurf smiled at the big man, who looked as if he was about to pass out.

"Back yo' fat ass up," Smurf ordered.

Buck nodded and did as he was told.

Smurf followed him through the door and secured it behind them. "Guess the tables have turned, huh?"

Buck tried to keep a straight face, along with his composure, as he nodded, but his knees wouldn't stop shaking. He'd gotten a thrill out of savagely fucking Gloria and kicking the shit out of her kid, but it didn't seem worth it at that moment.

"Listen, boy," Buck pleaded. "I know you're angry, but—"

"Shut the fuck up!" Smurf ordered. "You don't know how I feel, so don't say another fuckin' word."

The more Smurf talked, the more unsteady his hand became. He had never held a gun up to somebody before, let alone used one. He was just as scared as he was angry. Smurf looked at Buck and saw that Buck was even more frightened than he was. The sniveling coward before him wasn't the same beast who had beaten a woman and her son.

"You ain't so muthafuckin' tough now, is you?" Smurf asked with an insane-looking grin. "You felt like a big man when you was hittin' on a woman and a kid, but now you ain't shit . . . fuckin' coward. Why you ain't popping that shit now?"

"I didn't mean it," Buck said, crying freely. "Shit just got out of hand. I was angry, man. I didn't mean to hurt you and your moms. I swear to God."

"You lyin' muthafucka!" Smurf scream[ed] ping Buck with the gun. Buck crumple[d] ground, holding the side of his head as poured from the wound. Karma was a bitch.

Seeing Buck humbled in such a way sent through Smurf. He was the only thing that s between Buck living and dying. He felt godlike sense. He felt a surge go from the back of his h and through his arm, before it eventually mo to his hand, which began to stiffen. Finally, powerful sensation spread to his finger.

The first shot hit Buck in his chest. Smurf trie gain control of his hand, but he couldn't. Whate evil lurked within the firearm possessed him. arm jerked over and over, filling Buck's body lead. Buck's screams mingled with the soun the barking gun, threatening to drive Smurf When it was all said and done, the only thin could be heard was the squeaking spring gun's hammer.

Smurf stared at Buck's bullet-ridd[en] and nearly threw up. He forced his din down long enough to admire his hand' was hit up real ugly, but it was a s for a man who'd done such ugly took a moment to spit on Buck' disappearing.

Chapter 3

Money, Cash, Hoes

"I need some loot," Lisa said, plopping down on the worn-out leather couch next to Nay-Nay.

Spring was on its way out the door, and summer was around the corner. All the girls were at Lisa's house, shooting the breeze, which was what they usually did when their pockets had the shorts. When a bitch didn't have money, all she had was conversation.

"I'm tired of sitting around this house, lookin' at you hoes," Lisa continued. "I wanna go out, but hell, I'm broke. I ain't heard from Dink in two days, so I can't even get nothing from him. I hate not having ends."

"You ain't never lied," Monique cosigned as she lounged in the beat-up leather recliner. "A sista's pockets are tight." She leaned forward and squeezed her hands down into the back pockets of her size eight jeans. She wore a size ten, if not a twelve, all day long, but she refused to buy clothes in the double digits.

Monique wasn't one of those chicks in denial about her weight. But she was one of those girls who thought that once she started buying big clothes, she'd get too comfortable in them. A little discomfort served as her motivation to lose weight. However, if she didn't hurry up and lose weight, she was going to end up with chronic yeast infections from wearing those tight-ass, coochie-cutter jeans. She wasn't fat—just plain ghetto-girl thick. She had pretty brown eyes that slanted slightly. Her eyes weren't hazel, but they were a couple of shades lighter than the average Black person's brown eyes. She was a pretty brown girl with long micro-braids, which she always wore in a ponytail down her back.

"Damn, I know all of us bitches ain't broke," Nay-Nay said in her authoritative voice. "Yo, Lisa, you ain't get no money from Dink?" she asked, putting her hands on her hips.

"Girrrl, did you not just hear me say that I ain't seen or heard from that nigga in two days?" Lisa rolled her eyes. "What about you?" she asked, flipping the question on Nay-Nay. "I know you juicin' Dame's hustling ass."

Nay-Nay twisted up her mug. "Lisa, you know Dame's scrooge ass," she said in disgust. "That nigga got me ridin' PT. And you know I can't stand the fucking bus."

"Well, all my extra money goes to my son," Shaunna said, jumping into the conversation as she entered the living room from the bathroom. She stuck her hands out and wriggled her fingers, implying that she hadn't even been able to get her nails done. She waved her tattered fingernails, trying to remember the last time she had had a manicure. That definitely wasn't like Shaunna, with her wannabe-diva attitude. She was very pretty, with fair skin and long jet-black hair. She sort of resembled Alicia Keys, as she always maintained a fancy braided hairstyle. Shaunna had kept her hair in long braids ever since middle school. They had become her trademark—like Alicia's.

Coming up, Shaunna Parker had never had it easy. Her mother and father had died in a car accident, leaving her to be raised by an uncaring grandmother, her father's mother. Shaunna's grandmother had never approved of her father's choice for a wife. This was something that she had taken out on Shaunna regularly. As Shaunna had got older, so had her grandmother. The old woman had eventually become sickly and had had to loosen the noose on Shaunna. As a young girl, she had always secretly had a fascination with the streets, but now she would be able to run free in them. Get up close and personal with them. With a crew of equally anxious girls behind her, Shaunna had stepped onto the stage.

Shaunna and her team made it their business to be at all the hot spots, parties, clubs, and events. Quite a few hustlers always wanted a taste of the pretty, young, thicky thick girl from around the way. Shaunna made sure that nearly all of them got a sample of what she had to offer, but only if their paper was long enough. Dealing with these hustlers and pimps, she had acquired a taste for the finer things in life.

Shaunna thought that by the way she was moving, she was gaining popularity and prestige, but she was really developing a reputation. After most of the dough getters in Queens, as well as ballers from other hoods, had knocked the bottom out of young Shaunna's pussy, she had become old news to them. Like most of the other fresh faces, Shaunna's had become one of many. By the time Shaunna had turned sixteen, she'd found herself pregnant and jobless, with no education.

"And any other dime I get," Shaunna continued, sitting down on the love seat next to Laci, "is going to go on shit for this new baby." She rubbed her pregnant belly; she was six months along.

"And that's exactly why you should have your own money," Laci said matter-of-factly. Her big brown eyes swept the room as she looked for one of the girls to back her statement.

Laci had always been athletic, and her shapely build made that apparent. She'd run track up until high school. She had always been very outgoing, and she had sung in the choir and been a member of the drama club. By the time Laci entered the ninth grade, all of that had changed. She had been burnt out and thus had chosen to focus solely on her academics.

"Bitch, please. You get all your money from Mommy and Daddy!" Monique snapped, not appreciating how Laci was pretty much calling them birds. When Monique became angry or animated about something, her large nostrils flared. With her flat, round face, this gave her the appearance of a bull. "Don't even try to front like you do for self. I hate it when you do that shit, Laci. We ain't all got parents feedin' us money like you do."

"Monique's right," Shaunna said to Laci, poking out her lips and bobbing her neck. "You always tryin' to make us feel like we nobodies. Like we just some fuckin' squirrels runnin' around in your goddamned world, trying to get a nut."

Laci sat there with a puzzled look on her face. For the life of her, she couldn't figure out why the girls acted like they adored her at times but then turned around and showed her nothing but contempt and jealousy. This hurt Laci, but for some strange reason, she loved them. Being an only child, she viewed these girls as the siblings she had never had. Laci felt that maybe this was what it was like to have sisters: liking each other one minute, then fighting the next. And she figured that whatever it was about a person that made people love them was also the same thing that made people hate them.

It was no secret that Laci was definitely the most fly one in the clique and would probably be considered the prettiest. Guys always tended to holla at Laci first, not only because she had a sophisticated, good-girl aura about her, but also because she was the only one out of the crew who didn't have a known reputation.

"You know what, Laci? Forget about your parents," Lisa said, standing up and walking over to her. "What I really want to know is, How come I ain't never seen you with no dudes? You don't even *talk* about no dudes, and when they try to holla at you, you never holla back." Puckering her lips, she got right up in Laci's face, as if she was conducting an interview. "What's up with that?" she asked.

Once one person started in on Laci, it was an open invitation for the others to join in. But surprisingly, Monique came to Laci's defense.

"Lisa," Monique said with a disapproving look on her face.

"Lisa, nothing," Lisa replied, rolling her eyes. "Don't act like y'all ain't never thought about it, either." She turned her attention back to Laci. "So, tell us, if you don't like dudes, then what *is* your flavor?" Lisa tauntingly twirled one of Laci's curls around her finger.

"I'm more of a private person—" Laci said, grabbing her curl from Lisa's fingers and turning away.

"What you mean, *private*?" Nay-Nay said quickly, cutting in, as she glared at Laci.

"She means she's a down-low ho," Lisa said. She and the rest of the girls began to laugh. Lisa went and sat back down.

Not finding a damn thing funny, Laci responded, "Private, you know? I don't put my business all out in the streets. It's not ladylike to be running around spreading news about what you do. That's how girls get reputations."

"So what the fuck you trying to say?" Shaunna said, taking offense. "You trying to say we got reps?"

"Yeah," Lisa said, jumping in without hesitation. "Say the shit."

"You sayin' we ain't ladies?" Shaunna asked with major attitude.

"No, Shaunna," Laci said, enunciating Shaunna's name. "Lisa asked me a question, and I answered it."

Lisa folded her arms, ran her tongue along her lower teeth, and looked over at Nay-Nay. She had a "Should we let this shit ride?" look on her face.

Nay-Nay nodded her head in the affirmative. It was better to fall back for a minute, before shit really got out of hand, like the last time.

A few months earlier, Nay-Nay had had to hold Lisa down to keep her from going off on Laci. Laci had said something that Lisa took as being fly and threatened to cut every last curl off Laci' head.

Laci sat there now, with the same puzzled look on her face she always displayed when the girls were tripping on her. Lisa felt as though Laci was in no way threatened by her actions, like she didn't take her seriously. It was Laci's nonconfrontational approach that pissed Lisa off the most. Lisa always brought the drama, and Laci was a naturally laid-back chick. Laci believed that acting the fool only made people look bad. Lisa was right. Laci paid her no mind. She never even flinched at Lisa's bullying tactics. And that definitely made Lisa feel pissed and powerless at the same time.

Suddenly, Lisa got up and walked into the kitchen. She returned with a pair of scissors in her hand. She charged at Laci like a bat out of hell. Laci didn't attempt to defend herself, and she didn't run, either. She just sat there like she was Stevie Wonder and couldn't see the shit coming. Lucky for her, Nay-Nay cut in front of Lisa and grabbed her by the wrist. Nine times out of ten, Lisa wouldn't do shit. She knew damn well that her girls weren't about to just sit there and let her take a pair of scissors to Laci's head, at least Nay-Nay wasn't, anyway. Everybody else sat there, waiting to see some curls flying. But nobody got one off on anybody else unless Nay-Nay was beefing with them, too, or gave the okay.

"This shit is crazy," Shaunna said, looking over at Laci. "This ain't even about you, Laci. Let's keep it real. This shit is about us being a group of young, fine, broke-ass females."

"Uh-huh," Monique cosigned, nodding.

"What's the deal with the so-called men in our lives?" Shaunna continued. "We mad at Laci 'cause she ain't dealing with none of these sorry niggas around here. They quick to take some ass but slow on givin' cash. Fuck that!"

"They ain't shit," Nay-Nay said, getting half-way up off the couch. She reached out and gave Shaunna a high five.

"Most of these niggas ain't worth the sperm it took to get 'em here," Monique added. "It's all well and good when they're cracking for the pussy, but when a sista asks for some paper, they start acting all crazy."

"But at the end of the day," Nay-Nay said in a serious tone, "we the ones fuckin' *loco*. We crazy for lettin' them fools get away with it. Them niggas ain't gon' do no more than we allow them to."

"They still triflin'," Monique said, rolling her eyes.

"Yeah, but some of them make up for it in other ways," Lisa said, winking, with a sly grin on her face.

Nay-Nay sighed. "There you go, thinking with that stankin' pussy of yours again," she said, faking disgust. "Bitch, your whole life revolves around gettin' fucked. I don't even know why you call yourself having Dink as your man. Everybody know you ain't no one-nigga ho."

"Nay-Nay, you need to quit frontin', actin' like you some goddamned Virgin Mary or some shit," Lisa retorted. "Your pussy is just as raggedy as the rest of ours."

Monique and Shaunna snickered.

"It ain't my fault that the sorry-ass niggas y'all fuck wit ain't puttin' it down," Lisa said, adjusting her breasts. "No, Dink ain't the best dick I ever had, but he's my man, and he pleases me every time."

"Please," Shaunna said, snaking her neck. "My son's father had that good wood, but that don't mean his ass is off the hook financially. Like home-boy said in that movie, 'Fuck you. Pay me.'"

All the girls fell out laughing at Shaunna's crazy ass. Shaunna was the oddball of the posse. She was always saying or doing something that would make people ask, "What the fuck?" Shaunna was big boned. She was a little bigger than Monique but shapelier, which made her very sexy. And she had a sexy attitude to match. She simply seemed to breathe sex. Shaunna wore a 46 DD bra and still managed to rock a matching thong on her big ass. She would give the average skinny bitch a run for her money any day.

"Dink ain't the biggest baller, but his pockets stay laced. You hoes can pop all the shit y'all want to," Lisa said, folding her arms. "A nigga wit deep pockets is worth his weight, but a nigga wit a deep stroke is priceless."

"Let you tell it," Laci mumbled in disagreement. But who was she to talk. She'd never even worn a tampon during that time of the month, let alone let a dick up in her. If Laci's parents had taught her anything at all, it was to respect herself and, more importantly, her body. She took heed of their words.

"I'm wit cha on that one, Laci," Monique said. "I can't see no dick being worth more than money."

"That's because you ain't had the right dick," Lisa stated. "I can remember this one dude . . ." Lisa began fanning her private area. "Mercy, mercy me!"

"Shit, don't stop there," Nay-Nay said, turned on by all the talk about dick. "Do tell."

"Go 'head wit that." Lisa blushed. "Don't nobody wanna hear my slide story."

"Bullshit," Shaunna said, sitting up to pay better attention. "Go ahead, Lisa. Tell us about this so-called stud of yours."

"Yeah," Monique added. "Shit, now I wanna hear about it too."

By now, all the girls, with the exception of Laci, were on the edge of their wet seats in anticipation of Lisa's sex tale.

"All of y'all nasty." Laci giggled. "Telling fuck stories and all."

"Bitch, please," Shaunna said, then sucked her teeth. "You probably got more *private* fuck stories than any of us. Wit yo' prep-school ass."

Shaunna couldn't have been any further from the truth. Laci was as fresh as a cherry on the tree. As a matter of fact, hers had never even been picked.

"I do not," Laci said defensively.

"Don't even front, ho," Monique said, twisting up her lips. "Come on, tell the truth, Laci. You a closet freak, ain't you, Ma? Come on, girl. I know you be around a lot of them young niggas with cake at ya parents' little jump-offs, so just go on and tell it."

Laci gave Monique a blank stare. "Whatever," Laci said, not falling into Monique's trap. Monique was provoking her to say something, even if it was a lie, but Laci wasn't falling for it.

"So, what up, Lisa?" Nay-Nay said, eagerly to get back on the subject. "Ain't nobody forgot about your ass. Get to tellin' the story, you little griot."

"Damn," Lisa said with a smirk. "You all up in my mix." She paused, and a mischievous grin covered her face. "Okay already. I'll tell the story, since y'all ain't gon' let a ho be."

The vibe at Lisa's house started to change, and everyone looked as if they were all digging into their memory bank to pull out something wild to follow up her story with. They all had had experiences, some more erotic than others, that made their kittens purr. And for some, it was nothing more than a perfectly planted kiss in just the right spot. But they all had them, nonetheless.

"And we want full, explicit details," Shaunna said, rubbing her stomach. She always enjoyed Lisa's fuck stories, and Lisa enjoyed fucking in order to provide them. Lisa had plenty of them to cure Shaunna's appetite. She might as well have had a tattoo drawn underneath her belly button, with an arrow pointing downward that read ENTER HERE. It seemed as though every nigga who winked at her eventually found his way there.

Most of the other girls enjoyed Lisa's sex tales, as well, but Shaunna was one of those chicks who really got off on listening to other people's sexual encounters. There was no shame in her game when it came to the flesh. The stories were inspirational and motivational, giving her ideas and perhaps a few tips when it came to her own sexual endeavors.

Even though Lisa did a lot of fucking, Shaunna was still probably the most sexually liberated woman in the group. Shaunna would swing episodes with men or women, depending on her mood. And Laci lived vicariously through all the girls.

"A'ight, a'ight," Lisa said, then began her story. "His name was Maurice."

"Maurice!" everyone yelled in unison.

"Maurice? What kind of name is that?" Monique asked. "I thought you was gonna say something like Chico or Bang or something."

"You know," Shaunna said, "I'm trying to hear some thug passion. He ain't have no street name?"

"Shhh. Just let her tell her story," Nay-Nay ordered.

"Yeah," Laci added, forgetting that she wasn't supposed to be interested in such conversations.

"Now, if there are no further interruptions . . . ," Lisa declared before clearing her throat. "I hadn't seen Maurice in a hot minute when I ran into him at the store. I was in the back, getting a two-liter, and he was copping some brew. My pussy got wet at just the sight of him. He and I had kicked it a few times, but the last time I had kicked it with him and we were about to fuck, his pager went off. It read nine-one-one. He jumped up and said that he had to go take care of some urgent business. He was pissed 'cause he had eaten my pussy out and everything and was just waiting on his payback. But, anyway, the next time we bumped heads, we were still feeling each other. The fact that we got to see each other in spurts only made it worse. See, Maurice was married."

"Lisa, you messed with a married man?" Laci asked, shocked.

"Damn right," Lisa answered. "I looked at his dick, and it didn't have nobody's name on it, so I said, 'Fuck it.' Then that's exactly what I did."

The girls laughed at Lisa's pun.

"You know," Monique said, reaching over and giving Lisa a high five.

"Besides," Lisa said, "it wasn't my fault that his wife's shit wasn't tight. Plus, Maurice had that good dick. That's why I was just as pissed as he was that we didn't get to finish up where we had left off. I knew how good that nigga could handle his little dude, or should I say *big dude*? Girrrl, I had lust in my eyes and larceny in my heart. The two of us were horny just thinkin' 'bout it. We didn't even waste time trying to find a hotel."

"You didn't fuck him in that store?" Shaunna asked, with her mouth open.

"Girl, no," Lisa said. "Not that I wouldn't have. That nigga could have slammed me up against the cooler door and fucked the shit out of me, leaving my ass print on the glass for days."

"I heard that shit," Monique said, crossing her legs, trying to hide her throbbing clit, which she felt everybody could see.

"He drove me to the field," Lisa continued, with a smile on her face, as she thought about her and Maurice handling their business in broad daylight on a piece of unoccupied land. "That nigga massaged my pussy the whole way there. I could see his dude 'bout to burst out of his pants. His shit was rock hard and bulged in his jeans. Now, I know why niggas startin' to bust sags with they jeans." Lisa wiggled her ass into a more comfortable position as she continued. "Once we parked, he got a blanket from the back of his Blazer, and we walked over to the middle of the field. Maurice laid the blanket out, sat down, and pulled me down next to him." Lisa paused to fan herself with her hand.

"Come on, bitch," Nay-Nay said playfully. "Finish the damn story already."

"You know," Shaunna said, sighing, "I don't know about any of y'all, but this shit is making me . . . ooh!" Shaunna moaned and rubbed her inner thighs. Every time the girls talked about sex, Shaunna got excited. On a couple of occasions, she had actually slid her hand down inside her panties and taken care of herself with them sitting right there.

"How you over there horny, with your pregnant self?" Laci asked jokingly.

"Girl, pregnant chicks like to fuck too," Shaunna said, with an "I thought you knew" look on her face. "Pregnant pussy is the best. This shit be ripe."

"Let her finish," Monique said, putting her index finger over her lips. Everyone drew their attention back to Lisa.

"I was wearing this cute little one-piece denim dress, and I just lifted it up above my hips. Maurice got in front of me, spread my legs, and pushed my panties to the side. That nigga didn't waste time trying to taste it first. I was so wet that you could hear my pussy talking to him when he touched it with the tip of his dick. The tip alone damn near plugged me up. I kid you not when I say homeboy was packin'. His daddy had to be a horse," Lisa said, not realizing that she was squirming.

She went on. "I wanted to just fuckin' melt when he started teasing me with the head. He took it easy at first. He knew he was packin', and he had probably beaten up many a pussy. Then he plunged that monster shit as far as it could go. That nigga's dick almost split me clear to my ass."

"I know that hurt," Shaunna said, remembering the labor of her son and how his head bursting out of her pussy had felt.

"He entered my pussy with that big-ass dick in one stroke, but I took it all in like a real bitch," Lisa said proudly. "I squirted so hard that I thought I was going to faint."

"You lying," Laci said in disbelief.

"I wish I was, Laci," Lisa said. "I was a two-minute sister, please believe it. But unlike a minuteman, I wanted, and was good and ready for, some more."

"So did you fuck him again?" Shaunna asked eagerly.

"Please believe it," Lisa said, rolling her eyes. "Maurice turned me over onto my stomach, clamped his hands onto my shoulders, and tried to wire my shit from the back. That nigga was like a lion in the jungle, just walking up to a lioness and fuckin' her wild. The sound of his body smacking against mine as he fucked me sounded like he was beating the shit out of me."

"He was," Nay-Nay laughed. "He was beatin' that pussy up."

"Okay," Lisa agreed. "He literally fucked tears out of my eyes. When he finally busted a nut, that nigga's dick jerked off inside me like a loose water hose from a fire truck. He came all up inside me. After he busted, he fell out in typical nigga fashion."

The girls sighed and relaxed their bodies, which had been so tense with ecstasy.

"That was a'ight," Shaunna said, yawning, "but I don't see the originality of the story."

"That ain't the end." Lisa smiled. "That was only the climax—literally. Now I need to bring y'all down slowly off the high."

"Go ahead, then," Shaunna said anxiously.

"I stood to straighten myself up, and I noticed that we weren't alone," Lisa said.

"Oh no," Laci said, putting her hand over her mouth. "It was his wife, wasn't it?"

"Will you let me tell the damn story, please?" Lisa said, putting her hands on her hips. "No, it wasn't his wife. Anyway, a car was parked a few yards away. Once I focused, I realized that it was a fuckin' state trooper. His ass had been watching the whole thing."

"Shit. Did he lock y'all up?" Laci asked, now more interested in the legalities of the story then the sex episode itself.

"He threatened to but decided to take a trade instead." Lisa smiled and ran her tongue across her top lip. "I sucked his dick like a porn star, even jerked his shit off on my face. Need I say that he let us walk?" Lisa wiped her hands as if she had just taken out the trash.

"Lisa, you's a crazy ho," Nay-Nay said, laughing. "You always set things off right. However, I'm gon' bring it up a notch. I hope y'all ready for this one."

What had started as one person telling a story turned into a contest. Each girl searched her memory for the wildest sexual experience she had ever had, trying to outdo the others.

"Tell your story already, then, Nay-Nay. Stray talk fucks up the mood," Shaunna said, taking their sex-talk session dead serious. At the end of the day, she didn't care if one of the girls exaggerated her story or not, just as long as her pussy got wet.

"Whatever," Nay-Nay said to Shaunna, waving her off. "Now, me and my ex, Gary . . . Y'all remember Gary, right?"

Shaunna sighed and gave Nay-Nay the look of the devil. Taking her cue, Nay-Nay continued.

"Gary and I were going through the motions. I was tired of his dog ass and decided to be rid of him, good dick and all. Even the best bitch has her breaking point, so I packed up the few things of his that he had at my place and told him to come get his shit. I was taking a shower when he rolled through. He had been out there knocking for a minute by the time I heard him. When I did realize that I heard someone knocking, I turned the water off to make sure. Lo and behold, by now he was knocking like the police, yelling, 'It's Gary. Open the damn door.'

"I hurried up and got out of the shower to answer the door and let him in—soaking wet. When I opened it, he was standing there with two of his friends, and both of them looked good as hell, especially Spanish Lou. There I was in the doorway, wrapped in a skimpy pink terry-cloth towel. Nipples were hard as hell from the cool breeze that hit me while running through the house to get to the door. I let them in and went back into the bathroom to finish my shower.

"A couple of minutes into lathering up my body, Gary walked in the bathroom naked. He had this puppy-dog look on his face and asked me if he could join me, wash my back one last time. I never could resist Gary's sexy ass. He was standing there, dick swangin', looking like a chocolate God. I kept imagining his shit as a Snickers bar and me being high with the munchies. I opened the shower door for him, letting him know that one last time was cool. Once he stepped in and the water started pounding on his brown skin, he didn't have to say two words before I was down on my knees."

"Nasty," Laci mumbled.

"Shut up and let her finish," Shaunna snapped.

"Gary took one hand and grabbed me by the back of my head." Nay-Nay gasped. "While I sucked fire out of his dick, he fucked my mouth until we had a nice little rhythm going on. I could feel his hands clutching my head like it was his favorite bowling ball. I continued pleasing him."

"That's my bitch," Monique said proudly.

"I had that nigga's knees about to buckle. I didn't want him to cum yet, so I stood up and start tonguing him down. His hands were all over me," Nay-Nay said, closing her eyes and rubbing her hands down her body. "He wanted to fuck me right there in the shower, but I knew we were about to get buck wild with the breakup sex, so I led him to my bed. He was lickin' me up and down like I was a melting Bomb Pop. All I could do was lay there with my eyes closed and let him use my body as his playground. You know what I'm saying?"

The girls nodded.

"And then, out of nowhere," Nay-Nay said, opening her eyes, "I felt another set of hands on my ass. I sat up so fucking quick. When I turned around, Spanish Lou was glaring down at me, stroking his rod. At first, I was fittin' to clown, but his shit was looking on point. He had this look in his eye like he knew."

"Knew what?" Laci said out of pure curiosity.

"Knew what I had told Gary," Nay-Nay answered, staring off into space, as if she could see it all going down right before her very eyes.

"Told Gary what?" all the girls yelled at once.

"About my threesome fantasy," Nay-Nay answered sharply, as if they should have already known. "One time we were telling each other our sexual fantasies, and I told him that I wanted to have a threesome with two guys. He said that if we ever did, it would have to be with one of his boys. He asked me which one of his boys I would want to get down with and, of course, a bitch said Spanish Lou."

"So did your fantasy come true?" Lisa asked.

Nay-Nay gave her a "What the fuck do you think?" stare. "Hell yeah," Nay-Nay said. "Once Gary and Spanish Lou saw that I was down, Gary laid down on the bed and started stroking his dick. That was my sign to finish what I had started in the bathroom. I got on all four and proceeded to bob for dick. Spanish Lou climbed on the bed behind me and started drilling away at my pussy. The shit was so in sync. When I went down on Gary's dick, Spanish Lou was plunging inside me. When I slid back up off of Gary's dick, I threw that ass back at Spanish Lou."

Nay-Nay went on. "All you heard was slurpin', smackin', and just pure wetness. I got so caught up with all the moaning and whining and carrying on, I didn't realize it was my ass making all that noise. I had never felt that good in my life. My moaning turned them niggas on so much that the more I moaned, the more they put their pelvis into it. The next thing I knew, Gary was exploding in my mouth. And I let out one last whine as I came all on Spanish Lou's dick. A bitch was so caught up that I swallowed." She licked her lips in delight. "Damn, Gary tasted good."

"Shit, I'm thirsty now," Shaunna said, then smacked her lips.

"Gary closed his eyes and had a big-ass Kool-Aid grin on his face. I was still on all fours over him as Spanish Lou continued pounding away," Nay-Nay added.

Lisa squirmed and moaned. "Damn, he was hitting that shit like that?"

"Girl, yes," Nay-Nay answered. "Spanish Lou had the blueprint to my shit. When he pushed my ass cheeks up, his dick slid even further into my stomach. That shit hurt, but it hurt good as fuck."

"Do you mean you really felt him in your stomach?" Laci asked in amazement.

"Spanish Lou went deep." Nay-Nay moaned at the memory.

Laci rested her hand on her tummy and imagined what it felt like to be penetrated by someone who really had the goods.

"Spanish Lou had this thing," Nay-Nay added. "When he made a bitch cum, he wanted to see the look on her face. That nigga spun me over onto my back, put one hand on the bed and one hand around my neck, and just start pounding like I had done him wrong. I grabbed at his hand with both of mine as he tightened his grip around my neck. I don't know. There was something about the pressure that heightened the sensitivity of him being inside me.

"He looked into my eyes and started kissing me passionately and deeply. You know, most niggas don't like to kiss a chick if she ain't their top bitch, but we were into it. I swear, I came four times, and he was still stiff as hell, with no intentions of going soft. My eyes shed tears. My mouth drooled. My nose ran. My pussy dripped. Gary was upstaged by his own boy. That nigga was up at the corner of the bed jacking off, bustin' nuts down his thigh. That's how heated the shit was. Now, deal with that!" Nay-Nay crossed her legs and rolled her eyes.

"Nay-Nay, I have to admit, sometimes your stories aren't that good," Monique said, shaking her head, "but that Spanish Lou shit . . . whew!"

All the girls, except for Shaunna, who didn't feel like waddling up, high-fived Nay-Nay. Lisa gave her props for her encounter. Laci sat back and watched the girls. Laci never talked about sex with the girls. She was the quiet one, the less experienced one, and never felt like any adventure she had to share could compete with what the girls had going on. She never had a desire to talk to them on an intimate level. After listening to them air their dirty laundry, though, Laci felt the sense of sisterhood that had been missing in her life.

"Excuse me. Hey," Laci said softly.

The girls were still too busy giving Nay-Nay props for her threesome, so none of them paid Laci any mind.

"Excuse me. Hey," Laci repeated in a louder tone.

"Wasssup, Ma?" Nay-Nay said after everyone had fallen silent to see what Laci had to say.

Laci smiled and put her head down. She bit down on her lip, then looked up at the girls. "That Spanish Lou story makes me want to finally open up to you guys and tell you my stuff."

Every last girl had their full attention on Laci. She couldn't get any more excited about all the attention being on her. In that moment she was the most comfortable that she had ever been with her friends.

"Well, go ahead, Miss I'm Private and Ladylike," Lisa teased. "Open up that closet and let out some of those skeletons, Laci. I know you got a grave-yard."

Laci got up from the love seat and went and sat in the middle of the living room floor, next to the glass coffee table. She plopped down Indian-style and proceeded with her tale.

"All right, are you guys ready?" Laci wanted to make sure everyone was listening. It was like she was going to tell the story only once, and if they missed it, they missed it.

"I'm on the verge of cummin' in my maternity drawers," Shaunna said, stretching out. "Laci, I hope your story does it for me."

Laci cleared her throat. "I had fallen asleep on the couch at Mark's house."

"Mark?" Monique asked. "Who the fuck is Mark?"

"Just let her tell the goddamned story before you fuck up my nut now. Shit," Shaunna's nasty ass said.

Laci continued, "Mark woke me up by eating me out. He flicked his tongue across my clit, blowing it up to the size of a marble. I had never felt that kind of tingling in my body. Mark sent me there."

Laci appeared to be in la-la land. Every girl's face wore the same look of surprise. Laci had never spoken like this before. As Laci told her story, for the first time she felt like she was being fully accepted by the girls. It motivated her to continue.

"After Mark made me cum," Laci said, "I played with his dick until it got good and swollen. I teased him by just licking on the head, but not letting him inside me. He pleaded, but I still wouldn't take him."

"That's right, girl. Make that nigga beg," Monique said, leaning over toward Laci to give her a high five.

"When Mark's eyes began brimming with tears," Laci said, "I finally gobbled him up. He was surprised at how much muscle control I had. I opened my throat and took all of him. Now, Mark wasn't very thick, but he was long as hell. I felt like gagging, but I held it down." Laci paused, making sure the girls were still into her story. "I didn't want him to cum in my mouth, so I ended up jumping on top of him in a straddling position and placing him inside me. He grabbed my ass while he humped me back. I started to lose my mind."

"Ride that dick, Miss Prissy," Nay-Nay chimed in enthusiastically, grinding her hips.

Laci smiled and continued. "I came so hard and fast, it felt like someone kicked it out of me. Things just got harder and more violent. He smacked me on the side of my ass—not hard enough to hurt me, but hard enough to make my clit jump. The pain felt so good that I screamed out, 'Hit me harder.' The sound of him smacking my ass pushed me over the edge. That was the first time I had ever cum, merely by the sound of my ass getting smacked."

Monique pretended to wipe a tear from the corner of her eye. For the first time, she was proud of Laci's yellow ass.

Laci could see the excitement in the girls' eyes as she told the story. She couldn't stop there.

"This is kind of embarrassing," Laci said, "but the sensation made me erupt and, strangely, start to urinate at the same time. I could've died from embarrassment, but Mark seemed to get more turned on." At this point in the story, Lisa twisted her lips up and had a look of disbelief on her face. She knew that no matter how hard she had tried to piss during penetration, the piss didn't come out.

Laci went on telling the story, caught up in her own drama. She was on the edge of her seat, eager to find out what in the hell was going to come out of her mouth next. "He told me to stand up and let my pee run all over his body," Laci said, shrugging her shoulders, embarrassed that she was even telling the girls this kind of stuff. "Mark started to squirm and moan under the stream of piss. He gulped and blew his wad all over the place. He loved it."

Laci had the girls' undivided attention. At first, her story had had all the girls horny, but then it had got weird. Now Laci had eight pairs of eyes on her that never once lost focus.

She felt compelled to proceed. "So I wiped him off with a towel, and then he threw me on the floor and pushed my legs back to my ears. I lay there, helpless, while Mark dug into my guts. Then, oh my God, he started hitting a spot that I didn't even know I had. I started screaming at the top of my lungs. He knew he was tearing it up, and that excited him so much that he erupted inside me. He then just rolled off me and fell out. Me being naive, I thought he had passed out. Hell, I thought he might have had a heart attack or something. "I started whispering his name. I wanted to tell him how good he had made me feel, but he wouldn't respond. I started nudging him, and he wouldn't budge. Fear set in, and I sat up and started rubbing him on his chest while continuing to call his name. Still, he didn't move," Laci said, with such intensity, as if she was reading one of Stephen King's novels to the girls.

"His body didn't feel right," she continued. "I began to get nervous, so I checked him for a pulse. Nothing. Mark had died in the pussy. It wasn't until later that I found out he had a bad heart. See, he had been born with some crazy heart condition." She paused for a moment. "You know what I mean," Laci said in a tone that sounded as if she might be trying to convince herself and not just the girls.

For a few moments, the room was silent. The girls just sat there looking at each other. Then they looked at Laci. For the first time, these bitches were speechless. It took everything inside Laci not to burst out laughing, but then she couldn't hold it in any longer. Out of nowhere she started laughing uncontrollably.

"You lying bitch," Monique said as she began to chuckle.

"What?" Laci said, still laughing, but acting like she had no idea what Monique was talking about.

"I don't believe you just fucked up my nut like that," Shaunna said, trying to hold back her laughter. She let a slight chuckle slip out. "Hell, you actually fucked me up once you started talking about a dead muthafucka. I ain't into hearing about fucking a dead corpse and all."

The girls all started laughing.

"I'll admit," Lisa said, "Laci, you had me with you in the beginning. You even had me at the golden shower part, but you's a lying ho. You know damn well you made all that shit up."

"Gotcha!" Laci said, pointing.

Nay-Nay picked up one of the pillows from off the couch and threw it at Laci. "I can't believe you," she said. "Had us all caught up. Somebody else could have been talkin' 'bout some real shit."

"You know," Lisa added, "real bitches do real shit."

"My bad, ladies," Laci apologized after she got her laughter under control. "I wanted to be a part of the storytelling for once."

Monique was fed up. "I don't know 'bout y'all hoes, but she ruined the sex shit for me."

"Ditto," Shaunna agreed. "You got some food up in your kitchen, Lisa? My baby is hungry."

"Bitch, *your* fat ass is hungry," Lisa said jokingly. "That baby don't know what the fuck food is."

"I ain't pregnant, but I'm eating for two, anyway," Monique said as she stood up and stretched out. "What you got to whip up?"

"I don't know," Lisa said, getting up off the couch. "Come into the kitchen and see what you have a taste for."

All the girls followed Lisa into the kitchen.

"What's up for the summer?" Monique asked no one in particular as they entered the kitchen.

All the girls looked at each other but said nothing.

Monique tried again. "Let's not all answer at the same time," she said sarcastically. "No one has any plans? Nay-Nay, what about you?"

"I ain't really got anything planned," Nay-Nay said, shrugging her shoulders. "Hell, I'm living just enough. You know how I get down. I play it on a daily. I was thinking about maybe trying to take some classes for that stupid-ass GED again."

"Evidently, it ain't the GED that's stupid," Laci said, hoping to make a cute joke. She instantly wished she could take it back once she saw Nay-Nay's reaction.

Nay-Nay stopped in her tracks. What she wanted to do was haul off and slap the shit out of Laci, hell, maybe even take one of them butcher knives from the block in Lisa's kitchen and cut her fuckin' throat. But something told her to let it go, so she did. She looked at Laci and forced a fake grin. "Ha ha. That was real funny, Laci."

Lisa rolled her eyes at Laci, shook her head, and opened the refrigerator door.

"Sorry," Laci said, putting her head down. "I was just kidding. You know I would never come at you like that."

"Yeah, I know," Nay-Nay said insincerely. But she let it go . . . for now, anyway. "Lisa," Nay-Nay said, moving on, "what about you? What you got going on for the summer?"

"You know I just want to chill," Lisa answered as she examined the contents of the refrigerator. "But I'm also thinking about summer school. Maybe there won't be as many guys as there were in high school to distract me." Lisa closed the refrigerator door and opened the freezer.

Monique interjected, "Well, I don't have to worry about a GED, high school diploma, or none of that. I gots my high school certificate of completion."

"You mean attendance, don't you?" Shaunna said jokingly. "You got a certificate for just showing up every day."

"You stupid," Monique said. "I got my high school diploma. I passed the son of a bitch with flying D minuses." The girls started laughing. "But seriously, if y'all hoes gon' be all caught up wit gettin' an *edumacation*, then maybe I should do the community college thing. Lisa, you trying to go to college someday?"

"Nah, I just want my diploma," Lisa said with a shrug. "Dink said if I get it, he gon' take me out to celebrate anywhere I want to go. You know I'm trying to go to that fancy-ass steak house downtown. Y'all know the one with valet parking and shit."

"I know you glad you got him," Shaunna said. "He be takin' care of you. That's why I don't know why you ever crying broke. You know all you got to do is ask that nigga to hold something, and you straight."

"I know," Lisa said, pulling out a frozen pizza from the freezer. "I don't like to always have my hand out. Niggas get tired real quick of a beggin' bitch. If he don't give it to me on his own, I usually only ask him when I really, *really* need to hold something. But not once has he not come through for me."

"I wish I had a muthafucka holdin' me down like that," Shaunna said, reflecting on her own situation. "I wish I'd done my thing in school, instead of poppin' babies out by no-good niggas. Seems like you can't do shit without a diploma."

"Fuck that," Nay-Nay mumbled, sounding frustrated. "If I get it, I get it. That shit don't hold no weight for Black folks, anyhow. Once you get a diploma or GED, muthafuckas start talking about you need a bachelor's degree to make some real paper. Then the next thing you know, that ain't even good enough. Now you need a master's degree. The system ain't built to work for us."

"Got a point there." Monique nodded. "I mean, I think I wanna go to college, but who the hell wants to sit through another four years of school? That shit ain't gon' get me no paper. I should probably just get a job and say, 'Fuck it.' I need a Fourth of July outfit and a new leather jacket."

Laci looked at her friends and shook her head. Monique had no job experience and didn't have the temperament to work for anyone. Besides that, she had too much pride to apply at the places where she was qualified to work. There was no way she was going to fill out an application anywhere.

"You awful quiet over there," Lisa said to Laci as she put the pizza in the oven.

"We already know that bitch probably gon' die in school." Monique laughed. "She's probably going to be one of those career students who as long as they stay in school, Mommy and Daddy will flip the bills."

Laci ignored the comments and said nothing.

"I don't know what I'm gon' do aside from have this baby," Shaunna commented, looking down at her stomach. "I know someone in housing, and they supposed to hook me up with a two-bedroom apartment. Hopefully, by the time the baby comes, I'll have more space. But y'all know how the system works." Shaunna sighed and rubbed her stomach.

The girls stood there staring at her, feeling her pain.

"Y'all want some red Kool-Aid while the pizza cooks?" Lisa asked to break the monotony.

The girls all nodded or mumbled yes.

Laci addressed Shaunna. "Do you know what you're having?" she asked, still trying to dodge the college bullet, but at the same time, feeling concerned about Shaunna.

Shaunna's face lit up. "No, I want to be surprised." She smiled. "I already have a boy, so it would be nice to have a girl. But only God knows."

Laci walked over to Shaunna and held her hand up to her stomach. "Can I?" she asked, exercising caution.

"Yeah, go ahead," Shaunna said with surprise in her voice. None of the girls had ever seemed to want to vibe with the little life inside her.

Laci placed her hand on the center of Shaunna's belly and pressed softly. It was an amazing feeling to Laci. Shaunna's belly was as hard as a rock, and she could really feel the baby. It was surreal.

"Who's the father?" Laci asked innocently.

It was like a record started to skip and the DJ snatched the needle off. There was dead silence. Shaunna disregarded Laci's question and asked one of her own.

"What about you, Laci?" Shaunna said, removing Laci's hand from her stomach and walking over to the snack table to retrieve her drink. The other girls followed her lead. "What are you getting into this summer?"

Laci's inquisitiveness had set her up for the fall. She didn't know how to answer the question without starting an argument. For some reason, she could never get shit right. She always managed to say the wrong thing. If she told the truth, the girls were going to start trippin' on her. If she didn't tell the truth, they'd know. Those bitches were like Superman when it came to Laci; they could see right through her. Her lying to them would only piss them off even more.

"Uh, nothing much. Just going to Puerto Rico before I leave for school," Laci said nonchalantly, as if traveling out of the country was no big deal, despite the fact that most of the girls had barely traveled out of their own neighborhood, let alone the country.

Lisa wasn't about to let Laci get off so easy. "Oh, so little Miss Thing's parents are paying to broaden her education?" Lisa said. She batted her eyes and puckered her lips. "Figured as much. Too bad the rest of us don't have caked-up parents."

"I got a scholarship," Laci said, shutting Lisa up. "*I* got this—not my parents."

"Scholarship?" Monique asked, confused. "You ain't no athlete. I ain't never known you to play ball, run track, or nothing."

Laci shook her head. "I received an academic scholarship," she said slowly, as if she were talking to a child.

"Academic?" Monique asked, still a little baffled.

Lisa helped Monique comprehend. "Duh. Yeah, stupid," she teased. "When you get good grades, colleges give you a free ride to their school. It ain't like she, of all people, needs it, though."

Trying to cover up her jealousy, Nay-Nay joined in on the conversation. "What school are you going to, Laci?"

"Boston University," Laci said proudly.

"That's supposed to be a pretty good school," Shaunna said.

"How the hell would you know?" Monique asked before taking a sip of her drink.

"Fuck you, slut," Shaunna shot back. "I got an uncle who went there, so now."

"So now," Monique mocked Shaunna, then stuck her tongue out at her.

"You keep playing, and I'm gonna put that pretty tongue of yours to some use." Shaunna winked.

"Ooh, can I watch?" Lisa joked as she finished up her drink and sat the cup down on the kitchen counter.

"Anyway," Nay-Nay interjected, "forget about that school shit. What's this about Puerto Rico?"

Laci swallowed down her Kool-Aid fast. "My dad is sending me as a graduation present. He told me that I could do whatever I wanted before college, so I chose a trip to Puerto Rico."

The girls looked at each other with a mixture of jealousy and hatred. All of them wished they could travel anywhere other than the five boroughs, but they weren't as blessed as Laci. The only thing that saved Laci from a round of "bash the rich girl" was Lisa's boyfriend, Dink, sneaking in the house unnoticed by no one but Lisa.

Dink was a few years older than the girls. They were all eighteen and nineteen, with the exception of Laci, who was closing in on her eighteenth birthday. Dink was twenty-four. He had a baby face, though, and could easily pass for a high school student. He was a tall cat with a tight frame. Dink liked to keep his body tight so he could front for the ladies. He wasn't the typical man whore that most hustlers were—most had to have two or three different bitches a night—but he had his share of pussy. He managed to protect himself, though, which kept him from having any baby mamas to contend with.

All the ladies found Dink attractive. His medium Afro was always kept neat and trim. He wore an angel's grin to hide his devil's agenda. Dink was a true hustler.

He crept into the kitchen, with his index finger over his lips as a sign for the girls not to say anything. Lisa had just taken the pizza out of the oven and was setting it on top of the stove to cool off. Her back was to Dink, so she didn't see him coming.

"Guess who?" he said, placing his hands over Lisa's eyes.

"I can smell your Lagerfeld cologne," Lisa said as a smile crept across her lips. "Baby, where you been?" she asked in a little girl voice as she turned around to face him.

"Working, baby," Dink said before kissing Lisa on the cheek and sweeping the room with his eyes to see who all was in there. They managed to freeze on Laci. "You know that I have to take care of my business."

"You couldn't call me?" Lisa moaned. "You know I missed you, baby."

Lisa's whines made all her friends' stomachs turn. It showed on their faces as they stared at the scene from a poorly scripted ghetto soap opera.

"I'm sorry," Dink said to the girls. "I didn't mean to be rude. How's everyone doing?" He had yet to take his eyes off Laci. It was almost as if no one else was in the room.

"Fine," they all answered simultaneously, but none of the girls wanted to look Dink directly in his eyes. It was safe to say that Dink had four out of the five pussies sopping wet.

Dink knew it, too. That was why he deliberately made eye contact with each and every one of them to see where their minds were. Most of them were on his dick. The only one unimpressed by his presence was Laci. This made Dink curious. He knew all too well that challenging pussy was the best pussy.

"Hey," Dink said, nodding toward Laci, "I haven't seen you around before. What's your name?"

"Who? Me?" Laci asked in surprise.

"No," Lisa said rudely. "He's talking to Casper the muthafuckin' Friendly Ghost. Yeah, you. Who else is he looking at?"

It was beyond obvious that Lisa didn't appreciate the attention Dink was giving Laci.

"I'm Laci," she said softly.

"You got a last name, Laci?" Dink asked with a smile.

"Casteneda," Laci replied, not understanding what the interrogation was about. She was too naïve to really know when she was being hit on.

"Nice to meet you, Laci Casteneda," Dink said, walking over and holding out his hand. "A friend of Lisa's is a friend of mine."

Just when Laci held her hand out to shake Dink's, Lisa made contact with Dink and broke that shit up with the quickness.

"She's been around," Lisa said to Dink. "You just obviously never noticed her. Now, baby, I haven't seen you in two days, and you not showing me no love. You too worried about the house guests."

"My bad, girl," Dink said, trying to hide his irritation. "How you doing, Ma?"

"Could be better," Lisa said, rolling her neck. "The girls were asking me if I wanted to go out with them, but I ain't got no paper." Lisa had decided to hint around instead of straight out asking for money.

"Is that why you're so uptight?" Dink asked nonchalantly.

"Now, baby, you know I keeps it tight," Lisa said in a sensual whisper. "Uptight, never. But you know, I was just saying and all that I wouldn't mind going out with the girls."

"Say no more, Ma." Dink reached in his silk blazer and pulled out a huge knot of money that was wrapped in a rubber band. Taking his time, he peeled off ten one-hundred-dollar bills and laid them in Lisa's palm with a kiss.

Lisa wore a look of surprise. Usually, he would just hit her off with a few hundred.

"I hit you with a little extra, just in case you and your road dawgs . . . and the new little puppy here," Dink said, nodding toward Laci with a wink, "decide to pop a bottle or something."

"I don't drink," Laci said, unknowingly fluttering her innocent eyes. "Plus, none of us are old enough to even buy alcohol."

Dink snickered. "Where'd you find this one, Lisa? She's cute. *Not old enough.* Yeah, that's real cute."

The girls laughed.

"I didn't find her," Lisa said, twisting up her mug. "That's something else the cat dragged into the clique." Lisa pointed Nay-Nay out as the culprit. After all, Nay-Nay was the one who had brought Laci around the first time.

Nay-Nay, Lisa, Shaunna, and Monique were at the movie theater. They had actually just blazed one right in their seats. Once the munchies hit their asses, Nay-Nay decided to go to the concession stand to get some snacks. Laci just happened to be standing in line behind her. After getting her snacks, Nay-Nay paid the clerk and walked away. Laci noticed that there was $29.25 lying on the counter. Nay-Nay had forgotten to take the change from her fifty-dollar bill.

Laci scooped up the money and chased Nay-Nay down to give it to her. Nay-Nay was both shocked and impressed. Most muthafuckas would have had snacks for days compliments of her change, but Laci was different. Nay-Nay had never met anyone that honest. Most muthafuckas in New York would take your shit right from your muthafuckin' hand, not to mention if you left that shit laying somewhere.

"You ain't originally from here, are you?" Nay-Nay asked Laci.

"No." Laci blushed. "I'm from Pennsylvania. But I've been living here a few years now."

"What school do you go to?"

"Oh, I don't go to any of the public schools."

"Never seen you around," Nay-Nay said, peepin' Laci up and down, noticing she was wearing a couple of labels.

"I never really go anywhere. I still don't know my way around like I should. I just go to school. That's about it."

"You don't roll with no crew?" Nay-Nay asked.

"No," Laci said, shaking her head. "I haven't really made any friends. I've come to learn that New York isn't home to the most friendliest folks in the world."

Nay-Nay nodded and thought for a minute. Laci definitely didn't look as though she had anything in common with Nay-Nay and her clique. But she did, in fact, look as though she had money. Maybe she was exactly the type of person they needed to open their doors to. She seemed nice, too, and maybe she'd be nice with her money.

"Well, I'm up here now with my crew," Nay-Nay said. "We gon' get into something after the movie. You're free to join us. As a matter of fact, you got a drink coming on me. What do you drink?"

"Coke or Pepsi," Laci said, throwing her hands up. "It doesn't matter to me."

Nay-Nay put her head down and tried not to laugh in Laci's face. She and her girls had been copping alcohol since middle school. Coke and Pepsi were for babies. Nonetheless, Nay-Nay still extended her invitation.

"Well, we gon' be right outside when the movie let's out," Nay-Nay said.

"Okay," Laci said, smiling. "I'm here with my mom, but after she meets you, I'm sure she won't mind me hanging out with you and your crew for a minute."

Looking at her in her designer Liz Claiborne getup, Nay-Nay figured that if this girl's chance to get with her and the rest of the girls was based on her mother's approval, then nine times out of ten she wouldn't be joining them.

Nay-Nay snickered. "I'm sure she won't mind at all. She might even want to join us herself. I'll check you out later. By the way, I'm Nayandra, but my peeps call me Nay-Nay."

"I'm Julacia, but you can call me Laci. My dad gave me that nickname." Laci's face lit up when she thought about how special she had felt when her father gave her that nickname.

"*Your daddy gave you that name, huh?*" Nay-Nay said, bobbin' her head up and down.

"*Yep,*" Laci replied.

"*That what your friends call you, too?*"

"*Like I said, I really don't have any.*"

Nay-Nay stared at Laci for a moment, as if she was analyzing her. "*Laci,*" Nay-Nay said.

"*What?*" Laci asked, with a puzzled look on her face.

"*I'm your friend now, so I'm calling you Laci. Besides, that Julacia is too much to be trying to say,*" Nay-Nay said, insinuating that Laci wasn't nothing special to come up with. Her daddy had probably just got tired of saying that long-ass name was all.

Laci ignored Nay-Nay's slight and was glad to have made a friend. A huge smile covered her face.

That was the beginning of her future with Nay-Nay and her crew.

Right now all Nay-Nay could think about was the extra ends Dink had given Lisa to buy something to sip on. She didn't want Laci's Coke-or-Pepsi-drinking ass to fuck up their chances of getting tipsy.

"Who the fuck cares if you don't drink and how old we are?" Nay-Nay told Laci. "Just say thanks. Damn. Plus, we been getting muthafuckas to cop liquor for us since we grew titties. All we gotta do is stand outside the bodega and wait for some old man with a hard dick to come by and ask him to go in and cop for us." Nay-Nay felt that Laci was being disrespectful and trying to act like a Miss Goody Two-shoes. When a baller offered you money, you took it, no matter what you were gon' spend it on.

"Hold on, Nay-Nay. It's cool," Dink said, licking his lips seductively and rubbing his hands together. "So, Miss Casteneda, you don't drink, huh?"

"She's one of them pure bitches," Lisa said in a stink tone.

"Pure, huh?" Dink said, trying to hide the excitement that Laci's presence brought out in him. "You blaze?" he asked Laci. Assuming that she might not understand what he meant, he rephrased his question. "Do you smoke?"

"I know what you meant," Laci said, moving the curls from her face. "I don't drink or smoke." She sucked her teeth.

"I find that hard to believe," Dink said. "It's rare that you find a girl that ain't got at least one habit. I know you do something." He gave Laci a mischievous look. "What do you do, Laci? What's your habit?"

"Nothing, really," Laci said, shrugging her shoulders. "I like to sing, and I used to do a little acting in drama club—"

"She's going to college," Monique interrupted. Laci's naiveness was starting to embarrass her.

"College?" Dink said, raising an eyebrow. "Where you going?"

Monique jumped in and answered for Laci like she was a proud mama. "Boston University."

"Larry Bird's school, huh?" Dink said, as if he knew what he was talking about. Dink was a smooth cat on the streets, but he had no game with the ladies whatsoever. Most of the women who approached him were chicken heads and hood rats, whom he didn't have to have game with to impress. Pimp definitely didn't run in his blood. He didn't even know how to be discreet with his shit. All the girls could see that Dink was feelin' Laci, and he was trying to get at her right in front of Lisa.

The average broad would have checked his ass, copped for another grand, and gotten her pussy eaten or something. But, unbelievably to the other girls, Lisa was lettin' that nigga slide. Lisa figured that Dink was just a man. Besides that, how did she expect him to react with Laci just standing there, trying to be cute, acting like it was all good that her man was trying to get at her? Lisa saw it as Laci trying to rub her looks and purity in her face. At the end of the day, it was Lisa whom Dink came home to and spent his money on. Besides that, he hadn't been home in two days, and she missed him. She didn't want to get mad at Dink and ruin a perfectly good night of fucking. But deep down, what she really wanted to do was get even with Laci. And if all went as planned, she would.

Chapter 4

Am I My Brother's Keeper?

The only three things Sonny knew about his father were that he was seldom home, he never had any money, and he loved jazz. At a time when Sonny's peers had been shooting spitballs or beginning to play rock 'n' roll music, he had been forced to assume the role of man of the house. By the time Sonny was in his late twenties, back in 1965, he was not only a Black militant, but he was also the breadwinner of the house and the only father figure his twenty-two-year-old brother, Jay, had ever known.

A number of factors led Sonny down the road to hell, but there were too many to mention them all. But the more obvious factors were his mother's never-ending struggle and the weight of having to help raise his kid brother. Sonny internalized his problems and let shit just eat away at him continually. Finally, he shot all his problems into his veins.

It took only a week for the junk to cloud his mind and have his life spiraling out of control. Sonny quickly became a socially functioning heroin user.

"Sonny!" Jay called out as he went up and down the hallway, looking into the rooms. "Sonny, where the hell are you? You don't hear Mama calling you?" Jay then entered the kitchen, where his mother was sitting at the table. "Mama, I don't know where he's at. I didn't see him leave."

Jay had checked the entire house, to no avail, in hopes of finding his brother.

"Sonny been acting strange, Jay," his mother said to her youngest son. "He's not himself. He ain't even give me no money for the rent this month. Sonny always gives me money on the rent."

"He's probably just going through something, Mama," Jay said, rubbing his brown cheek.

His mother simply sat there, with a look of despair on her face. "Jay, I hope your brother ain't got caught up in them streets," she said with tearful eyes. The last thing she needed was for the streets to get her boy. "I work two jobs, barely making ends meet. I depend on Sonny to help out around here. If my boy is caught up . . ." She lowered her head, unable to complete her sentence.

She had been trying to take care of her two sons ever since her husband had decided that he wasn't cut out for family life four years after the birth of Jay. What kind of man left his wife and two sons for dead like that? With Sonny forced to mature before he was ready, she wanted more for her sons than what she saw the young men in their neighborhood amount to. She had done everything in her power to keep them away from menial jobs and in the classroom.

"What do you mean, Mama?" Jay asked inquisitively. He hadn't noticed anything different about Sonny. Then again, he hadn't paid much attention to him lately, either. With all the studying and exams that freshman year of college involved, Jay had been lucky to find the time to sleep.

"I don't know. He just ain't been around as much as he used to."

Jay saw the hard years etched in his mother's face, and all he could think of was kicking his brother's ass. Who better than Sonny knew the condition of their family, to what degree their mother slaved away, and how important his help was? To Jay, his brother's behavior was unacceptable, a violation of an unspoken family pact.

Jay tore through the house a second time, screaming for his brother, praying to God that he didn't get his hands on him. He envisioned his fingers squeezing the life out of Sonny until he lay motionless. He saw this as Sonny's payment for causing their mother undue heartache.

"Sonny!" he shouted repeatedly, angrily charging through doors.

Jay went into his brother's room, and as he was rummaging through his personal belongings, he heard something move inside the closet. He ran over and opened the closet door. Inside the closet was Sonny, in a deep nod. He was sitting on the floor, with a piece of fabric tied tightly around his left arm and a hypodermic needle still stuck in his skin.

"Sonny!" Jay said, lightly slapping him across the face in an attempt to snap him out of his zone. "Wake up! Oh God. What the fuck you doing, man?"

"Hey, man," Sonny slurred. "What the hell is your problem?"

"Get your jive ass up," Jay said. "What the fuck you doin'? You gettin' high? Mama know you gettin' high, Sonny? Do Mama know you getting' high in her house?"

"Get the hell outta here, man," Sonny said. "I'm still your big brother, and I'll kick your little ass if you don't ease up."

"Sonny," Jay sobbed, "you gonna kill yourself with this shit. Then that's gon' kill Mama. Then what the hell am I gon' do? What the hell are you thinking, Sonny?"

"Quit asking so many damn questions," Sonny snapped. "You're killin' my high, square." Sonny looked at the needle in his arm as if he was noticing it for the first time. He removed it and threw it on the closet floor. He untied the fabric, scratched at his arm, and began to nod again.

"I'm gonna kill you my damn self, muthafucka!" Jay snapped, grabbing Sonny up. "You don't give a damn about Mama. She's worked hard for us, nigga! Ain't that what you've always told me? This is how you repay her, Sonny? Huh? This is how you repay Mama? Fuck that, Sonny! You gettin' the hell outta here."

"Jay," their mother called from the kitchen, "what's all that noise?"

"Nothing, Ma," Jay answered calmly, though he was fuming. "Nothing."

"Is that your brother you're talking to? Did you find Sonny?" she called.

Jay ignored her.

Jay got Sonny to his feet, and after their brief game of tug and pull, he whispered to Sonny, "You get your shit together and go find you someplace else to get high. It ain't gonna be in this house no more."

"Who the fuck you think you are?" Sonny roared. "You can't kick me out of my own house, you shade-tree nigga. Joe College, how you think you were able to get those good grades you get, huh? How you think your books were paid for? Where do you think the coins came from? The sky? You better watch who you talkin' to."

"If you don't get out," Jay said through clenched teeth, "I'm gon' knock you out and then throw you out. It's your choice."

Sonny and Jay stood face-to-face, squaring off. Usually, Jay would be the first to back down, but this was a different day. He was either going to kick some ass or get his handed to him, but the odds were in his favor. Sonny wasn't at his best.

"What, nigga?" Jay stood his ground.

"*Man*," Sonny said, waving Jay off.

"I don't fucking believe this," Jay snapped. "Look at yourself, man." Jay grabbed his brother by the arm, closed the closet door, and forced him to look at himself in the mirror that was bolted to the door.

For the first time since he had started chipping at the heroin, Sonny took a long, hard look at himself. His skin looked as if it was sagging from the merciless pull of gravity. His clothes weren't filthy, but he wasn't his usual crisp self. His eyes wore deep circles from long nights of being up in search of a hit. Sonny used to love to look at his handsome face in the mirror. Now he couldn't bear the sight of what he had become. Where a man had once stood, a dope fiend had taken his place.

"Shit," Sonny said under his breath.

"Shit is right," Jay said, turning his brother around to face him. "That's just what you look like right now—shit. I used to be proud of you, big bro. I used to look at you and say to myself, 'Damn. I wanna look just like Sonny when I grow up. I wanna walk just like Sonny. I wanna talk just like Sonny.' Now I can't stand to look at you. Just take your shit and get out."

Although the effects of the heroin had Sonny scatterbrained, he was playing himself. After looking out for his family all these years, he was becoming the same kind of monster that he had tried to protect them from. Sonny's current condition would break his mother's fragile heart. He couldn't bring himself to face her the way he looked, so he did the honorable thing. After packing his meager belongings into a green duffel bag, he crept out the side door.

It hurt Jay to talk to Sonny the way he did, but it hurt him more to watch his older brother kill himself. Sonny used to be his hero, the man who had the answer to all his problems. He had been more of a father to him than a brother, but things were different now.

It was as if the torch had been passed. Jay would now have to take on the role of man of the house and look after things. He prayed that Sonny would get himself together and come back home and take care of things. Deep down inside, Jay knew it was a long shot. Sonny was a slave to the horse that coursed through his veins.

The same week that Sonny left, Jay got a job as a short-order cook to replace the income his brother had brought home. It would be a tough road juggling school and a full-time job, but he didn't have a choice. Jay put his nose to the grindstone, and when it came time to hand out degrees, Jay graduated at the top of his class. He went on to earn a master's degree from Syracuse University and then headed to medical school in Pennsylvania.

Unfortunately, his mother wouldn't live long enough to see her son become what she had sacrificed so much for him to be. She died shortly before Jay finished medical school. By then his estranged brother was too far gone to even come to the funeral. Jay eventually shut out the rest of the world and continued his journey. And he still held a grudge against his brother twenty-plus years later. As far as Jay was concerned, he didn't even have a brother. His family ties had died with his mother, and so had any hope of Sonny ever coming back.

Chapter 5

All Fall Down

Dink couldn't take his eyes off Laci. There was something about her that wouldn't allow him to look away. She was pretty, but not enough to trip over. He had seen pretty girls come and go. This one, though, just had a certain air about her that he couldn't shake. She had his nose open without even trying.

Lisa was his boo-boo, but he wasn't in love with her. If anything, he liked her a lot and had love for her, but as far as being in that unconditional love bullshit, it wasn't happening. When it all came down to it, Dink saw Lisa as not being much different than the rest of her crew. She was okay to look at when she dressed up, but she was not wifey material. Laci, on the other hand, had something about her that Dink needed to know more about.

Lisa read Dink's eyes like they were a kinder-garten spelling test. She wasn't the sharpest knife in the drawer, but she was hardly stupid. She was well aware of what the look that Dink was giving Laci meant, 'cause that was how he had caught her ass. This muthafucka could bat his eyes and lick his lips all he wanted, but Lisa was determined to show both of them who the queen bitch was.

Lisa kissed Dink full on the mouth and whispered, "Can I taste the magic stick, Daddy?" For emphasis, she grabbed a handful of his crotch.

"Damn, Lisa," Dink said. He held her at arm's length. "There are people here." He fronted like he was embarrassed, but Dink really loved that kind of shit. Lisa was a freak and a half, which was part of the reason he kept her around. He thought about the last time she had sucked him off and let him blow in her mouth. Just thinking about it made Dink want to wet himself.

Lisa and Dink's fooling around made Nay-Nay uncomfortable, or perhaps *jealous* was a better choice of words. She figured it was time to block Lisa's action.

"Lisa," Nay-Nay said, then coughed.

"Okay, okay." Lisa giggled. "Y'all know how I get when I see *my* man." Lisa shot a look at Laci, hoping that she understood where she was coming from, just in case she had any ideas.

Dink unzipped his jacket and flipped it behind him like Michael Jackson, exposing his gold rope chain and medallion. He was in stunt mode now. "So, what you ladies getting into tonight?"

"Nothing really," Shaunna said, rubbing her stomach. "We'll probably keep it local. Besides, I can't go too far with this belly."

"You probably don't need to be going nowhere," Monique said. "Why you always gotta be the pregnant girl at the club?"

The girls snickered. Shaunna stuck her middle finger up at Monique.

"Do you know what it is yet?" Dink asked, walking over to Shaunna and placing his ear against her stomach.

"What the fuck you think you gon' hear?" Lisa said, jealous that Dink was that close to Shaunna. "You think it's gonna bust out freestyling or something?"

"I don't know if it's a girl or a boy," Shaunna said, running right over Lisa's comment. "I want to be surprised."

Even though Dink had no intentions for Shaunna, the attention he was giving her made her feel warm. Her own children's fathers didn't pay that kind of attention to her. She wasn't used to it, and this only made her crave it more. As Dink began to rub her stomach, she imagined that he was her man instead of Lisa's.

"That's cool," Dink said, smiling. "Did you eat yet? You know you gotta keep your strength up—"

"Damn, baby," Lisa interrupted. "Since when do you love the kids? She's fine. Would you want someone all over you like that?" Lisa walked over to where Shaunna was sitting and pulled at Dink's arm. "C'mon now. I ain't seen you in a minute. I missed you. Shit, nigga. Come rub on me."

"I missed you too," Dink said, patting Lisa on the ass. "You think I don't think about you when I'm out handling my business? C'mon now. You know you're always on my mind. Stop actin' like that."

Dink hugged Lisa and lifted her off her feet, but with her back turned, it meant that he could study his prey—Laci.

When Laci realized that Dink was burning a hole through her with his eyes, she blushed and turned her head. She used her tongue to scoop a piece of ice from her cup. Her smile let Dink know that she was finally onto him. And although he was involved with her peoples, time and opportunity were a muthafucka. All he needed was opportunity and, hell, he'd make the time.

Dink released Lisa.

"I'll see you girls later," Dink said, quickly eyeing Laci. "Y'all be safe. Lisa, you go on and have a good time with your girls, Ma. I'll be back later to check you out." Dink licked his lips and spared a last glance at Laci. There was no mistaking what his intentions were.

This time Laci didn't turn away or look down. She stared right back at him. Dink nodded his understanding and left.

When the girls were sure that Dink was out the door, Monique began speaking.

"Dink is a classy-ass nigga," Monique said, picking at her nails. "He fine too. You better watch him, Lisa. One day one of these loose-ass sluts are gonna try you. You can trust his ass all you want. It's these hoes you can't trust."

Lisa nodded in agreement. Typically, it would have struck a nerve for some other female to call her nigga fine. Monique and Lisa were the tightest, like sisters, so Monique was the only one out of the crew that could make the comments she had without Lisa hitting the roof. The other girls just stayed silent and stewed in their own juices, romanticizing the forbidden idea.

Laci looked down at her watch. "Well, ladies, it's been real, but I'm about to bounce," she said, stretching. "I'm gonna go home and lay it down."

Lisa looked over at Nay-Nay. Her eyes bulged.

Nay-Nay shrugged her shoulders, as if to say, "Handle yours."

Then Lisa quickly said, "But, Laci, you're always on some leaving shit. You be acting like you're too good to be with us after a certain hour."

Laci was surprised at Lisa's comment. She was usually a two-fingers bitch—peace. But perhaps this was a sign that she was really starting to appreciate Laci's company. Most of the time Laci split if the girls were getting ready to go party, but this time she really was tired and was ready to call it a night.

"C'mon, you know that's not true," Laci assured her. "If I didn't want to be around y'all, I wouldn't be. But a sista got to go home and get her beauty rest."

Lisa rolled her eyes and twisted up her lips.

"That's fucked up, Laci," Shaunna said.

"How do you figure that?" Laci asked defensively.

"Forget it." Shaunna waved her off. "Leave then."

"Yeah, leave if you're going," Monique added.

All of sudden, Lisa surprised Laci yet again with her comment.

"I don't know about them, but I'm not letting you off so easy this time. I want you to stay, Laci. See, unlike our crew, I ain't afraid to speak my mind. How I see it is that you sit up around us while we drink, smoke, and all that shit, and you even listen to us talk about our *real* sexual experiences. But you don't do none of that. Sometimes it seems like you using us as lab rats. You sit around taking notes on what you don't want to do. It's like you're sitting back and judging us."

Laci's jaw dropped. She couldn't believe this was how she made the girls feel. Finally, this explained why they were so sometimey with her.

"You think I've been judging you guys?" Laci asked in disbelief. "Is that how you all feel?" Laci looked around the room, waiting for someone else to speak up.

"Yeah, I guess that sounds about right," Nay-Nay replied. "I mean, how would you feel? While we're passing blunts and bottles, you're on some chill shit. Like you're propped up on a pedestal. You even act like being around weed smoke is gonna kill you."

"But you know I don't do drugs," Laci explained.

"That's some sad shit," Shaunna said. "Weed ain't even a drug. It's a natural herb from the ground, baby—like fuckin' oregano or some shit."

"If anything, I would say alcohol is more of a drug than weed," Lisa added. "Who you know smoke a joint, jumps in a car, and takes out a family of five on the expressway?"

"You know?" Shaunna said, giving Lisa some dap.

"I know you don't drink, Laci," Nay-Nay said. "And I can totally dig that. But why you stunting on the weed? A li'l smoke ain't gon' hurt you."

Laci stood there silently.

"Nay-Nay, I don't know why you wasting your time," Monique interjected. "Laci ain't gon' smoke with us. Privileged kids ain't got no time for us hood rats. She's too good. I say let her go get her beauty sleep. That bitch can be pretty, and we can be high."

"Why don't y'all fall back?" Lisa said. "Laci is part of our crew, and y'all treating her like an outsider."

Monique and Shaunna looked at each other with confused expressions on their faces.

"Since when did you become Laci's best friend?" Monique asked with an attitude.

Lisa gave Monique a "Shut the fuck up!" look. Knowing Lisa like she knew Lisa, Monique knew that look better than anybody. Right then and there, she knew that Lisa was up to something. The reason for Lisa insisting that Monique call Laci back to make sure that she joined them tonight was starting to come together.

"I ain't say we were best friends or nothing like that," Lisa responded. "I just don't know why my bitches is tripping over some fucking smoke. I don't believe that Laci thinks she's too good to smoke with us. As a matter of fact, I'll bet that she'll hit the weed just to shut you hatin'-ass bitches up. Ain't that right, Laci?" She shot Laci a knowing look.

"You must be crazy," Shaunna said. "Either that, or you smokin' on some different shit. If she won't hit a little drink, she sure as hell ain't gonna smoke."

The fact that Lisa seemed like she was on her side made Laci feel obligated to at least take one puff. She didn't want to let Lisa down. This was the first time any one of the girls had stood up for Laci. *One pull can't hurt. It is just marijuana*, Laci thought. Maybe this would stop the girls from always riding her. If one puff of the magic dragon was all it was going to take to show the girls that she could be a down-ass bitch, then it was worth it. Once her virgin lungs made love to the herb, she'd be in.

"You got some?" Laci asked Lisa.

"Some what?" Lisa asked.

"Some weed, a joint," Laci said. "I was thinking that I might need a little something to make my rest just that much better."

Laci smiled a mischievous smile. The girls returned one.

"As a matter of fact, I just happen to have some," Nay-Nay said. "It's in my purse in the living room. Hold on. I'll go get it." Nay-Nay winked at Lisa and headed into the living room to retrieve the goods.

Shaunna looked at Monique in amazement. They had to admit that Lisa was good. Never in a million years would they have thought that Laci would ever jeopardize her pureness. Sure enough, Lisa was able to sway the naive girl. Now it was time to sit back and watch the show.

Nay-Nay rejoined the girls in the kitchen with the blunt now in her hand. "Ta-da," she said with a smile.

She handed it to Laci, who looked at it as if it were a foreign object. Laci had never actually held a joint, not even to pass it on to one of the other girls if she was sitting in the line of fire. As Laci examined the blunt with curiosity, Lisa started to get impatient.

"What are you waiting for?" Lisa asked, moving the pizza, which they'd all forgotten about at this point, out of her way and then turning on a burner on her gas stove. "Just blaze."

"Why don't one of you guys light it and then pass it to me?" Laci said nervously. The last thing she wanted to do was burn off her bangs while trying to light a blunt on the stove.

"Quit playing with the weed," Monique said, egging her on. "Either light the shit or pass it off. See, Lisa, I told you."

Seeing the smug look on Monique's face made Laci angry. That little ghetto bitch thought she knew everything. Laci was sick of all of them doubting her and was now more determined than ever to show them that she could hang.

Laci approached the stove and then cautiously leaned over the flames and lit the blunt.

"That's a girl," Lisa said with a smile. "Now come on in the living room."

The girls followed Lisa into the living room as if they were going to watch a pay-per-view movie. Laci sat down on the couch, and all the girls huddled around to watch her like she was in a glass box in a sex-toy store and they had all inserted quarters in a slot to witness her fuck for the first time.

Laci looked at the girls looking at her, and then without hesitation she took two baby pulls.

"Give me a fucking break." Lisa laughed.

The other girls stood watching in amazement. They were impressed. They hadn't thought Laci had the balls.

"Did you see those sucker-ass pulls?" Lisa said. "Look, Laci. That is some good shit, and I don't want to see it go to waste. If you gon' do it, do it. Don't be wastin' the shit."

This was the Lisa whom Laci was used to, but it was also the Lisa she wanted to cleanse away. Laci took two more pulls, only these were deeper. Her throat immediately constricted, causing her to cough. Laci began to feel light-headed. The girls started to laugh. To shut them up, Laci took two more deep pulls, only this time she didn't cough out the smoke. She blew it out. The smell of the weed began to fill her nose. She thought that something was different about the smell than before, when she had inhaled it secondhand.

Laci looked at Nay-Nay with glassy eyes. Nay-Nay nodded, and like a good little soldier, Laci continued to hit the blunt. Laci could feel her face getting numb and her jaw trying to lock. Her ears began to ring, and she could've sworn she heard "The Star-Spangled Banner" playing in her head. Laci looked at the blunt and smiled. All this time she had been avoiding something that felt so good. A little toke on the Mary Jane wasn't that bad at all.

"My nigga," Nay-Nay said in amazement. "She did the damn thing. And that's some ole chronic shit that we ain't never had our hands on before." Nay-Nay winked at Lisa.

Laci smiled as she took another long pull. She had inhaled secondhand smoke while being around the girls when they blazed. She had even caught a buzz from the smoke before, causing her to act a little silly. But she didn't remember ever feeling like this.

"Damn, you blunt hog. Now, we said smoke *with* us," Shaunna said, reaching for the blunt.

"No!" Lisa was quick to say. "Don't smoke that. As a matter of fact, you shouldn't even be around the smoke."

"Bitch, I smoked with every last one of my kids, and you know it," Shaunna said. "Keeps me from getting sick."

"No, Shaunna," Nay-Nay insisted. She turned her head and gave Shaunna a stern look. Shaunna threw back a puzzled look. "This one is *especially* for Laci," Nay-Nay revealed.

"Oh . . . ," Shaunna said, nodding. A grimace stretched across her lips. "My bad. You right. I shouldn't be smoking, anyway."

Shaunna just sat there in the chair, decoding the cryptic language and actions. All of a sudden, the smell of the blunt began to fill the air. Just as Laci had thought, it had a different stench to it. Instantly, the girls shot each other looks. Lisa began to shake her head. She was amazed at just how naive Laci really was. She was almost finished with the blunt and was none the wiser that it wasn't the average blunt. How could she be?

Nay-Nay looked over at Lisa. Lisa cracked a broad smile, like she was doing a good deed. Nay-Nay turned her attention back to Laci and watched her take another puff. She was starting to feel like shit. She sat there watching Laci get higher than high, and she didn't do a thing to stop it. She felt like a coward for not telling Laci the real deal at this point, but Lisa was her homegirl. Laci was just another stuck-up bitch, or at least that was what Nay-Nay tried to convince herself of to wash away some of the guilt.

Laci rolled her head back and looked up at the ceiling. The cracks in the plaster turned into little streams, which Laci tried to follow, but she couldn't stay focused. Her eyes felt like they were going in two different directions at once. She looked at Monique and saw her lips moving, but she could only partially make out what she was saying. All she could see was her teeth, which seemed to be sprouting from her mouth at several odd angles. She thought it was a side effect of the potent weed and kept pulling on the blunt roach. In her high-ass state, it never occurred to her that none of the other girls were putting up a fight or even reaching for the blunt.

Once she was too far gone to comprehend anything, all the girls sat down and had their own private jokes about the hell they had just introduced young Laci to.

Laci awoke in the middle of the night with a headache to end all headaches. Her eyes throbbed as she stared down at her watch. She had been out of it for at least four hours.

That was some bomb-ass weed, she thought. That must be what they meant when they were talkin' about the chronic.

She tried to stand, but her legs gave out under her. Laci flopped back down on the couch and clutched her head in an attempt to stop it from spinning. She searched for something in the room to try to focus on. It was then she realized that she was still at Lisa's.

Laci staggered to her feet and proceeded to look around the apartment. She searched the kitchen, both bedrooms, and the bathroom, but there was no sign of the girls. As Laci passed back through the living room, she noticed a note on the coffee table, with a blunt lying on top of it. She moved the blunt to the side. then picked up the note and read it:

Tried to wake you. Went to the club.
The Girls

Laci sucked her teeth. She really wished that she had been awake earlier, because she had been looking forward to partying with the girls for once. A night of dancing and laughing was what she needed to get rid of that strong-ass buzz. Oh well, at least they thought enough of her to leave some more of that chronic.

Laci put the note down, then picked up the blunt. She stared at it for a minute before she started fishing around for a book of matches. She couldn't find any, so she went into the kitchen and turned on the stove. She lit the blunt and looked at it.

"Practice makes perfect," she said to herself before taking a hit.

This time the smoke didn't hit her as hard as the first time. She still gagged, but she was able to hold it in her lungs. The rush from the smoke went directly to Laci's brain, almost making her dizzy. She inhaled the stench from the blunt and realized that this one smelled even less kosher. She could smell the weed, but there was something else that she couldn't quite place. In all the times she had previously smelled the girls' blazing weed, it had just never had this type of odor. She simply chalked it up as Nay-Nay having a connect for that real chronic shit.

Laci finished the blunt and tried to figure out what to do next. For some odd reason, she couldn't seem to sit still. She felt alive and wanted to do everything at once. It was as if all the sleep had drained from her body and she had a second wind.

Now, had Laci been a regular weed smoker, certain things would've tipped her off that something was not quite right. Weed was a depressant, but Laci felt hyper. Marijuana also had a knack for giving folks the munchies, which Laci didn't have. Actually, she didn't have an appetite at all. The signs were clear for someone who knew what to look for, but Laci didn't, so she didn't heed the warning going off in the back of her mind.

Laci circled Lisa's apartment three or four times, trying to burn off some of her excess energy. This went on for a little bit before she started to feel herself coming down off the high. The girls didn't appear to be coming back anytime soon, so she was on her own for the rest of the night. She put Lisa's door on slam lock and headed into the streets.

"Did you see that bitch tweekin'?" Shaunna asked as she sipped her Absolut and cranberry. They had managed to find some older dude outside the store to cop them some alcohol. They had decided to go to the field, drink, and clown on Laci.

"Girrrl, I thought I was gonna fall out when her jaw locked." Monique laughed. "That bitch was *so* gone. Lisa, did you peep when she started steaming that shit?"

"Huh?" Lisa asked, not really paying attention.

"Earth to Lisa," Monique said, trying to snap her out of her daze. "Damn, you been on some quiet shit since we left the crib. I know you ain't still tripping on how Dink was up on Laci?"

"You peeped that too, huh?" Lisa asked.

"Who didn't?" Monique said with a snicker.

"Nah, I ain't stunting that bitch," Lisa lied. The truth was, she felt terrible about what they had done to Laci. Giving her a regular blunt would have been evil enough, but lacing it with crack was some medieval shit. Lisa had an aunt who fell victim to the pipe. She watched her aunt go from a hard-working mother of four to a base head who sucked dick for her next high.

"Fuck the dumb shit," Monique said. "That li'l bitch deserves a reality check. I'll bet her mommy would have a fit if she knew her little girl was up in the crib smoking a woo."

Nay-Nay, who hadn't said too much, either, decided to jump into the conversation. "Oh, my precious Laci," Nay-Nay said with a horrible British accent. "A crackhead? Well, I never!"

The girls laughed.

"She's probably gonna feel like shit when she wakes up," Lisa said.

"You don't know the half," Nay-Nay said. "That second one we left her . . . double the lace."

"Girl, you crazy!" Monique shouted hysterically. "You see this crazy bitch, Lisa?"

"What the fuck were you trying to do? Kill her?" Shaunna said, shaking her head.

"If she's gotten a taste of our reality yet, she probably wishes she were dead. Ain't that right, Lisa?" Monique laughed.

"Yeah." Lisa chuckled half-heartedly.

Nay-Nay didn't miss the fact that Lisa was acting strangely. She knew about her aunt and could see how Lisa probably felt funny, but fuck it. It was too late now. It was a cold world, and fucked-up shit happened every day.

The girls couldn't wait to see Laci so they could find out firsthand what the drugs had done to her. They laughed every time they thought about Laci trying to speak through locked jaws. She sounded like a mush mouth. They'd see how much she talked about her parents and college and shit now. Maybe this was just what Laci needed to keep that trap closed. Perhaps she had had it coming.

Though the plan was something Lisa and Nay-Nay pretty much made happen, all the girls went along with it. Nay-Nay was their leader. Once she was down, it was a go. Whenever she gave shit the okay, the others fell in line behind her like good little soldierettes. What the crew didn't know was that Nay-Nay harbored a secret—a dark, ugly secret. Everyone assumed that Nay-Nay didn't like Laci for the same reasons they didn't much care for her, but that wasn't the case.

Nay-Nay actually admired Laci's manner. That was another reason why she had pulled her into the clique in the first place. Laci was polite and very pleasant to be around. Laci was the young lady that none of her hood-rat-ass friends could ever even fathom becoming. It was this same admiration for Laci that made Nay-Nay often despise her.

Laci came from a nice home and had loving parents. Nay-Nay had been running the streets ever since she could remember. No one had ever given a shit about her, especially not her drunken-ass mother. Ever since her father had left, all her mother had cared about was the bottle and getting a shot of dick here and there. Nay-Nay had always run around unsupervised, getting into this or that. Her mother didn't too much care, as long as she got a check for her twice a month. Nay-Nay, like most girls, looked toward men to get the love that she so desperately wanted. That was how she had got involved with Dame's foul ass.

Sometimes just looking at Laci or watching her interact with her mother made Nay-Nay want to break down in tears. She felt so cheated, not having a mother to love her, or anyone else, for that matter. There were times when she would close her eyes and imagine that Margaret was her mother. She would fantasize about them staying up until all hours of the night, having girly talks. Then when she opened her eyes, reality would always hit her, making her accept the fact that Margaret wasn't her mother—she was Laci's.

"Fuck that bitch," Nay-Nay said, downing the rest of her drink.

Laci couldn't get off the train soon enough. The ride from Queens to Manhattan had been a less than pleasant one. When she'd left Lisa's house, she'd been fine, but after being on the train for a few minutes, she'd begun to feel sick. Her stomach had begun to cramp, and she'd got light-headed.

When the train reached Ninety-Sixth Street, she was all too happy to get off. The musty train had done nothing to alleviate her nausea. She trudged up the few stairs and was greeted by a gush of night air. The chilly breeze felt good against her face. Slowly, Laci's head began to clear, and she realized that she probably needed to eat. Perhaps that would make her feel better. She had been at Lisa's all day and hadn't eaten since breakfast. She should have eaten that frozen pizza when she had the chance. But it was too late now.

Laci took a detour toward Broadway to grab a bite from the diner. She crossed Columbus Avenue and was halfway to Amsterdam when she had a brilliant idea. She thought how much better her food would taste if she smoked a blunt before she ate it. She made a left and headed toward the projects on Ninety-Third Street. She remembered Nay-Nay taking them there one time when all the girls had wanted to cop.

It didn't take Laci long to have one of the local hard heads approach her, trying to push up. He was a short kid with a nappy 'fro and gold teeth across the bottom of his mouth. His jeans hung off his ass, showing way too much of his boxer shorts.

"What up, Ma?" he asked, flashing his gold teeth. "Can I talk to you for a second?"

"Nada," Laci said with a sassiness she had never had about her before but felt compelled to express. "I'm kind of in a rush."

"You don't look like you're rushing to me," he said, moving a little closer to Laci.

"Well, I am," she said, backing up a bit. "I'm actually out here waiting for my man." Laci had to think quick on her feet. She was on a mission and didn't have time to fuck around with this loser.

"My bad, sis," he said, raising his hands in surrender. "I didn't mean no disrespect. I'ma bounce, but tell ya peoples that he's very lucky."

"I will," Laci said to his back as he walked away. Laci could've kicked herself for appearing to be such an easy mark. The girls had warned her time and again about walking through hoods looking like she didn't belong. That was like dripping blood in a pool of sharks.

As Laci watched the young man get farther away, it occurred to her that she had never bought drugs before. She was all up in someone else's hood and didn't even know whom to ask. The young man whom she had brushed off might've been her only hope to score. Laci swallowed her pride and went for it.

"Hey!" she called behind him.

The young man looked around, as if he wasn't sure who she was talking to.

"Yeah, you," Laci said, pointing her finger at him. "Come here for a minute."

The young man flashed a grin and headed back in Laci's direction. He knew she would come to her senses. He was young, handsome, and getting a little paper. What woman in her right mind would turn him down?

"What da deal, Ma?" he asked, looking her up and down, now cockier than ever.

"Listen, sorry about the brush-off thing. I thought you might've been trying to rob me," she half lied.

"Me?" he said, slapping his chest. "Baby, I'm totally harmless—at least outside the bedroom, anyway." He winked. "Say, what's your name?"

"Tina," Laci blurted out. One thing she had learned from her girls was never to give a potential mark her name.

"Nice to meet you, Tina," he said, extending his hand. "My name is Tee."

"Tee?" Laci asked, looking quizzically at his hand.

"Yeah, baby, short for Terrance. So, what you doing out here this time of night, other than checking for me?"

"Uh," Laci stammered, "I feel kinda funny about this."

"What's to feel funny about?" he asked, getting in Laci's space. "Two young people having a conversation? What, you think ya man is gonna catch you talking to me?"

"No, not exactly," Laci said, looking down at her shoes. "I kinda lied about that part."

"Damn, shorty," Tee said, shaking his head. "Lying ain't exactly the best way to start things off, but I forgive you. I knew you were kinda square when I peeped you. Now, this brings me back to the original question. What you doing down this way, Ma?"

"I'm trying to get something," Laci whispered.

"Oh, hell nah," Tee said, disappointed. "You fuckin' wit them rocks, shorty?"

"No," Laci said defensively. "Do I look like a crackhead to you? I just want to buy some weed."

"Oh, you had me shook for a minute. I thought you was strung out. That would've been such a terrible waste of flesh. You should've just asked, instead of comin' round on some spy shit."

"Do you know where I can get some?" Laci asked with hope in her eyes.

"Sure do," Tee said, pulling two bags of weed out of his pocket. "You came to the right place, Ma. I got whatever you need."

"I guess I'll take ten dollars' worth," Laci said after digging into her purse and seeing that all she had was a ten-dollar bill and a couple of ones.

"Hold on, boo. Your money is no good here," Tee informed her. "Besides, all I got is twenties."

"I ain't that naive," Laci said, then sucked her teeth. "Ain't nothing free."

"I never said it was free, Tina. I just said that your money ain't no good here. I'll take it in trade, though." Tee looked her up and down like a hungry animal.

"I don't think so," she said, rolling her eyes, putting her money back into her purse. "What the fuck do I look like to you?"

"A'ight," he said, a little surprised to see the hood come up outta Laci. "I ain't even mean it like that, shorty. You can have the weed. Just come upstairs and blow an L with me."

"I got a better idea. How about I give you the ten bucks and we can sit right out here on the bench and smoke together?" Laci was hardly stupid enough to go off with a strange man. Her girls didn't teach her that little piece of advice. It was something her mother had instilled in her.

"Shorty, you're crazy," Tee chuckled. "A'ight. We can sit right out here. That way we can see if the police are coming while we're rolling."

"Police?" Laci asked nervously.

"Easy, shorty. It ain't like that round here. Police only pass through this part of the world every so often. Niggas on this block ain't making enough moves to draw attention. It ain't like the block is hot. We'll be good," Tee said, leading Laci over to the bench, where the two sat down.

Laci was hesitant as she sat down on the bench next to Tee. She looked on in amazement as he split a cigar, dumped the guts behind the bench, and then crushed up the weed. It was a good thing that she had run into Tee. In addition to not knowing whom to cop the weed from, Laci couldn't roll. She had seen the girls do it hundreds of times, but she had never done it herself. She was just glad Tee had volunteered to roll, 'cause had he asked her to, she would've surely fucked it up.

"So, where you from?" Tee asked.

"Queens," Laci lied. "I came out here to visit a friend. If you think I'm square, you should meet her. She doesn't smoke, so she didn't know where to get any weed. That's why I'm out here in the middle of the night like a damn fool."

"Don't even trip, Ma," he said, sealing the blunt with one last lick. "Tee got the best green around here. You're gonna be high as a kite." Tee proceeded to light the blunt, took a hit, and then passed it to Laci.

"I hope so," Laci said before taking two deep drags. "Me and my girls in Queens only smoke the best shit. You know, the chronic." Laci almost laughed at how silly she sounded. She was fronting for Tee like she was really a part of something. She was glad the girls weren't around, because they would've surely clowned her for trying to sound hip.

The blunt went back and forth between Laci and Tee until it burned down to a roach. The weed had Laci buzzed, but it was nothing like the shit Nay-Nay had let her taste. Now she was mostly sleepy and hungry.

Definitely not as good as Nay-Nay's, she thought.

"Well," Laci said, standing, "I better get going."

"You gotta leave so soon?" Tee asked.

"Yeah, I got something to do in the morning."

"A'ight, shorty," Tee said, standing up alongside her. "Can I get a number or something? Maybe we can hang out again?"

"I don't think so, Tee," Laci said, yawning. "Look, you're cool and all, but you're not really my type."

"What you mean, I ain't your type?" Tee asked defensively.

"Check it," Laci said, feeling the effects of the weed. "You stand on the corner and grind all night.

On top of that, you're grinding for someone else. Let's be real, Tee. Ain't no future in that."

"That's some cold shit, shorty," he said in almost a whisper. "I was good enough to get you high, but I ain't good enough to go out with?"

"It ain't personal, Tee. That's just how it is. I'll see you around, though." Laci gave him a girly wave and walked off, giggling.

Tee looked at Laci with a mix of hurt and anger. He was about to pick up the bottle that was sitting on the ground next to the bench and throw it at her, but he changed his mind. All that would do was make him hot if the bitch decided to call the police. He would see Miss Tina again, though. There was no doubt in his mind about that. But the next time, she'd be the one getting played.

Chapter 6

Training Day

Dink and his partner, Marco, were posted up on the Ave, enjoying the weather. All the honeys who passed by were checking for the two hustlers. Business was good, and everyone knew it.

"Fuck is this li'l nigga at?" Marco complained. "Got a muthafucka sitting out here waiting."

Marco was a short, fat dude with a chemical wave. His clothes were always fresh, and his jewel game was tight. Marco wasn't the most handsome dude in the hood, so he had to depend on material things to boost his appearance.

"My li'l man will be here," Dink assured him.

"I don't even know why you fuck wit that li'l nut," Marco said. "Muthafucka is angry all the time. That shit ain't normal."

"Smurf is cool," Dink said and snickered.

"Cool my ass. That little trigger-happy bastard is dangerous, D. You better keep a leash on that fool."

"I don't need a leash with Smurf. I got a different way of controlling him."

"And how the fuck is that?"

"Books," Dink said before spitting on the ground.

"Books?" Marco replied, twisting up his mug.

"Yep. The li'l nigga likes to read. When he's feeling antsy and I ain't got no work for him, I give him a book to occupy his time."

"That li'l muthafucka can read?" Marco asked in disbelief.

"Don't judge a book by its cover," Dink warned. "If you took the time to get to know him, then you'd see he's got some sense."

Marco and Dink had known each other since the third grade and had always argued like husband and wife.

"That's what you say. I say the nigga's got issues." He knit his brow. "What is he reading now?" Marco asked.

"I loaned him *Behold a Pale Horse*."

"Dink," Marco said, getting serious, "I know you ain't give him *my* book?"

"Why you always bitchin'?" Dink sucked his teeth. "He gon' bring the shit back. Damn!"

"That ain't the point," Marco said, rolling his eyes.

Dink turned and faced Marco. "Okay, then, what *is* the point?"

"The book wasn't yours to give away."

"If the nigga don't bring it back, I'll buy you another one. Matter of fact, how much is it? Never mind. Here." Dink dug down into his pocket and pulled out a roll. He peeled a couple of hundreds off and gave them to Marco. "Buy ten of 'em."

"That ain't the point. You just don't respect people's shit," Marco said, putting the bills in his pocket.

"What you talkin' 'bout? I keep all my shit tight."

"Yeah, just like you said. *Your* shit," Marco pointed out.

"Whateva, yo. Hey, there he go," Dink said, spotting Smurf heading their way. "Yo, Smurf! What's up, baby?"

Smurf nonchalantly looked around and assessed everyone in the area. He made it his business to know exactly how many people were with Dink and what route would provide the best exit if something popped off. He always paid close attention to his surroundings.

"Ain't nothing," Smurf said, giving Dink some dap. "Another day in the hood."

"What did you think of the book?" Dink asked.

"Yo, that shit is serious," Smurf said, wild eyed. "The muthafuckin' government is grimy."

"That's the world we live in," Marco said. "Now, give me back my book, shorty."

"C'mon, yo. I'm almost finished," Smurf said. "I wanna read the rest of it."

"So, you dig it, huh?" Marco asked.

"That shit is dope," Smurf replied.

"A'ight, you can hold it a little longer. Just make sure you give it back to me when you finish," Marco said reluctantly.

"Bet," Smurf said, giving him a handshake.

Although Marco seemed cool to Smurf, there was something different about him that he couldn't quite put his finger on. He had gotten used to Marco being around Dink, but he couldn't get used to the man himself. Something wasn't kosher.

"What y'all gettin' into?" Smurf asked.

"Why? You wanna roll?" Dink said, looking over at his Honda.

"Hell yeah," Smurf replied. "I ain't got nothing to do." Dink looked at Marco and nodded.

The two men walked toward Dink's car, and Smurf happily followed them. Smurf made it a point to sit right behind Marco. He didn't trust the man, no matter how cool he and Dink were. If Dink gave the word, Smurf would gladly choke the man from behind.

Marco had been on the scene since before Smurf's time, but Dink had only recently let him into the business. The vibe Smurf got was that Marco was down only because of the years he'd known Dink and nothing else. Marco didn't look like he added anything to the mix. Dink just wanted to make sure his man ate. Smurf respected his boss's call, but he didn't like it. Dink caught the look Smurf was giving Marco, so he decided to break the silence.

"Smurf, this been my main man since, like, third grade," he said, referring to Marco. "He get on my nerves, but this one of the real niggas out here. You know what I'm saying?" Dink looked at Smurf though the rearview mirror.

"I hear you," Smurf said and nodded nonchalantly.

"Do you?" Dink asked, making sure that if Smurf really did hear him, that the shit was loud and clear.

"Yeah, I got you," Smurf said, gazing out the window.

"It's hard to find good dudes," Dink said. "And never trust any bitches, no matter what they tell you. Whatever you do, never let a female know your business."

Smurf didn't reply.

"I wonder if bitches will change their style in the nineties. New decade, new attitude maybe," Dink said, thinking out loud. "Nah, they ain't gon' be no different." Dink continued talking as if either Smurf or Marco was dying to hear what he had to say. "This shit will also change you as a person," he said.

"What you talkin' 'bout up there, man?" Smurf asked, confused.

"The game," Dink replied. "It makes you callous to a lot of shit the average person gets all emotional about. Because you constantly hustlin' and have it on the mind, you always think people hustlin' you."

"Huh?" Smurf said.

"I'll give you an example," Dink said, clearing his throat. "Sometimes when I hear someone say somethin' I don't understand at the time or agree with, my antennas go up and I lose it because I think they tryin' to swindle me. That doesn't mean that they are. It's just the shifty shit that you do makes you defensive like that. You have to be careful. You can ruin a lot of relationships with that bullshit. I'm still battling with that. It ain't easy."

"He right, Smurf," Marco added, finishing off the Devil Dog he was eating. "Niggas'll try to glaze you all the time, but you have to be sophisticated enough to be able to differentiate between the straight shooter and the one tryin' to take you. You have to work on that balance."

"Balance?" Smurf questioned.

"Yeah," Dink said. "Niggas mistake kindness for weakness, so you have to be cool breeze but yet rule with an iron fist. You got to know when to go hard and when to finesse shit."

Smurf absorbed every word. He knew how to be still and let the teachers teach. This was a plus.

"I can tell by what you just said that you's a smart nigga," Marco said, turning down the car radio.

"Smart? I ain't said nothing," Smurf protested.

"That's the point," Dink said casually. "Most niggas know too much, and they can't take direction. They always tryin' to get you to believe how true they are. You just listen and sop it up like a mop."

Smurf had no comment.

"That's why I gave you that piece back in the day. I don't just give niggas I don't know shit, especially without seeing any paper. In you, I saw loyalty and someone truly willing to do whatever it takes to rise above the dumb shit. That's why I put you down. You still got a long education ahead of you, but you're a good student. I wish my nigga Earl was here to meet you."

"What happened to him?" Smurf inquired.

"Oh, he ain't dead or nothing like that. He doin' life right now," Dink said sorrowfully.

"Life?" Smurf said with a deep sigh, lowering his head. "Shit, nigga might as well be dead. What did he do, anyway?"

Marco and Dink looked at each other.

"What you've been doing for the past two years," Dink said. "You came along not long after he got knocked. Earl was thorough too. You got big shoes to fill, kid."

"Sounds like this conversation is long overdue," Smurf said.

"Well, then, I guess it's better late than never," Dink said. "But listen up. You've got an edge over

Earl, and that is your age and size. People don't even think you're old enough to piss straight, let alone drop a nigga. Even though you 'bout to be eighteen, you look like a baby. That's why they never see it coming. Police wouldn't even give you a second look. And if you do get bagged, it's a slap on the wrist. You won't even have a record."

Marco turned the air conditioner up to max, and a frigid wind swept through the car. Dink looked at him like he was crazy. The weather was nice, but it wasn't summertime yet.

"Marco, turn that shit down," Dink ordered.

"Damn, it's hot in here," Marco complained as he turned the air down. There were three things Marco always was: hungry, hot, and out of breath. "You know it's hot in this bitch," he continued. "If you open the glove compartment, you'll see the devil in there sittin' on an ice cube."

"Crazy muthafucka," Dink said with a slight laugh.

"Say, let me ask you something," Smurf said. "I've been down with y'all niggas for a minute, right?"

"Your point?" Dink asked.

"My point is, when am I gonna get to meet the rest of the crew?" Smurf said, leaning forward to the point where his head was almost perfectly positioned between Marco' s and Dink's. "So far I've only met a couple of cats."

"Yeah, and you don't need to know the rest," Marco said. "You're the best kept secret, so to speak. The less niggas you know and the less they know you, the better off you'll be."

"That's right," Dink cosigned. "They're gonna know who you are, but they ain't gotta know why you wit us. That's my business. Plus, those low-level, bottom-of-the-totem-pole niggas get replaced a lot. Never can tell who's gonna make it and who ain't."

"What about the cat Dame I've been hearing so much about?" Smurf asked.

Dink and Marco exchanged glances.

"You'll meet him soon enough," they answered in unison.

Rick Young, otherwise known as Dame, was well known for outsmarting the police a couple of years earlier. They thought they had him, but he had mastered a trick that some of the young hustlers weren't up on yet. When the police searched him, the drugs were nowhere on his person. Frustrated, they had to let him go. They couldn't figure out what the hell he did with the drugs. He stuffed them in his ass. It was a trick he had learned from his brother while he was up North.

As a boy, Rick was made fun of by his peers. He was called ugly, and females paid him no attention. His family ignored him, and his teachers neglected his needs in the classroom. If that wasn't enough, his chest was flabby and underdeveloped. People said it looked like he had breasts, which resulted in people calling him Tittie Ricky. Many fights were started over this nickname. Rick's psyche took a beating during his adolescent years, in part because he had no father to turn to. Tyrone, Rick's father, was a below-average-looking country Negro with no talent. Rick saw him only twice in his life. He favored his mother, though, and blamed her for what he was told was his repulsive appearance. And it wasn't just Rick's outward appearance that caused him so much pain. It was the fact that he secretly craved love from a woman, which he had never got as a child. He despised his mother on account of both things, along with any female that reminded him of her. He eventually became violent, and his aggression was mostly directed toward women.

By the time he reached his late teens, peddling illegal drugs had made Rick's confidence soar. He was the man when he was on the grind. For the first time, he had the attention of females, and he treated them all like shit. Any time a female pushed his buttons, he took his deep-seated personal frustrations out on her.

Rick also had a reputation as being somewhat extra. He was doing his own thing out in Brooklyn before joining forces with Dink. He was a good earner and brought a multitude of talents to the team. Most notable was his lust for violence. But he was a hothead who believed in doing things only one way—his way. He and Dink constantly butted heads, but the money they made together overshadowed all the bullshit.

"Yo, speaking of Dame, that nigga tryin' to run whores now on the sneak tip. Muthafucka always doing some sideways shit. Yo, we need to check him, Dink," said Marco.

Marco had never liked Dame, because Dame had a file on him. He wasn't sure exactly what he knew, but Dame was always giving Marco a look like "I got yo' ass, nigga." This made Marco insecure, and he felt as if Dame carried this information around like an ace of spades. This gave Marco the feeling that Dame would show his hand at any given moment. A feeling that was justified, indeed.

Chapter 7

Still Down For Me

It had been a couple of days since Laci had seen her girls. None of the girls wanted to make the initial contact. They chose to sit back and allow Laci to get at them so they could see where her head was at. Laci couldn't have cared less about who made contact first. She had spent the past forty-eight hours fantasizing about getting high, wanting that feeling back.

The morning after Laci went on her quest for a high, she started to feel a little under the weather. Her mother even walked into her bedroom and found her keeled over. They both thought Laci might be coming down with the flu. So, Margaret kept Laci home from school a couple of days.

Laci tried to stay in bed for those couple of days, but as the hours ticked by, she became more and more restless. For some reason, she couldn't stop thinking about getting high. Not the high she had got from Tee's weed. That had just made her the three *S*s: sleepy, silly, and starved. Laci needed that high she had felt from her first hit ever. She feared that like sex, it would never be like the first time.

The weed she smoked at Lisa's had stunk to high hell, but it had taken Laci to paradise. She shivered just remembering the feeling.

During the days she spent at home, Laci's mom tried to make small talk, but Laci only half listened and half responded. All she could think about was getting high. Her mother went on and on about graduation and Puerto Rico. Laci wasn't trying to hear that shit, not unless the principal was going to hand her a rolled-up blunt instead of a rolled-up diploma, or unless her parents were sending her off to Puerto Rico with a suitcase full of weed. Fuck clothes. Laci would lie around buck naked, blazin'.

After two days at home, Laci was damn near ready to climb the walls, which seemed to be closing in on her. The high was calling her, and she couldn't resist. In her mind, she thought it was the cool thing. Now she had a weed habit, just like the girls. Laci had no idea what tune the devil was about to play for her on his fiddle. She didn't care, either. She was just content to be dancing at all. Now she knew why the girls couldn't fly in the world without getting high.

When she thought about the girls, her mind went back to Nay-Nay's weed and the high it had provided her. She kinda missed the girls, or maybe it was the weed she knew they could get for her that she really missed. Either way, she was missing something inside. Laci decided to shoot Nay-Nay a call. Maybe Nay-Nay could help her fill the void. Laci picked up the phone and dialed the number.

"Who dis?" Nay-Nay answered on the second ring, with a stink attitude.

"Hey, it's Laci," she said sheepishly. "What you doing?" Laci spoke as if nothing was up, so Nay-Nay did the same.

"Nothing. I'm waiting for Shaunna's pregnant ass," Nay-Nay said. "Where you been hidin'?" Nay-Nay waited for Laci's response. If Laci was going to clown, this was going to open the door for her to do so.

"I've been a little sick," Laci told her.

"Really?" Nay-Nay sighed a sigh of relief. "Everything cool?"

"Yeah, probably just getting a cold." Laci sniffed.

"Say, how did you like that weed?" Nay-Nay asked, again opening up the door of opportunity.

"It was the bomb," Laci said excitedly. "I was actually gonna ask if you had any more."

There was a pause.

"Well, do you?" Laci asked, impatient.

Nay-Nay's mouth dropped open. "Listen to little Miss Pothead." Nay-Nay smiled cunningly. "Sorry, girl. The last of that got smoked up."

"Damn," Laci said, sounding defeated.

"But I know where to get more," Nay-Nay told her. "But it's a little expensive."

Fuck it, Nay-Nay thought. The shit must not have fazed her like they thought it would. It didn't kill her, either, so everything was all good. Anything this bitch did now, she was doing on her own.

"How much?" Laci asked, looking over at her purse, which was sitting on her dresser.

"Depends. Usually you've gotta buy it in bulk. For about a hundred, I can probably do something for you."

"I don't know if I've got that much on me," Laci said. All she had left was what was in her purse the night she met Tee. She walked over to the dresser, opened her purse, and thumbed through her cash.

"Don't sweat it," Nay-Nay said nonchalantly. "We can get some regular green."

Laci thought about the weed she had smoked with Tee, and got turned off. That green shit was whack. She needed to get exactly what she had had the other night. Anything less just wouldn't cut it.

"Give me a little while to try to scrape up that hundred," Laci said.

"Okay. Meet us at the Parsons Boulevard stop on the F line at, like, four o'clock," Nay-Nay instructed. She hung up before Laci could answer. There was no need to wait for a reply. She knew the girl would be there.

Right after Nay-Nay got off the phone with Laci, Shaunna showed up at her house. She wobbled into the house and flopped down on Nay-Nay's couch. Shaunna, several months along in her pregnancy, was starting to look run down. Trying to live the life and carry a child at the same time was starting to catch up with her.

"Girl, you're just in time," Nay-Nay said to Shaunna.

"In time for what?" Shaunna asked.

"To see some funny shit," Nay-Nay said, like she was in possession of a top secret. "I just hung up the phone with you-know-who."

"Who?" Shaunna asked.

"Who you think, yo?" Nay-Nay said, placing her hand on her hip. She sucked her teeth.

"Word?" Shaunna said, leaning forward. "Did you call her? What did she say? Did she cuss you out?"

"Listen to this," Nay-Nay said, sitting down next to Shaunna. "We're about to take her over on Hillside to get some rock."

"No way," Shaunna said in complete disbelief. "You need to cut it out. Don't you think one time is enough? You're gonna give the girl a fucking habit."

"It ain't on me," Nay-Nay protested. "That ho called and asked me to get it for her."

Shaunna shook her head in disagreement. "Nay-Nay, I think you're going a li'l too far with this shit. I mean, ha ha, jokes over. We all had a good laugh. The bitch passed initiation, or whatever you want to call it. It's over."

"Damn, you starting to sound like Lisa," Nay-Nay said defensively. "I called her to let her in on what was going down, and she tried to throw salt too. Fuck is everybody so worried about Laci now? I didn't see anybody taking that blunt from her the other night."

"Whatever," Shaunna said.

"Yeah, whatever," Nay-Nay said, waving her off as she got up from the couch. "Just bring yo' ass on so we don't miss her when she shows up."

Reluctantly, Shaunna pulled herself up from the couch and followed the leader.

By the time Nay-Nay and Shaunna got to the Parsons stop, Laci was already waiting. She still looked like her normal stuck-up self. Her hair was pulled back in a big, curly, puffy ponytail, and she was wearing a pair of creased blue jeans with a crisp white shirt. She might have looked like the same Laci on the outside, but Nay-Nay could tell by the way she was antsy, dancing in place, that something totally different was going on, on the inside.

"What up, girl?" Nay-Nay asked, with a fake sisterly grin.

"Hey, girl," Laci said, hugging her. "What up, Shaunna?"

"Hey," Shaunna said flatly.

Laci caught Shaunna's bland-ass greeting and made a mental note of it. It never failed. Every time she came around, one of them found a reason to have an attitude. She was so happy to see Nay-Nay that she didn't even care. Let Shaunna have her attitude. All Laci was thinking about was chilling and getting her smoke on.

"So, where to?" Laci asked, getting right to the purpose of the meeting.

"Right to the point, huh?" Shaunna mumbled.

"Shut up," Nay-Nay warned her. "It's only a few blocks from here. Come on, y'all."

Nay-Nay led the way up and out of the station. The streets had a light sprinkling of people, but it wasn't too hectic. Car dealerships lined one end of the strip, while gas stations and fast-food joints dotted the other. The girls cut up into a block that was filled with short brown buildings. Some were leaning, and some had just fallen down completely.

People moved up and down the block, trying to hustle this or that. Nay-Nay waved them off and headed directly for the man she was looking for.

Marvin was an older man who looked like he had seen better days. He sat on the hood of someone's car, rapping to a cracked-out-looking chick. Nay-Nay made eye contact with Marvin and waved him over.

"Gimme your money, Laci," Nay-Nay said, extending her hand.

Laci placed five twenties in her palm.

"Hold up, y'all," Nay-Nay said, excusing herself from the two of them. She walked over to Marvin and started speaking in a hushed tone.

Laci looked around the neighborhood as if she was scared to death. She was afraid that someone might spot her and tell her parents. But no one that her parents knew would be caught dead in that particular area. That only alleviated Laci's fear a little bit. She had been through many such hoods, but that was in a car or just passing through; she had never actually lingered in broad daylight in a hood like this one. Being in such close proximity to so many addicts made her uneasy. It was crazy what she noticed under the sun's watch that she hadn't noticed under the moon's.

Shaunna noticed how noided Laci was acting. She simply shook her head. Laci was afraid of the very thing she was becoming.

"Let's go, y'all," Nay-Nay said, walking past her friends.

"Did you get it?" Laci asked hopefully.

"Just bring yo' ass," Nay-Nay said, continuing her stroll.

Laci scrambled behind her like a lost puppy. Nay-Nay got a kick out of stringing Laci along. It made her feel good to be on top for once. Laci had tasted the drug only for a short time, and she was already starting to jones from it. Miss High and Mighty would be put in her place.

"Let's hop in a cab," Laci said, looking around. "I wanna get up outta here."

"What's the matter?" Shaunna teased. "Ain't got no stomach for the hood?"

"No, I just want to get off this hot-ass block," Laci lied. Between all the activity and her urge to get high, Laci felt like she was going to go bananas. When a gypsy cab pulled to a stop in front of the girls, Laci was the first one to hop in.

Nay-Nay was slick with her shit. When they got in the cab, Laci asked to see what her hundred dollars had bought her. Nay-Nay fed her a bullshit excuse about the area being too hot to flash it for her. During the ride Shaunna engaged Laci in conversation while Nay-Nay discreetly rolled the woo. By the time they reached their destination, Laci was presented with two freshly rolled blunts.

***

The sun set in the hood, and the locals began to stir. Nay-Nay and her crew had been in the same spot for the past couple of hours. Laci sat on a bench, higher than high. She was looking off into space and having trouble feeling her tongue. The bullshit green that Tee had lit with her didn't have shit on what she was feeling at that moment. This was the kind of high she had been craving.

By this time Monique and Lisa had joined them. When Monique first walked up on the girls, she immediately knew what time it was. She had seen Laci with that glazed-over look two days prior at Lisa's house. She looked at the stupid-ass grin Laci had, and had to turn her head to keep from laughing in her face. One time, maybe. But how the hell had they gotten Laci to smoke on a second occasion without her sensing that something was up?

Laci, being the kindhearted fool that she was, offered to let Nay-Nay spark the second blunt. Nay-Nay told her that she was trying to go for a city job over the summer and didn't want to piss dirty. Shaunna used the pregnant excuse again. Smoking with Monique was out of the question. Laci did pass the blunt to Lisa a couple of times but was too busy talking and carrying on to realize that Lisa never once hit the blunt as she held it between her fingers. It ended up just being her and the two laced spliffs.

The more Laci smoked, the more she fell in love with the drug. Nay-Nay had put more crack in the blunt than weed, but Laci didn't notice. All she cared about was sucking in the death mist that had become the object of her affection. Laci had been officially introduced to her monkey.

The girls pretty much just sat around watching Laci make a fool of herself. The crack had her bugging. First, she kept pacing back and forth, talking about how much energy she had. Then the fool started singing "Cloud Nine" at the top of her lungs. Shaunna felt like she was going to go into premature labor from trippin' off Laci.

"Yo," Laci said, hopping up for at least the fifth time. "I'm mad hyped. Any other time y'all would be trying to talk me into sneaking into a club or something. But now everybody just wants to sit around and look at each other. We need to do something, anything. Let's just make a move."

"Why don't you just chill," Lisa said. She had enough of observing Laci's condition. She wished she had just kept her ass at home.

"Fuck that." Laci snapped her fingers. "We need to be in the streets, y'all. Why are we wasting the night?"

"Listen to Miss Worldly," Monique said, then sucked her teeth. "You been standing in the mirror, practicing from your ghettosaurus? Why don't you sit yo' high ass down?"

Laci paused for a moment, getting ready to follow Monique's orders, like she normally would have done just to keep things down. But this time she decided against it.

"You know what?" Laci said, putting her hands on her hips. "Fuck you! Every time you come around, you bring your bullshit with you. Take that shit home with your tired ass."

Everyone got silent, and mouths dropped open. This was the first time they had ever heard Laci come out of her face. The crack had her acting outside of her character, and Monique didn't like it. Instead of trying to quell the situation, the girls looked on in anticipation.

"Fuck you say to me?" Monique asked, standing up.

"You heard me," Laci said defiantly. "You stay coming at me wit the rah, rah. You need to check yaself, bitch."

"Ain't this a bitch?" Monique said in disbelief. "This ho has been sitting back, taking notes. Well, write this down . . ."

Monique lunged from where she was standing and grabbed Laci by her shirt. Laci was caught totally off guard. Monique slammed her fist into Laci's face like it was a pillow. Laci tried to defend herself, but she was short. And Monique was a street fighter, while Laci had hardly ever been in a fight. Actually, she had never been in a fight. She was just the pretty girl who always got picked on and beat up. It didn't take long for Laci to start bleeding and for Nay-Nay to break it up.

"Cool the fuck out!" Nay-Nay shouted into Monique's ear.

"Fuck that," Monique barked. "I'm tired of this bitch. You ain't shit, Laci."

"Fuck you," Laci said, patting her lip. "You got some nerve. Low-life bitch, you're just hating, and everybody knows why."

"Low-life?" Monique said in a serious tone. "I got ya low-life, you fucking crackhead."

The other girls started to get antsy. Anger made a muthafucka speak the truth. They crossed their fingers and prayed that Laci wouldn't keep pouring on the truth serum.

"Bitch, you wish," Laci said. "I could never fuck wit that shit. I got too much smarts, unlike your dumb ass. And weed ain't hard core. Y'all said it yourself that it's a natural herb."

"You so green that it's almost fucking pitiful." Monique chuckled. "You think you so muthafuckin' street, but you ain't nothing but a prissy bitch. A street bitch would know the difference between crack and weed, dummy."

At that moment one could have heard a pin drop. The leaves on the trees rustled, while a basketball bounced, unattended, somewhere in the distance. Monique's statement froze the entire crew. Laci looked over at the girls. Shaunna had her head down, rubbing her belly, and Nay-Nay was looking away.

Laci closed her eyes and took a couple of deep breaths. "Wh-What?" she said, almost in a stutter.

No one had an answer for her. Nay-Nay shot a murderous stare at Monique, letting her know that she would answer for her dumbass move. Shaunna shook her head, and Lisa turned away. Things were falling apart fast, and someone had to step up.

"All y'all do is fuckin' run y'all's mouth," Laci said, both fury and fear starting to set in. "Now you mean to tell me that not one of you bitches have shit to say?"

Laci ran her hands down her head, as if she was tightening her ponytail. She began to pace in a panicked stride. "Oh, my God. Oh, my God," Laci repeated.

"Laci," Nay-Nay said, "Mo is tripping, girl. Why the fuck would we give you crack? We're your fam."

"Y'all my family, huh? My fuckin' fam?" Laci asked, teary eyed. "Fam doesn't try to hurt each other, not like the way y'all do me. All I've ever wanted to do was to fit in. The way y'all have each other's back—the unspoken love y'all have for one another—that's all I've ever wanted to be a part of. I've allowed y'all to do damn near everything but shit on me. Y'all talk about me like a dog in my face. I can only imagine what y'all say about me when I'm not around. Fam?"

Laci shook her head as tears poured down her face. "Fam doesn't try to condemn one another for wanting to be something in life more than just somebody's baby mama or somebody's bitch. Fuck kinda fam is this?" Laci spun around and ran off.

Nay-Nay sat there for a second before saying, "Fuck this. I can't let the shit go down like this." Nay-Nay blinked away the moistness from her eyes and called behind Laci.

"Laci!" Nay-Nay shouted. "Laci!"

But Laci was long gone. She was so far gone from the Laci everyone knew just a few days ago, and that would soon become evident.

Chapter 8

New York's Rising Stars

Similar to pumping iron, packing heat shot steroids into your heart. The first time Smurf felt the kickback of his .32, he was hooked like Floyd Patterson. Since then, he had been putting in work for Dink. Smurf looked at it as getting his degree in gun busting instead of anything he might've learned in school.

This suited Dink just fine. He was one of New York's rising stars and was destined for great things. Dink had a way with ladies and paper. Besides that, he had a dedicated crew behind him. Even with all this, Smurf was to be Dink's trump card. The boy was young and had a fresh mind for Dink to cram with whatever he chose.

"Oh shit," Smurf said, closing his borrowed copy of *Behold a Pale Horse*. He held the book at arm's length and examined the cover. When Dink had first let him hold the book, he hadn't even wanted to read it. It had been stupid to him, but as Smurf had got into the book, he'd found himself blown away. He was only halfway through it, but the book was already fucking with his head. Smurf dog-eared the page where he had left off, and stuffed the novel inside his coat pocket. He then high-stepped to the Ave. He had only an hour before it was time to meet Dink.

***

Many would say easily scoring 1440 on the SAT meant that you were brilliant and were on the way to doing something great with your mind. For Daryl Highsmith, it meant absolutely nothing. He had all his teachers throughout his school years dumbfounded by the genius that had sprouted from his lack of effort. More concerned with women and coming up with schemes to make ends, Daryl left school at sixteen, taking his scholastic achievements as serious as a mosquito bite. Taking after the only father he had ever known, he became a full-time hustler.

When Daryl was a child, he had no idea who his real father was, and he was nothing more than a bargaining piece for his heroin addict mother. When he was only two months old, she traded him to a pusher named Bruce for an ounce of heroin. It seemed only fitting that Daryl become a product of his environment.

With a pusher for a father and the streets for a mother, it was understandable how Daryl could be swayed by the lure of the streets. To Daryl, school and thoughts of the White American dream were nothing more than a distraction. Genius or not, when it came to school, he was jaded.

Although Bruce, also known as Bop, wanted a son, it was all for the wrong reasons. Not having had any paternal nurturing himself, there wasn't much Bruce could transmit to his boy, Daryl. Instead of a rose, to be tended to and nurtured, Daryl became a weed, growing in whichever direction the streets blew him. Through it all, though, he was determined to make his own way. By the time he was fifteen, Daryl was sitting on 250 grand of his own scratch and had no driver's license but owned three cars.

From there, it took him only three years to move from small-time pimp to minor-league pusher. Eventually, he became the man to see. Daryl had made his choice in life, and there was no turning back. It was around this time that he met a female hustler named Lisa. It was Lisa who had given him the nickname Dink.

It was inevitable that upstart street crews would try to contend with Dink and his troopers. Just before the summer of 1989, Dink gathered his executive branch together to discuss how they were going to rid themselves of a growing headache that called himself Titus.

"Who the fuck is this Titus nigga?" Dink asked his execs, fuming. "All I keep hearing is Titus this and Titus that. Somebody tell me something." Dink was to the point of raving now. It took a lot to get him angry these days, but some things got under his skin like tattoos.

"Y'all niggas is out there, right?" Dink continued. "Fuck is going on? Everywhere I turn, a nigga is telling me Titus stories, but my boys don't know shit? Fuck is up?" Dink slid down the window of his Honda to let some air in. Four bodies in a car could build up a lot of heat.

"Yo, I'm like you," Marco responded. "I don't know who the fuck he is. But what I do know is that he's on one of our blocks, gettin' money. At least that's the word on the street."

Dame didn't see Titus as the threat everyone else in the car did. He figured since it was his block that dude was violating, he should be the one stressing. Dame would handle things like he always did, his way.

Dame cracked a chipped-tooth smile as he began to speak. "I think y'all overreacting. It ain't even that serious," he said nonchalantly.

Dink turned in the direction from which the silly comment had come. He looked at Dame as if he had lost his mind. Dame had a bad-ass habit of testing Dink, and now wasn't the time for that. Dink took out his burner and placed it on the armrest between Marco and himself.

"Repeat that," Dink grumbled. "I want to make sure I heard you right."

Dame loved a challenge and feared no one. When he saw Dink's attempt at intimidation, he countered by pulling out his own piece, cocking it, and resting it in his lap. "I said it ain't that serious," Dame answered with a daring tone.

"How the fuck you figure?" Marco spat.

All eyes were focused on Dame.

"Because," Dame continued, "I seen that nigga around, and he ain't moving nothing major. He small and can be taken out in a second. I ain't sweatin' that fool."

"Where you seen him at?" Smurf asked.

"And why you ain't say that shit when I asked?" Dink added.

Dame had no respect for the seventeen-year-old gunman and resented the fact that he felt like he was in a position to ask him anything. The li'l nigga was a nobody to him and didn't deserve to be answered.

"Where?" Dink asked.

"Baisley," Dame said. "Around my way."

"Okay, so this is your problem?" Dink said, scratching his chin. "How long has this nigga Titus been violatin'?"

"Only a couple of months," Dame said, picking at his nails.

Dame's nonchalant demeanor angered Dink. "Two months?" he barked. "You got muthafuckas disrespectin' the hustle for months, and you ain't say nothing? Other cats lookin' at that like our team ain't keeping it funky. Soon one of them smaller crews is gonna try to climb up the food chain."

Marco wanted to say something, but he had a governor on his comments, and only he and Dame knew why.

"Look, man," Dame said, clapping his hands together. "If I felt the nigga needed to be seen, then it would've been done already. That's my spot. I know what I'm doing, kid. If his hand call for it, then he goes. When I off the muthafucka, niggas gon' know what the truth is. Right or wrong? Right now he comfortable thinkin' that he movin' in, but he can always be touched. I got it covered."

"Dame, I understand that you do shit different," Dink said. "But we countin' on you to keep it tight where you at. Forget about Titus for now. What's the deal with these bitches you fuckin' with? They runnin' their mouths, and niggas tellin' me shit they ain't supposed to know."

Two years wasn't much time in the game, but Smurf knew what Dame represented. He was a cancer to their crew. Bigheaded niggas like himself were always the downfall of the great dynasties. His gut told him that he would be called on to put Dame to sleep sooner or later.

"Believe me, I got this," Dame assured Dink. "I'm gonna take care of the bigmouthed bitch and some mo' shit in a hot one. I know just what bitch you talking about, though. Fucking dumb bitch. I told her to play her cards right and she would be good, but a fucking bitch is always gonna be a bitch. I was actually kinda digging her too. Bitch got crazy one time, and I almost killed her. If it wasn't for that crazy ho Quita walking in, I probably would've bodied her."

"That's why I always tell y'all to leave them hoes alone," Dink said, shaking his head. "Dame, you're either gonna hustle or pimp. You can't swing both, 'cause it's fucking up our action."

No sooner had Dink finished his sentence than two of Dame's girls walked up to the parked Honda.

"What up, Daddy?" Julie said. "No wonder I ain't seen you. You spending all your time with these cats." Julie was one of Dame's best pieces of ass, and she got away with just as much as his main girl, Quita.

"Go wait in my car," Dame said to her flatly.

"Hey, Dame," Naomi said, licking her lips. She usually stayed quiet, but the sight of Marco had her talkative. "Your friends looking for a date?"

"Yo, Dame," Marco said. "Call your bitch before you be pickin' her up off the ground."

"Damn, big man." Dame smiled. "Talk to her, nigga. It ain't gon' cost you nothin'."

"Yeah, what you afraid of?" Naomi asked. "Don't tell me that you scared of little ole me, big man," Naomi crooned in her clear stilettos and skintight tube dress, which was so short that the hairs on her pussy were damn near showing.

"Pshaw, scared of what?" Marco said, shooing her away. "Get the fuck out of here. I'll blow your little back out," he fronted.

Smurf sat in the back seat, confused, as he watched Marco turn down what he thought was a nice piece of tail. And it was free at that.

"*Shit*. If that was me, I'd know what to do," Smurf said. "She wouldn't have to say that shit twice."

Dame began to chuckle. "Yo, even li'l man back here ready to do the do," he said. "You supposed to lead the younger niggas by example. You ain't showing him shit, Marco."

"C'mon, big boy," Naomi begged. "Take me somewhere. I like you." Naomi ran her hand along Marco's cheek. "I'm clean, and I know this pussy is good. C'mon, baby. I ain't had no good dick in a while. Show me somethin'."

"Ooh wee," Smurf said, then whistled. "If he don't want none, hook me up." Smurf addressed Naomi. "Hey, girl. If he don't want none, I'll take care of you."

"You cute too." Naomi winked at Smurf. "But you a little young, sweetie. Come back in a couple of years, when you grow some hairs and start drinkin' beers."

"What? You crazy?" Smurf said, offended. "I know what to do. I wouldn't be sittin' there, stupid. I'd be all up in that ass."

"Smurf, you want a taste?" Dame asked.

"Hell yeah," Smurf responded.

During this rare moment, Dame's heart went soft.

"Uh, girl," Dame said to Naomi, "leave that fat nigga alone and give my boy Smurf here a shot of somethin'." Dame looked at Dink and said, "Dink, we done here?"

"Yeah, we finished for now." Dink nodded. "Do me a favor, though. Get these bitches the fuck off the block."

"Naomi, Julie," Dame called out the window, "go sit in my car." Dame threw Naomi the keys. "Smurf, it's on you. Go with them to the car. I'll be there in a second."

Before Dame got out of the car, Dink made sure that he understood how serious he took the situation.

"Yo, I don't want to have to hear about this nigga Titus no more, man," Dink said. "I'm trustin' that you gon' take care of business. If you can't handle it, let me know and I'll fill your position with someone who can."

"What did I say?" Dame frowned. "I told you I got it. I'm gon' take care of the nigga. You startin' to doubt me, yo?"

"And them girls?" Dink added.

Dame sighed out of frustration. "You don't even have to say it. I got it. You got my word on that. My word is bond."

Dame got out of the car and joined Smurf and the girls. Marco and Dink glared at him as he walked away.

"It ain't the fact that I'm starting to doubt your word," Dink said, addressing Dame as if he was still within earshot. "I'm just wondering if I ever should have held weight to them in the first place."

"I guess we'll find out soon enough," Marco said.

"Or not soon enough," Dink replied.

Chapter 9

By the Dawn's Early Light

Laci walked through the streets of Queens, trying to stop the tears from falling. All she had wanted was for the girls to accept her, and she had ended up playing the fool. But she couldn't fully believe Monique's confession. A falling-out was a falling-out, but to slip her crack? Her brain couldn't and wouldn't process it. Finding that shit out seemed like it would be equivalent to finding out that she had AIDS. Either way, she felt that her life was over.

She continued to wander the streets until a thought entered her mind. She needed a blunt to ease the drama. Yeah, after a blunt all the dumb shit would go away. Laci thought about the numbing effect of the drug and began to shiver.

What the hell was she thinking about? It seemed that getting high was all that was on her mind as of late. No matter what she was doing, the thought of getting high would come to mind. This made her wonder if there was any truth to Monique's confession.

Laci tried to tell herself over and over again that her peoples wouldn't go out like that. In all actuality, if Nay-Nay had wanted to slip her something, she had had every opportunity. Laci had never watched her roll the blunt, but she had trusted Nay-Nay so there had been no need to. But the more she thought about it, the more possibilities came into play.

Laci continued her walk and tried to push the insane thoughts from her head. She was just being paranoid. She had read somewhere that smoking weed did that to you. A blunt would help her relax.

Laci caught herself in mid-thought. There she was, thinking about getting high again. For some reason, she couldn't seem to focus on anything else. She wasn't a seasoned smoker like the rest of the girls, but she had smoked enough weed over the past few days to notice the difference in the highs. When Nay-Nay had first set her out, Laci had felt like she was on top of the world. It was the best feeling she had ever had. She had tried to reach that special place time and time again, only to fall short. She couldn't seem to get that blast that she had had the first time, but she was determined to keep smoking until she did.

Before Laci even realized it, she was back in the neighborhood that Nay-Nay had taken her to when they got the weed earlier. She didn't know exactly where she was, but she recognized Marvin. Suddenly, Laci had a thought. Maybe Marvin would score some weed for her. With getting high on the brain, she didn't hesitate to approach him.

"Hey," she called over to him.

"Who that?" Marvin asked through slit eyes.

"I came over here earlier with Nay-Nay. Remember?"

"Oh," Marvin said, scratching his chin. "What's up, redbone?"

"Chilling. I wondered if you could do me a favor," she said.

"What ya need, miss?"

"The same thing you got for Nay-Nay earlier."

"So that was for you?" he asked, surprised.

"Yeah," she said, looking at the ground. "I don't smoke all the time, just when I need to relax."

"Sure, kid," Marvin said. "Okay, let me get your bread."

"Is this enough?" Laci asked, handing him forty dollars. "Can I get something with this?"

"Yeah," he said, stuffing the bills in his pocket. "Gimme a minute." He then walked up the block and whispered something to one of the kids that was standing on the corner. A few minutes later, he came back to where Laci was standing.

"Come on," he said, motioning for her to follow him. Marvin led Laci around the corner and handed her four cellophane bags with rocks in them.

"What's this?" Laci asked, looking at the bags. "I didn't ask for this. I asked for what Nay-Nay copped earlier."

"What you think I just gave you? That's what Nay-Nay copped when she came through earlier."

Laci felt like she went blind and deaf at the same time. She couldn't believe what Marvin was telling her. It was just like Monique had said. Laci had been smoking laced weed. She felt like screaming, but the onlooking addicts put her on pause. Laci walked away from Marvin without saying another word. All she could do was look at the crack and cry.

Laci rode the train into Manhattan but didn't feel like going home yet. Instead, she hopped on the A train and got off at West Fourth Street. She walked up and down the side streets in a crisscross pattern. She didn't have a destination, but she felt the need to keep moving.

She found a little store off to the side and ducked in to get a few things. Laci picked up a bottle of water and a pack of gum. When she got to the counter, she asked for a pack of Newports and a lighter. Laci had never smoked, but she was stressed out and willing to try the cancer sticks.

As Laci scanned through the racks behind the counter, she noticed a variety of little corn pipes. She picked one up and looked at it. She had seen Lisa smoke weed out of these pipes before and had always been curious. She added the pipe to her purchases.

Laci found a little park near a basketball court and decided that it would do. The jungle gym had been long abandoned, so Laci had it all to herself. She climbed the metal ladder and sat on the lip of the platform. Laci pulled a cigarette from her pack and placed it between her lips.

She flicked the lighter, and the flame stood at attention. The orange serpent swayed back and forth, waiting for its mistress's command. Laci slowly placed the flame to the cigarette and inhaled. She gagged from the horrid smoky taste and spat on the ground. Laci tossed the cigarette and scratched tobacco from her mental things-to-have list.

There went her only reasonable method of calming her nerves. A moment later Laci pulled out the bag of rocks. She held one of the tiny stones between her thumb and index finger and twirled it. She couldn't believe how something so small could reshape a person's life. Round and round she turned it, becoming more fascinated as it went.

Laci couldn't believe her girls had been grimy enough to slip her crack. But if there had been more than weed in the blunt, wouldn't she have noticed it? Shouldn't she have noticed it? There were countless possibilities running through her head, but she couldn't be sure which one was accurate.

"Crackhead," she mumbled. "Yeah, right." Laci knew there was no way that Nay-Nay could've slipped her crack without her noticing. It was laughable at best. Laci decided to get rid of the rocks and be done with it.

Laci tossed the rock she held on the ground and then shook the rest of them onto the iron platform. For lack of anything better to do, she decided to burn the rocks that lay before her. She took her lighter and lit them. The rocks fizzled and popped, producing a sickly yellow smoke. Laci smiled at the melting pile and then froze in place.

At first, the stench burned her nose, and then it became strangely familiar. She started to bug, because her nose wasn't lying to her. She leaned in closer to get a better whiff, and sure enough, it was the same smell that she had encountered at Lisa's house. This was her weed.

Laci's mind spun at a million miles per minute. *Me, a crackhead? How?* Her brain couldn't seem to process this. She saw crackheads in the streets, but she didn't fit the bill. Crackheads were degenerates who came from broken homes. She didn't fit the description at all.

Laci was brought out of her daze by a sticky sensation on her fingers. She looked down and noticed that some of the melting crack had got on her hands. She looked at the gooey substance and observed it. There was something beautiful about it—something that wouldn't allow her to look away.

Just the smell of it put her in a tranquil state. Her mouth began to water, and her hand moved involuntarily. Without even realizing it, Laci had the corn pipe in her hand. She looked from the pipe to the goo, as if she was figuring out some great math equation.

"I need to know," she said, teary eyed.

Laci packed some of the goo into the pipe and stared at it. Her hand shook uncontrollably as she raised the pipe to her lips. She couldn't believe what she was about to do. Her poor mother's heart would be broken if she could see her right now. Laci was bugging, but she put the flame to the pipe and took a hesitant pull. The smoke rushed to her brain, and there was no doubt in her mind this time that she heard "The Star-Spangled Banner."

Chapter 10

Satisfied With Nothing

Dink wasn't satisfied with the way Dame was acting and figured that he'd make a trip to Baisley Park Houses himself to see if he could get a line on Titus. During his drive there, all he could think about was leaving the game that put clothes on his back and food in his stomach. This micromanagement shit was starting to take its toll. Shit had been a lot easier when he didn't have to do shit but stand on the corner and sling. If he got taken out or locked up, it was all on him. But he'd be damned if he let another muthafucka be the cause of his downfall. Besides that, niggas were starting to get hardheaded. They was actin' like they were doing Dink a favor, even though if it wasn't for him puttin' they asses on, them niggas wouldn't eat. Yeah, the game was changing, and Dink's mentality wasn't. This didn't make for a successful empire.

"How much money is enough?" Dink asked himself out loud as he busted a right turn on Guy R. Brewer Boulevard. *Is there something out there better for me to get into? How long before I go to jail or get shot*? he thought. These were only some of the questions that floated around in Dink's dome as he scanned the boulevard, looking for anything out of the ordinary. It wasn't long before Dink was crossing Linden Boulevard and was driving past the bus depot. What he saw made his jaw drop.

Walking out from underneath the trestle was Laci. He beeped the horn, but she didn't seem to notice him.

"Laci!" he called out the window, but she kept walking. Dink checked for oncoming traffic. When he saw there was none, he busted a U-turn. He pulled his ride up alongside Laci and slowly followed her.

"Laci," he said, wearing a smooth grin. "Where you going, girl?"

Laci still didn't respond to him. She didn't even look in his direction. It was as if she was a zombie. This wasn't exactly what Dink had in mind when he'd decided to stroll the boulevard for anything out of the ordinary, but this definitely fit the category.

Dink pulled the car over, got out, and proceeded to catch up with Laci.

"Yo, Laci," he said, grabbing her arm.

"Get off me," she said defensively, snatching her arm from him. She then continued her stroll.

"Damn. What's wrong with you, baby?" Dink asked.

She could see that he was going to be persistent about this. So, ready to holla at this nigga, get it over with, and be on her way, Laci stopped in her tracks and turned to face Dink.

Dink looked into her eyes and noticed that they were glazed over like a doughnut. It was obvious that things weren't kosher. Although Dink had never really kicked it with Laci like that, he could still see that something was very different about her. Something that just didn't seem to go along with the girl he had held a conversation with the other day. Dink took a step back as all too familiar glazed eyes stared him down.

I know the streets ain't got her, Dink thought, giving Laci the benefit of the doubt.

Laci was in a dreamlike state. Between all that had gone on that night and the thought of getting high, she couldn't even function. She looked at Dink as if she were seeing him for the first time. Then, finally, she was able to focus for a minute.

"Dink?" she asked.

"Yeah." He smiled. "It's me, Dink. You a'ight? You don't look yourself."

Laci gave him a half smile, which he didn't take for granted.

"I'm just trying to get home," Laci said with an irritable tone. Not trying to seem obvious, she stated, "My mother is sick. I'm trying to get home."

Behind that half smile, Dink could see that something wasn't right with Laci. He didn't know her well enough to be able to read her like a book, but he wasn't quite convinced that it was her mother who was sick. Being caught up in Laci's physical beauty didn't allow Dink to analyze her frame of mind.

"Your mother is sick? Then what you doin' around here? Do you know where you at, girl?" Dink asked, looking around. "This ain't no place for a beautiful girl like yourself to be." He took hold of her arm once more.

"Yeah, I know," she said, fidgeting. "I just need to get home. I gotta go."

Laci tried to pull away from Dink, but he wasn't going to allow her to escape without telling him what the problem was. Plus, the longer she stayed, the more his heart fluttered.

"Laci, I have a car and can take you home faster than you can walk or get there by bus," he offered.

"That's okay." She brushed him off. "You probably have more important things to do."

"Laci, it's dark out here. You shouldn't be walkin' the streets alone. Now, quit playing, girl, and get in the car."

Laci wanted to be alone with her thoughts and her craving. Dink was cool. She could tell by the way he looked at her and the way he kept smiling at her that he liked her. By the end of his conversation with her in Lisa's kitchen, she had picked up on how he was feeling her. As a matter of fact, it had been a minute since a guy had looked at Laci the way Dink did. Well, it wasn't that guys hadn't looked at her. It was just that she had never taken notice like she did with Dink. Even so, she didn't feel like being bothered at the moment. Dink wouldn't easily take no for an answer, so she allowed him to lead her toward his car, but she had no intention of getting in.

"You still didn't tell me what you are doing around here?" he said, pressing the issue, as they approached his car.

"Damn, Dink! I just need to get home!" she snapped. "Enough with all the questions, please."

"Easy, shorty," he said in surrender. "Ain't nobody trying to get all up in ya shit. I'm just trying to make sure you're good."

She looked at Dink, who was only trying to help her. "Sorry," she said, embarrassed. "I didn't mean to snap. I'm going through something."

"It's cool." He shrugged as he opened the passenger door. "Come on," he said, holding the car door open for her.

"Nah. Think I'll take a rain check on this one. Maybe I'll see you later." Laci smiled at Dink and quickly walked away.

He stood there, deep in thought. He didn't feel played, but he was disappointed and thought that he didn't get the opportunity to be alone with Laci, to get to know her. It would have only been a drive, but it would have been a start.

A part of Laci had wanted to accept Dink's ride. For some reason, she felt safe around him. She had wanted to get in the car and tell him everything, but she hadn't. Another part of her had wanted to be alone to examine the remainder of her stash, and that part had won.

Dink realized that it was a no-win battle as he got into his car and watched Laci walk farther down the boulevard. He felt a longing in him grow, even though his ego was slightly bruised. But there would be another time, so he brushed off this encounter and proceeded down the boulevard.

But the more Dink thought about it, the more the situation with Laci really ate away at him. It wasn't because she wouldn't roll with him. Dink had more than his share of bitches. What disturbed him was that there was something not quite right about her. She didn't have that innocence and life in her eyes, which had initially attracted him to her. If he didn't know any better, he'd have sworn that she was on something. However, he couldn't waste time trying to figure out shit about somebody whom he had just met. He had bigger fish to fry.

Dink rode through Baisley, looking for the man called Titus. He had a description of the man, and from what he had heard, Titus shouldn't be hard to find. Soon enough he spotted his quarry entering a Spanish American restaurant.

Titus was truly a sight for the eyes. He was a tall man, but his body was shaped funny. He had a broad upper body but little toothpick legs. Titus's massive bald head was covered in beads of sweat, which he dabbed with a washcloth. The large medallion that hung on his chest looked more like a saucer than a piece of jewelry.

Dink found himself furious as the man walked through the block like he owned it. He was greeting people and nodding to shop owners like he was a fucking don. This nigga had invaded Dink's turf and made himself right at home. And to think Dame had said he wasn't bubbling. This made Dink rethink his relationship with Dame. Either that nigga was blind or had his eyes closed, because as far as Dink could see, Titus was on the come up in his territory.

Dink considered approaching Titus but decided against it. For the moment, he would just sit and watch. When Dink finally had enough of Titus's stunting, he decided it was time to take action. He picked up his car phone and called in the dog.

Smurf was surprised when he got a page from Dink. When he called back, Dink instructed him to come through Baisley and to bring his hammer. Smurf's dick immediately got hard at the thought of putting in work. Over the past couple of years, he'd become quite fond of it.

Dink silently watched Smurf as he slithered onto the block. Given that he was dressed in all black and was as small as he was, no one even seemed to notice him. Smurf pulled his black skully down and made his way across the street. Without being invited, he climbed into Dink's car.

"Sup, boss?" Smurf asked.

"Chilling," Dink said, lighting a cigarette. "How was shorty?"

"Man, she was proper. I bust it out."

"That's my nigga," Dink said, giving him dap. "Now, on to the business."

"What's good?" Smurf asked, leaning forward.

"Remember that shit I was getting at ya man Dame about?"

"Yeah, the shit wit the kid Titus."

"Right on, li'l man. That nigga violating, son, and Dame ain't handling his business."

"These niggas ain't built like that," Smurf huffed. "That shit should've been dealt with."

"That's why I called you." Dink smiled. "I want that nigga gone from here, son. Can you make it happen?"

"That's a dumb question," Smurf said, checking his nine. "Point that muthafucka out."

Dink flashed a broad grin at his pupil's enthusiasm. "In the restaurant." He nodded. "Fat, funny-looking muthafucka wit the big chain."

"Done deal," Smurf said, cocking his pistol. "Park up around the corner and keep this muthafucka running. I'll be back."

Smurf hopped out of the Honda and melted back into the shadows.

Titus came out of the restaurant, holding his bag of food. He had a big butt freak and a good basketball game waiting on him at the crib. The only reason he had even come out was that the girl had said she was hungry. He had never thought that a walk to the store would turn into the green mile.

Smurf came oozing out of a dark corner. He moved quietly through the sprinkling of people, tailing his target. He would've taken him out on the Ave, but there were too many people still about. Smurf was a patient hunter, though. When Titus turned the corner, it would prove to be his undoing.

Smurf quickly closed the distance between himself and the mark, never making a sound. Titus must've felt something was wrong, because he stopped and turned around. Smurf raised his pistol to the big man's chin. Titus opened his mouth to say something, but Smurf never heard it. He put two shots into Titus's gums. Before the man's body hit the ground, Smurf was gone.

"You should've seen my nigga," Dink said, passing the blunt to Marco. "Li'l nigga came running around the corner, talking 'bout, 'Floor this bitch.' This nigga was on his *Dead Presidents* shit." He leaned up against his car and nodded his head as if he was a proud papa.

"So, this li'l nigga get down, huh?" Marco asked after pulling on the blunt. "Niggas on the streets better know to steer clear of young Smurf."

"Come on, son." Smurf sucked his teeth. "Don't be putting my business out there like that. I like to stay on the low."

"Ain't nobody gonna blow ya spot," Dink assured him.

"I wasn't talking about you," Smurf said, cutting his eyes at Marco.

Marco caught the look that Smurf was giving him, and wasn't comfortable with it. The li'l nigga was giving him the same look that Dame had given him. He wondered if the two of them had discussed anything when Smurf popped shorty.

Dink saw the look that Smurf was giving Marco and wondered what the deal was. Ever since Dink had started having Marco around full-time, Smurf had been looking at him sideways. For some reason, Smurf just wasn't feeling him. This was something Dink would have to think on.

Before he could ponder it further, Dame came walking around the corner. Dink could tell that he had something on his mind, 'cause his nostrils were flaring. Dame pushed past the few cats that were standing around and stomped over to where Dink and the team were standing.

"What up, my nigga?" Dink asked with a smile, holding out his hand to show Dame some love.

"Don't gimme that shit," Dame grumbled, leaving Dink hangin'. "That was some bullshit you pulled."

"Fuck is you talking about?" Dink asked, faking confusion.

"Dink, don't play me like that, yo. You know just what the fuck I'm talking about. That muthafucka

Titus got hit." Dame paced back and forth a couple of times.

"So? That muthafucka was violating and had to be dealt with. Why you wetting why that nigga died?" Dink replied.

"I don't give a fuck why he died," Dame said. "I'm tight 'cause he got popped on my block. That shit was whack!"

"First of all," Dink said in a serious tone, "watch that bass in ya voice, nigga. Second of all, Titus was *your* fucking problem. I shouldn't have had to deal with it."

"Dink, you got no right to get in my business," Dame said. "You know what that makes me look like?"

"Wrong. I got every right when ya business is conflicting with mine. That nigga had to go. End of story." Dink looked off in the distance to let Dame know to drop it.

Dame's rage was mounting. He couldn't believe that Dink was coming at him as if he was some lame soldier. That didn't sit well with him. In all actuality, he didn't give a shit that Titus was dead. He had planned to kill him soon, anyway, but in his own time. Titus had been sending quite a bit of money Dame's way with the street tax he was paying Dame on the low.

"A'ight, yo," Dame said, sucking his teeth. "You got that, Dink. You got that." Dame walked away with his hands in his pockets. Part of him wanted to spin around and unload the Glock he was carrying, but he knew not to overplay his stroke. Dink would answer for his smart-ass mouth and cocky-ass attitude soon enough. Dame was content to bide his time.

"You better start watching these niggas, Dink," Marco said.

"You ain't lying," Smurf whispered under his breath as they each watched Dame fade.

Chapter 11

Slippin', Fallin', Can't Get Up

Once Laci lit the crack, it was out of her hands. After that first pull, she tried to pull away, but it was no use. As the crack burned, it began to sing in a whisper to her. The song was such a beautiful one that Laci couldn't hear anything else. It was a sweet melody that told her everything would be all right. Laci swooned to the rhythm while she inhaled the crack. She was in a total zone. When she finally came out of it, she was alone on a park bench, with a charred corn pipe in her hand.

Laci wasn't sure how long she had been sitting there, but her legs were asleep. She looked around, wild eyed, trying to gauge where she was. Sometime during her smoke session, she had wandered from the playground over to Washington Square Park. The park was empty, except for a few dope fiends and a lone crackhead, *her*.

Laci placed her head in her hands and sobbed. What the hell was she becoming? If someone had told her three days ago that she'd be sitting on a bench, smoking crack, she'd have laughed them out. For some reason, the light-headedness and the locked jaw didn't seem funny.

After working the feeling back into her legs, Laci got up off the bench. It seemed like when she stood up, her buzz began to fade. Without even thinking about it, she looked at the little corn pipe. The last of the crack was gone, and the pipe looked like it had seen its last days.

Laci tossed the pipe and began to stagger toward the train station. So much had happened in the past few days. So many things had changed. Laci felt some sense of normality returning as she entered the station. The pure crack still coursed through her system, making her feel awkward. Laci figured the only good thing was the fact that she hadn't done the drug long enough to get hooked. At least she hoped not.

The next day, Laci woke up sick as a dog. She didn't even remember coming home, putting on her pajamas, and getting in the bed. Her stomach was in knots, and she felt like she had to throw up. She credited it to being out until the wee hours. It never crossed her mind that she might be crashing.

Laci shuffled out of bed and headed to the kitchen. She rummaged around in the refrigerator but couldn't find anything of interest. She finally decided on a bowl of cereal. Laci took about three spoonfuls, then heaved the cereal back into the bowl. Milk splashed on the table and onto Laci's nightgown.

She coughed a little but managed to keep everything else in her stomach. She pushed the bowl away and proceeded to clean off the table. Her appetite had fled, but she was still craving something. Something she was sure she could keep down.

Laci washed the few dishes that were in the sink and proceeded to vacuum the house. After that, she cleaned her room. After doing all this, she still couldn't seem to sit still. This was one of those times when she wished her mother was at home so she would have someone to talk to. Talking would help keep her thoughts focused in the right direction.

Her mother was off at some meeting for a committee she was part of. Laci vaguely recalled her mother saying something about her missing another day of school and making a doctor's appointment. Everything was like a puzzle, though. Eventually, Laci thought, she would piece it all together.

She thought about calling the girls but immediately decided against it. After the bullshit they had pulled by lacing her blunt with crack, they'd be lucky if she didn't try to kill them off one by one. The girls were capable of some low shit, but never had Laci thought they would sink so low. What kind of friends slipped each other crack?

In a sort of twisted way, Laci enjoyed the high. It was a feeling she enjoyed. A part of her, the part that enjoyed the feeling the most, loved the girls for turning her on to the feeling. Shit was funny like that. The thing that made her now hate the girls was the same thing that made her love them.

When she'd smoked the crack mixed with the weed, the high had been out of this world. Laci thought that it was the best feeling ever. But when she'd smoked the crack alone, the high had been more intense. She had felt like every cell in her body tingled. It was a high she would never forget.

Just thinking about it made Laci moist. She felt ashamed of how the drug made her feel, but not ashamed enough to not want to go there with it again. She just would have never thought about putting crack inside a joint. But then Laci thought about this girl that Nay-Nay used to bring around named Quita. Laci remembered the girls never wanting to smoke any blunts that Quita had pre-rolled and was willing to share. They'd said her blunts were like a box of Cracker Jack. You never knew what surprise you were going to find inside them. But nine times out of ten, it would be crack.

Quita had never appeared to be strung out. Finally, Laci had a ray of hope.

Laci thought about calling Quita to see what she was up to, but Quita hadn't been around the crew since Nay-Nay had started fucking with Dame. Quita had been his on-again, off-again broad since before Nay-Nay was even thought of. In Quita's opinion, she still had claim over Dame. Nay-Nay didn't see it like that.

Although Quita had beef with Nay-Nay, she still spoke to the other girls when she saw them. But not once had any of the girls dared to stray from Nay-Nay in order to hang out with Quita. But now shit was different. All them hoes were on Laci's shit list. Maybe calling Quita wouldn't be such a bad idea. Being that she didn't fuck with Nay-Nay and didn't really plan on ever fuckin' with her again, Laci decided that she would go ahead and make that call.

Quita was hardly surprised when Laci called her up. Dame had beaten her to the punch by five minutes. There was already word surfacing about the fine-ass crackhead who was new to hittin' the block. Only one person that Quita could think of fit the description. Laci made small talk, but Quita knew there was more to her call. After getting tired of going back and forth, Laci finally asked Quita if she wanted to hang out. Laci was all too pleased when Quita accepted. She told herself that she just needed someone to talk to and nothing more.

When Laci arrived at Quita's house, she received a sisterly hug, something she had never got from her supposed homegirls. Quita opened her home and her heart to the young misfit. Laci thought that she might've finally found a friend . . . a real friend, whatever that was out here in the streets.

"Girl, I was so surprised when you called me," Quita lied. "It's been ages."

"I know," Laci said with a smile. "I had your number written down from that time Nay-Nay needed me to click you in on the three-way. Figured I'd see what you were up to. I felt like a change of pace."

"I know that's right," Quita said, pulling out a bag of weed. "You know I ain't the judgmental type, but I don't know what you see in them low-life bitches you run with."

"They're all right." Laci shrugged.

"Bullshit. Them some jealous hoes, and you know it. Come on now, Laci. Look at how them bitches treat you. They act all funny 'cause they're jealous. Tell me I'm wrong," Quita said, then waited on a response, which she never got.

Laci wished she could've given her one, a rebuttal at that, but Quita was dead right. That was what it all boiled down to, jealousy. Why else had they always tried to tear Laci down? She had always shown them so much love, and they had tried to flip it on her at every turn. Quita was right. Fuck them broads.

Quita continued to roll the blunt while Laci silently listened to her bash Nay-Nay and the crew. Seeing the weed gave Laci the urge to get high, but she was able to maintain her cool. It was when Quita pulled out the cocaine that she almost lost it. Being the virgin she was, she would have hated for her first orgasm ever to be right there on Quita's couch, but that was exactly what the sight of the cocaine made her want to do, cum all over herself.

Quita opened the tinfoil and began to slowly sprinkle the powder over the weed. Laci's mouth literally started to water. Quita finished rolling the blunt and lit it. The smell wasn't quite the same as Laci remembered it from the night she had smoked the blunt at Lisa's, but it was still quite similar. Quita saw the weakness in Laci's eyes and decided to play on it.

"I would offer you some," Quita said after slowly blowing smoke out, "but I know you don't get down."

"I'll hit it," Laci blurted out.

"What?" Quita said, pulling her head back to make sure she was seeing the full picture.

"I've tried some weed once or twice," Laci said.

"Sister girl, this ain't just weed. This is a woo. I don't know if you're ready to get this high."

"I'll try it. Just this once," Laci said, with greed in her eyes.

"Okay," Quita said, passing the blunt. She made it a point to hold it just out of arm's reach so that Laci would have to stretch to take it.

Laci could almost feel the pull of the drug. Her hands wouldn't even stop shaking when she reached for it. Laci took the blunt and inhaled deeply. When the smoke entered her system, the shaking stopped. She didn't hear "The Star-Spangled Banner," but she felt *normal* again.

Quita sat across from Laci, who had her eyes closed, enjoying her high. She could tell that was just what Laci needed. A fix. Whether little Miss Thing knew it or not, she had gone past the point of chipping and was developing a full-blown habit.

Nay-Nay and her crew were chillin' inside Crown Fried Chicken, watching the day go by. Shaunna was sitting on a crate, complaining about her stomach cramps. Lisa was on the pay phone, arguing with Dink, while Monique stared out the window. Monique had been unusually quiet for the entire day. Nay-Nay peeped it and wondered what the hell was going on.

Little did the girls know, but the night before, Monique had had an unforgettable evening with this Brooklyn cat named Sean, who pumped weed in Brooklyn. It was an evening that she wouldn't soon forget.

She had met him in the early afternoon, right after pulling off a boost. Monique had come out of Jimmy Jazz on Fulton and had tried to walk at a normal pace. She had just hit them for two outfits—two pair of jeans and shirts to go with them—and was trying to get away from the scene of the crime. Some of the girls would sell the stuff that they boosted to turn a profit, but Monique kept all her shit. Just because she was broke didn't mean she had to look the part.

After walking about four blocks, she ducked into a McDonald's and beelined to the bathroom to look over her goods. As she was coming out of McDonald's, she noticed a young dude sitting in a cherry-red BMW. He was wearing a black T-shirt and wore his hair cut close. A huge link bracelet hung from his arm, and a cross from around his neck. When he noticed Monique looking at him, he flashed a gold-toothed smile.

Dollar signs lit up in her eyes. Monique smelled money coming all off the boy, and she wanted in. She strolled past him, swaying her big ass and licking her lips. When he called her over, she damn near twisted her ankle getting to him. Monique never knew how to play her hand. After about five minutes of game, Monique was in the car.

They went out for dinner and drinks. By the end of the night, they were both feeling good, so the next logical stop was the motel. Sean and Monique went at it for a good while. She gave him head, and he piped her out. Sean's dick wasn't much to look at, but he knew how to work it. After they finished, he had an added surprise for her. He stepped into the hall to get some ice and came back with one of his boys. When his boy started stripping, she knew what time it was.

Monique had done two guys in a night on more than one occasion, but never two at once. That was Nay-Nay's thing, not hers. She tried to tell Sean that she wasn't wit it, but he laughed at her. He told her that for all the money he had spent on her, she would be down for whatever he said. When she tried to force her way between them, Sean slapped the shit out of her.

Sean and his friend took turns fucking Monique. She cried and asked them to stop, but they just laughed at her. After about an hour, they were done violating her. She was laid out naked, with semen all over her. Sean tossed her two hundred dollars and said they should hook up again.

Monique lay on the bed for another fifteen minutes or so before getting up. She took a shower with nothing but scalding hot water, then climbed into her clothes and left the motel. Using part of the two hundred, she took a cab back to Queens.

She felt disrespected and hurt, but at the same time she felt that she had no one to blame but herself. She had gone with Sean, hoping to get some money out of him, and that was just what she got.

"Anybody seen Laci lately?" Nay-Nay asked, skinning a chicken breast.

Lisa, who had just hung up the phone on Dink, replied, "I ain't seen her since the other day. Bitch is probably somewhere getting high." She laughed.

"You need to quit," Nay-Nay told her.

"Stop acting like you wasn't wit it, bitch," Lisa said, rolling her eyes. "You were the bearer of the bad news that got all this shit started, if you know what I'm saying."

"Yeah, well, we was all wit it the first time," Nay-Nay reminded everyone.

"But you kept the shit up," Lisa commented. "That girl could be really twisted behind that—"

"Fuck that bitch," Monique muttered, cutting in, angry at the whole fuckin' world right about now. "Serves her right for wanting to be so down."

"I still don't think it was cool," Shaunna said.

Lisa sighed, taking in Shaunna's words. "I don't know. Maybe you right and all."

"You didn't seem to feel like that when she was all up in Dink's face," Nay-Nay reminded Lisa.

"That called for an ass whipping, not a fucking addiction," Lisa said.

"Whatever." Nay-Nay waved her off. "What we doing tonight?"

"Shit, this li'l muthafucka is kicking my ass," Shaunna said, rubbing her stomach.

"Ain't nobody include yo' ass in the equation," Nay-Nay teased her.

"Fuck you," Shaunna shot back. "When I drop my load, it's on again."

Their conversation was broken up when Dink and Marco entered the restaurant. Dink was his usual handsome self and was wearing a pair of black Guess jeans and some construction boots. He spotted the girls and walked over to them. He nodded to all the ladies and kissed Lisa on the cheek.

"What up, Ma?" Dink asked with a smile, as if they hadn't just finished arguing on the phone.

"Don't try to be sweet now," Lisa snapped. "You wasn't sweet a minute ago on the phone." Lisa had hung up on Dink because he had seemed to have this stink, brush-off attitude, as if he had better things to do than to talk to her.

"Stop acting like that," Dink said, hugging her. "You know how you like to call when I'm handling business."

"Well, since you're handling business, can I get some money?" Lisa straight out asked.

"Damn." He sucked his teeth. Dink wasn't used to Lisa just coming straight out like that and asking for ends. "I ain't even been in this muthafucka for two minutes, and you're begging."

"Don't try to play me, Dink," she barked. "I hardly see you anymore, and when I do, your attention is divided."

"Look," he huffed, "I ain't got time for this shit, Lisa. Take this." He handed her a fifty. "Holla at me later." Dink walked away and joined Marco at the counter to place an order.

"What the fuck I'ma do with this?" she asked his back. Dink didn't even turn around. "That's a'ight," she mumbled. "You ain't the only nigga getting it round here."

Chapter 12

She's Gotta Have It

It had been fourteen days since Laci had declined Margaret's offer to celebrate her recent academic success. She had noticed a change in her daughter, and her intuition told her that they needed to have a heart-to-heart.

Laci had been keeping late hours and missing school. She had refused to go to the doctor or talk with her mother. The first thing Margaret had thought was that Laci might be hiding a possible pregnancy, although Laci was adamant about not having a boyfriend.

Worry had definitely taken a toll on Laci's mother. She found herself snooping through Laci's things and even trying to listen in on her phone conversations. It seemed to Margaret that Laci no longer belonged to a clique. The only person she appeared to want to be connected with now was some girl named Quita.

Quita was quickly tuning Laci on to the fast track. She had taught her that a crack high was cheap and that a coke high was better. Laci alternated as the mood struck her.

She and Quita had been getting higher than high for an entire week straight now. Laci and Quita snorted and smoked up anything they could get their hands on. It was to the point where Laci wasn't even mixing the shit anymore. She was straight up basing.

One night Margaret waited up for Laci to come home. It was three in the morning when she heard keys jingling. Margaret didn't approach her at first. She wanted to let Laci think she had pulled off sneaking in the house late again before she burst her bubble. When she thought Laci had settled in, Margaret went into her bedroom and found her about to change into her pajamas.

"Mom, why are you still up?" Laci asked, startled and a little disoriented. Attempting to hide her condition, Laci smoothed her hair and tried to straighten out her clothes.

She had been out for half the night, trying to score a decent blast. It had been almost three days since she had spoken to Quita, and her stash was all gone. Laci had found herself walking the streets with a jones and a half.

Margaret looked Laci up and down and wondered what had happened to her daughter. Laci's hair looked as if she hadn't run a comb through it in days, and her clothes looked like she'd slept in them. Laci was on fashion, so Margaret was sure something was wrong.

"Where have you been?" Margaret asked sternly.

"I was out," Laci stammered. "Out with a friend."

"Really?" Margaret said, with a raised eyebrow. "Which one?"

"Lisa," Laci said, blurting out the first name that came to her mind. "Lisa and I were hanging out in Manhattan."

"That's funny, because Lisa called here for you twice," Margaret said, using mother psychology. "Are you sure that it was Lisa that you were with?"

"Yeah," Laci continued to lie. "A couple of the other girls were with us too. Lisa left before the rest of us. She was probably making sure that I got home safe."

Laci was lying, but Margaret was going to see how far she was willing to go with the lies.

"Where did you say that you and Quita went again?" Margaret asked.

"I don't remember the name," Laci lied. "It was in the Village somewhere."

"I thought you said that you were with Lisa."

"Oh yeah, right." Laci smirked. "I meant to say Lisa. Quita wasn't even there."

"You know that Quita called you too?" her mother asked, continuing to play the game.

"Did she?" Laci said, getting excited. "When? What time? I need to call her back."

Laci headed toward the phone, but her mother stopped her in her tracks by grabbing her by the arm.

"Do you know what time it is?" Margaret asked, staring at her daughter. "What's wrong with your lips?"

Margaret held Laci's face in her hands and observed her.

"Nothing, Ma," Laci said, pulling away.

"Looks like their scorched. Like you've been smoking. Are you and your friends smoking?"

"Nooo, Mom!" Laci said, stomping away. "Look, some of the girls smoke, but I don't."

Laci hadn't told the truth since she stepped foot inside her house. In her condition, the falsehoods had started spilling out one after the other. She was also ridin' dirty and excused herself to go in the bathroom and dump the last flakes of coke that she had tucked in her hand. Her mother followed her and stood in the bathroom doorway and watched her daughter stagger.

"Laci?" Margaret whispered.

"Why are you sneaking up behind me?" Laci said, aggravated. "I'm in the bathroom."

Margaret wasn't going to give Laci three feet until she got an explanation.

"Talk to me, Laci, please," Margaret desperately pleaded. "What's going on, baby? Come on, Laci. You know that you've always been able to talk to me. That will never change."

"Fine, Mom. Cool. We'll talk," Laci said, trying to get rid of her mother. "Just give me a second to use the bathroom."

Laci started to panic. There was no way she could tell her mother that she was strung out. There was nothing she could say to her that would make her understand. Though it may have seemed a little rude, Laci walked over to the bathroom door and closed it in her mother's face.

Laci held the flakes over the toilet and hesitated. There were only a few scraps left, but it might be enough to fight off the sickness she was feeling. Laci ran her index finger through the coke and rubbed it across her gums.

"Laci, are you okay in there?" Margaret asked through the closed door.

Laci closed her eyes in shame. No way could she sit there in her parents' house with her mother outside the door and poison herself. She tearfully brushed the rest of the coke in the toilet. It hurt like hell watching her get-high disappear into the sewer system, but this was the price of attempting to live a double life.

"I'm okay, Mom," Laci called back. "I'll be out in a second."

Laci washed her face and splashed water on her curly hair, then slicked it down a little bit. She wanted to give the appearance that she had it together, but the mirror didn't lie for her. When Laci opened the bathroom door, her mother was still standing right there. No matter the trouble Laci was in, she was still her baby and Margaret was going to be there for her.

"Laci, I'm so worried about you," Margaret told her. "What's going on? You aren't acting like yourself. I mean, you're brushing school off and everything."

"Mom, I'm just tired," Laci said, rubbing her forehead. "You know, ever since I caught the flu, I haven't been myself. As far as school goes, Mom, you know the worst grade I've ever gotten since kindergarten is an A minus."

Margaret wasn't naive; she knew there was something more to Laci's story than what she was telling her.

"What about your trip to Puerto Rico, Laci?" Margaret asked. "Have you thought about that at all, or are you blowing that off like you seem to be doing with everything else?"

"I don't know. Maybe," Laci said, confused. Her mother was hitting her with too much all at one time.

Margaret watched her daughter tremble. "Are you cold?" she asked her, touching the goose bumps on Laci's arm. "You're shivering."

"No, I'm fine," Laci said, looking at her shaking arms. "I don't know why I'm trembling like this. Maybe I'm cold. I don't know, Ma." Laci began to laugh, though there was no joke made.

"All right, Laci," her mother said, sounding as though she was about to throw in the towel. "Like I said, I worry about you. You've been hanging out a lot, and I could tell that you haven't been eating much. You have to start eating square meals. You don't want to fall out dead out there, do you?"

"Don't you think that's a little extreme, Mom?" Laci said. "I'm not gonna die just because I'm not stuffing my face every five minutes. Besides, I do eat."

"Have you been thinking about college any?" Margaret asked, finding another subject to beat into the ground.

School wasn't on Laci's mind at all, and now her mother was really starting to piss her the fuck off. Why wouldn't she just let her be?

"Oh, Mom," Laci said, exasperated.

Margaret remained silent for a moment. The proverbial music had cut off, so it was time to stop dancing around. "Laci, are you taking any drugs?" she asked, just putting it all right out there on the table. She couldn't find an easier way to ask if her child was doing drugs.

"Why would you ask me that?" Laci asked defensively. "Do I look like I'm taking anything?"

Margaret dropped her head and sighed. "Laci, you answer my question."

Laci shook her head, acting like she was upset that her mother was accusing her of something foul without evidence. In her heart, she knew the writing was on the wall.

"Mom, I can't believe you," Laci moaned, flipping it. "Just because I've been hanging out a little more than usual, you think I'm doing drugs? You know how important fitting in with my friends is to me. Just because I'm hanging out more doesn't mean that I'm doing drugs. Summer is pretty much here. As far as these last couple of weeks of high school, Mom, even if I never went back to school another day, I'd graduate."

"This just doesn't sound like you, Laci," Margaret said, shaking her head.

"Well, it is me, Mom. People change."

Margaret sighed. "I'm so disappointed in you right now," she said emotionally.

"Mom, I swear to you," Laci said, walking over to her mother and gently placing her hands on her shoulders, "school is a breeze, and I'm not doing any drugs. I'll even take a drug test if you want me to. Dad's a doctor. I'll even let him administer it. Now, would I go through all of that if I were using drugs, Mom? You have to believe me."

Laci and Margaret stood there, having a minor stare-down contest. Laci was shouting out mental

Hail Marys that her mother wouldn't see the truth through her lies.

"Okay," Margaret said with a sigh, giving in but still not feeling 100 percent right about the situation. "If you say so, then I have to believe you. Here, let me help you into bed."

"Mom, I'm almost eighteen," Laci said, throwing her a friendly look. "I can put my own self to bed. I'm not a baby."

Margaret quickly pulled Laci up against her and hugged her. "You will always be my baby," Margaret said. "Sleep well, Laci. I'll make you a big breakfast in the morning. I want you to stay home and rest up this weekend, Laci. No excuses. You're going to school on Monday. Deal?"

"Deal," Laci said.

"Good night, baby."

"Good night," Laci said as she watched her mom head toward the door. "Mom," Laci called to her, "what has Dad said about me and school?"

"Nothing, dear," Margaret said, giving Laci that look she had whenever they were keeping something just between the two of them and away from her father. "Sweet dreams, Laci."

Laci watched her mother leave her room and close the door behind her. It eased her mind knowing that she had eased her mother's mind. Laci flopped down on the bed and let out a victory sigh. She then picked up the phone and quickly began to dial.

"Hello, Quita," Laci whispered into the receiver after Quita answered the phone sleepily. "It's me, Laci."

If it had been anybody else, Quita would have gone the fuck off for ringing her phone at that crazy-ass hour. But because it was Laci, she was cool. Quita and Laci exchanged necessary words, then ended the call. When Quita hung up the phone with Laci, she packed her pipe and lit up. She then picked up her phone and dialed Dame's number.

"Yeah," Dame said, answering the phone just like a hustler would. It didn't matter if you called a hustler at 4:00 p.m. or 4:00 a.m.; you best believe they were up hustling.

"Hey, it's your girl, Quita," she said, sitting back, blowing smoke. "It's taken some doing, but I finally got the bitch exactly where we want her."

Quita met Laci on the corner of Linden and Merrick Boulevard, by the gas station. The two quickly walked down Linden toward Guy R. Brewer Boulevard and headed in the direction of Baisley Park Houses.

Laci's eyes darted about as she scanned apartment buildings, parked cars, and people, who knew she was out of her element. She knew where she was, but she kept asking herself what the fuck she was doing there. She wanted to turn around and leave, but the promise of getting high was too tempting.

"Does Dame live over here, Quita?" Laci asked.

Quita snatched Laci by her wrist like a disobedient child. "Just follow me and stop asking so many fuckin' questions. Stop being paranoid and come the fuck on. My man ain't gon' wait all day."

"He's just going to give me some, right?" Laci questioned. "I mean, I don't have any money right now, but I'm good for it."

Quita didn't say a word. Her expression and tight grip around Laci's arm said it all. She knew that bringing Laci around Baisley would cause all the men on the street to inquire and hold them up, so she made a conscious effort to avoid them. There was no need to fully expose Laci to this world—at least not yet. For now, it was better that she remained nothing more than a rumor. And Quita had already violated one of her man's cardinal rules. Being late would double her punishment, and Dame was hard on bitches. As the two approached one of Baisley's back entrances, Quita gave specific instructions.

"Listen, don't act stupid while you up here, Laci. I'm doin' you a favor. Do exactly what he say, and we won't have no problems. Everything will go smooth."

"Okay," Laci said. "I trust you, Quita. You're not like the other girls. I know you're not going to let anything happen to me, right?"

"Nah, you my girl. I got your back."

They were lucky to catch a ride on the rickety elevator, being that it was more of a young person's sex and weed hangout than a means to transport people from floor to floor. Waiting to reach the fifth floor, Quita leaned up against the back of the elevator. She focused on how beautiful Laci was, even in her present condition . . . Her hair, skin, frame, and facial features looked fine. By the time the ding for the fifth floor sounded, disgust was evident in Quita's dark brown pupils.

Quita unbuttoned Laci's jacket. "Leave this shit open. He need to see."

Laci became nervous, and she began to mumble senseless things while continually straightening her already tucked shirt. Quita knew that the expected hit had her completely bananas.

"What the hell are you talkin' about, Laci?" Quita asked as the elevator stopped. "Don't you fall apart on me. We here now, so get your shit together." She gave her a hard look. "You ready?" she asked Laci.

"Huh?" Laci replied, dazed.

"Huh, hell! I asked you, are you ready?" Quita snapped.

Laci's eyes were empty, and she stood there like a zombie while Quita tried literally to shake enough life into her to get her to walk out of the elevator before the door closed.

Laci snapped out of her stupor and shoved Quita off her with attitude. "Stop shaking me, damn it! I hear you."

"Bitch," Quita said, putting her fingers in Laci's face. She thought about beating Laci's ass for biting the hand that fed her. But now wasn't the time. "Girrrl, you don't know. Just bring your ass."

Quita led Laci to a rusty blue door, knocked on it, and waited. Laci's constant pacing made Quita remember how bad she had wanted to get high before she learned to pace herself and became lightweight immune. In Laci's case, Dame had been rationing out the powder to Quita until she was able to turn Laci out completely.

After what seemed like forever, Dame answered the door. He wore a black bathrobe and was sipping Guinness. He looked at Laci and made a funny face. He'd never met her, but he would've known who she was had he passed her in the street, based on all the talk.

"Who the fuck is this?" Dame asked, as if he didn't already know.

"This is the girl I was telling you about," Quita said, walking into the apartment and pulling Laci behind her. "This is Laci."

"What up, girl?" Dame said, licking his lips.

"Hi," Laci said shyly.

"Fuck is wrong with you?" Dame asked Laci.

"Don't pay her no mind," said Quita. "She just needs to get right."

"Well," he said, pulling a bag of rocks and a pipe from the pocket of his robe, "she's come to the right place." Both girls' eyes lit up at the sight of the stones, but Dame pulled them back. "Hold on a sec. Let's talk finances. How much y'all got?"

"I don't have any money," Laci said sadly.

"You ain't got no money? Then you ain't got no rock," Dame said, putting the bag back in his pocket.

"Don't act like that," Quita pretended to plead. "We just wanna feel good, Daddy."

"Feel good, huh?" Dame smiled.

"Yeah," said Quita. "You be good to us, and we'll take care of you. Right, Laci?"

Laci didn't reply. She simply stared at the pocket where Dame had put the rocks.

"Come on, Daddy," Quita urged.

"Hmmm," Dame said, scratching his chin. "We're gonna have to work something out here."

Laci spoke up. "I can pay you back. I'm good for it. My parents have money. Tell him, Quita."

"Shorty, I ain't wit all that. No cash, no stash. But you know what? You a cute li'l bitch, so I'ma have a heart. Y'all get right," he said, taking the bag out of his pocket again and tossing it on the table. "We'll discuss payment later."

Laci and Quita damn near collided as they tried to get to the bag. Quita, being the more aggressive of the two, won out. She had first pick of the rocks. Laci took from what was left over. The two girls went to their respective corners and began their routine.

Dame studied Laci's internal battle from a distance and found himself aroused. Intercourse with Laci would be more than just sex. Dame's ego exploded when he imagined himself conquering high-yella ass with good hair and light eyes. Despite his success in the illegal drug market, his dark skin allowed him to play only in a certain league when it came to women. But today would be different.

"Don't get too comfortable with my shit, now, 'cause something got to give," Dame barked. Dame had been ranting for quite a while, but Laci had ignored every word that came out of his mouth. She looked around at the place she was in and wasn't even bothered by the fact that there were all kinds of drug paraphernalia lying around. All she could think about was getting high at any cost.

Laci's eyes rolled back in her head as the crack kicked in. Dame's shit was the bomb. It took only seconds before one whole side of her face was numb. It didn't take long for her and Quita to smoke up what Dame had given them. By then Dame had had enough of watching them get high off his shit. It was time to collect. He dropped his pants where he stood, then held his dick with two hands. He was feeling very confident.

"Yo," he said, "I know y'all bitches wanna get high, but we gots to come to an understanding. I ain't setting out no more rock till we discuss payment. What's up?"

"I told you I don't have any money." Laci shrugged.

"Li'l bitch," he sneered, "you think I'm holding my dick 'cause I want ya money? Nah, baby. I want it in trade."

"Go see him," Quita said, nudging Laci forward. "And remember what I said. Don't act stupid."

Dame was standing there naked, holding a bag of rocks. His huge penis swung back and forth as he shook the bag. Laci looked at him with disgust. There was no way she was going to do anything with Dame. No sooner had she had this thought than her legs started moving. As Laci slowly walked toward Dame, Quita started taking off her clothes. Dame told Laci to stop when she got only about five steps away from him. He wanted her to get on her knees and crawl the rest of the way.

"Get down and crawl," Dame snarled. "Crawl your ass over here."

"What?" Laci asked, thinking that she must have heard him wrong.

"I said crawl," he repeated.

"I will not," she said defiantly.

"Oh, you will," he said, packing a pipe and lighting it. He didn't pull on it. He just let the smoke float into the air. "You'll crawl, or you'll kick ya habit."

Laci thought about the pains that had rocked her body the last time she'd gone without a hit. It was something that she wouldn't wish on anybody. The thought of getting sick and the threat of sobering up made Laci weak. She would be degrading herself by being obedient to Dame and fulfilling his request, but the call was so strong. Laci started to bend down, but Dame stopped her.

"I want you to strip first," he said. "Take your clothes off."

"Go ahead," Quita whispered into Laci's ear. "Ain't nobody gonna know."

Before Laci bent down, Quita unbuttoned her shirt and unfastened her pants, then slid them down to her ankles. Laci's shapely hips and silky thighs made Dame shake his head and grunt in amazement. Never had he seen such creamy and tender flesh. Quita slipped Laci's arms out of her jacket and shirt and pulled her tank top over her head, exposing breasts that looked like they were dying to be fondled. There Laci stood, naked and in need of a serious high.

The combination of crack and sex, especially for beginners, drove them mad, so Quita loaded the pipe and kept it within Laci's sight.

"C'mon, bitch, crawl over here and get this dick."
Dame started to dance and shake his ass, as if
performing for a crowd.

Laci's insides boiled over with shame as she
made her way to Dame. Her knees burned on his
rug, but her addiction helped block out the pain.
She required what he had. Laci gently gripped
Dame's manhood in her right hand as her left one
cuddled his balls. Dame couldn't wait to feel the
inside of her hot mouth, so he hurried things along,
forcing her head to his crotch.

Quita looked on, rubbing her clit. Like Shaunna,
she went both ways. She wanted to eat Laci's pussy
just as much as Dame did.

As Laci performed the head clinic, Quita lay on
her back, slid her face underneath Laci's ass, and
began to lick and suck on her. Quita's experienced
tongue made Laci mash her pussy against her
mouth and briefly lay her face on Dame's stomach
in enjoyment. This was all some new shit to Laci.
The only person who had ever touched her clit was
her.

Dame knew what time it was. He reached for the
crack pipe and put it in Laci's mouth. Laci took a
man-sized hit and held it. The mixture of getting
eaten out and inhaling crack made Laci's pupils
disappear in her head. Dame began flexing like he
was the man.

After furnishing Laci with another rush, Dame went around to where Quita was lying and stuck two of his fingers between her legs and moved them in and out of her. Quita began to moan, and he swapped his fingers for his penis. Quita's moans weren't just a turn-on for Dame; they aroused Laci as well. Laci began to lick and suck at Quita's nipples. Laci figured that if she worked shit out with her tongue, then she'd protect her virgin pussy.

The sight of Laci getting into it made Dame wanna pop. Even high as a kite, the li'l bitch was still fine. Dame couldn't help himself from finding out what the little peach tasted like. He turned Laci around and started eating her from the back. Laci tasted like sun-dried peaches on his tongue. He had to have her.

Dame pulled out of Quita and backed Laci up toward his dick. Laci held back. She knew what was about to go down, and fear of pain set in. She had never even used a tampon before. She couldn't fathom something as big as Dame's dick running up inside her. But then she thought about the pain of not being high. Laci decided to go with the lesser of the two evils.

Dame proceeded to put his large penis into Laci's tight little vagina, but it ran into a roadblock. When Laci was about to scream, Quita put the pipe back into her mouth. Laci took a deep pull and exhaled as her eyes welled up with tears. Dame proceeded to enter her all the way. She took it all.

Laci's pussy felt like pure magic to Dame. He got only a couple of good strokes in before he had to pause. Laci was so warm and tight that he almost squirted prematurely. He stroked her slowly at first, and then he began to beast on her. He expected her to cry out, but she didn't. Laci banged her fists on the floor in both pleasure and plain. She started to beg for more, more of what, her mind couldn't decipher. Quita lay on the floor in front of Laci. She spread her legs and pulled Laci's face toward her pussy. But Laci and Dame were more into each other at this point. Quita's head was cut short because Dame's dick had Laci concentrating more on throwing her ass back into him than on how her tongue moved.

"Dame," Quita moaned. "Dame . . ."

He plowed into Laci. "What, bitch?" he responded, not missing a stroke. "Don't you see me working?"

"I know you ain't trippin' off no crackhead pussy. You in love already, nigga, ain't you?" Quita ran her hands all over her naked body. "You know this is the best pussy you ever had."

"What the fuck is you talkin' 'bout, bitch?" Dame said, holding Laci's hips, attempting to beat her precious goods to death. He pushed her knees to her throat. He needed that shit opened wide so that he could drill all the way up into it.

Dame gave Laci another hit as he continued pounding away at her. She came at the same time the smoke hit her lungs. She had no idea if it was Dame's pipe or the crack pipe that caused the eruption in her body. She didn't care. Dame continued to work her insides. The entire time he just kept thinking about how good Laci felt to him. He could feel himself getting ready to cum, so he pulled out and let it go all over Laci's chest and stomach.

Quita rubbed Dame's cum into Laci's skin like it was Jergens lotion and sucked the rest out of him herself. When Dame's dick was clear of sperm, he lit a cigarette. It was only halftime, and he was building up for another nut.

"You was lovin' that tight pussy, wasn't you?" Quita asked, shooting Dame an evil look.

"Bitch, pussy is pussy," Dame said after blowing smoke in her face. "I don't give a damn about that base-head bitch. I just wanted to beat, that's all. What? You jealous?"

"I brought the bitch here. How the fuck am I gon' be jealous?"

During Dame and Quita's back-and-forth, Laci lay on the floor, enjoying her high and the aftereffects of her orgasm.

"Shit, you actin' like you jealous," he continued.

"Look, I know she look good, and it's understandable if you hooked. I kinda think the shit is funny myself. I know if Dink and them knew how you was actin', they'd be crackin' on you for days. You should've seen yourself." Quita made faces, mimicking Dame's expressions during the sex.

Laci paid no attention to what was being said. She was in her own world, finishing what was left in the pipe. She couldn't give two shits about what they were arguing about.

"You forgot who the fuck you talkin' to?" The volume of Dame's voice warned Quita that she was about to get her head cut back to the fat meat. "Bitch, you got amnesia?"

"Nooo, baby," Quita said, massaging Dame's abdomen. She then kissed him on his neck to defuse any potential problems. "You know I love you, Daddy."

Laci sat on the floor, leaning against the couch. There was a vacant look in her eyes, and her mouth was halfway open. If it weren't for her chest heaving up and down, she could've been mistaken for dead. Laci was on cloud nine.

Dame looked at his cigarette and glanced at Laci. From the look in his eyes, Quita knew just what time it was. Dame was a cold nigga by nature, and Laci would soon find out what time it was too.

"Laci," Dame yelled. "Yo, baby girl, you ready for the second half or what?"

Laci kept up the mute act.

Giving Laci the benefit of the doubt, Dame walked over to her and posed the same question. "Hey, girl. I said, Are you ready for part two?"

There was still no answer from Laci, so Dame pressed his lit cigarette into her bare back. Laci jumped to her feet and tried to reach the burned spot on her back.

"Ouch!" she screamed. "What the fuck you do that for?"

"Your ass is talkin' now, ain't it?" Quita said as she laughed. "You'll be all right. It ain't nothin' a little smoke won't fix, right?"

Dame caressed Laci's breasts, then dropped to his knees and kissed her stomach. He wanted to be a gentleman, but he had to stay strong because Quita had already called him out. If he full out licked the precious now, there would be nothing that he could say in his defense. The more his tongue circled Laci's belly button, though, the more intense the feeling to lap her juice became.

"Light the shit, Quita," Dame ordered.

Quita loaded and lit the pipe on Dame's command and gave Laci a hit. As Laci pulled from the pipe, she pushed Dame's head between her legs. Much like the crack had Laci, the pussy had Dame. He let her lead him toward her pussy.

Quita looked at her man being humbled in disbelief. He could kick the shit out of her and call her out of her name, but he wanted to be suave with this bitch. She felt repulsed. Quita ground her teeth as her man pleasured Laci the same way he had her. Laci bucked and whined as Dame pleased her with his mouth.

Quita was red with anger and stomped out of the living room into the bathroom. She paced back and forth in a rage. There was no way that bitch was gonna play her out like that. The plan Quita and Dame had laid down was going to the left. It was time for Quita to make that shit right.

Dame got his second wind and pushed back up inside Laci. He was captivated by her beauty and her facial expressions as his dick slid in and out of her. He pumped away like a dog in heat while Laci threw it back like a vet.

Laci opened her eyes and took a good look at Dame. Here was this supposed hard drug dealer soft as Wonder Bread up in the pussy, whining like a bitch. His funny-ass face, coupled with the drug, made Laci giggle. The giggling soon turned into laughter.

Dame was trying to get his second nut off when he realized that Laci was laughing at him. He tried to close his eyes and act like he didn't see it, but he could feel her body shaking. Dame paused and looked at Laci like she was crazy. She was staring right back at him, laughing her ass off. Then, suddenly, Laci realized that Dame was on to her.

"I'm sorry, baby," she said, rubbing her hands across his chest. "I was just thinking that when you do your face like that, you look like one of those Sambo dolls." Laci began laughing again.

Dame couldn't believe that another side of him had finally shown its face. It was a side that allowed him to please somebody other than himself. And now here this bitch was laughing at him—a base-head bitch at that. Aiming at Laci's face, Dame drew back and smacked the pipe out of her hands and clear across the room.

Dame began to breathe heavily and growl. "So you think I'm funny looking, huh?" he said to Laci.

Frightened, Laci quickly pushed herself out from underneath him and crawled to the side of the couch for shelter. He grabbed her by her curly ponytail and pulled her back toward him. He forgot all about a certain part of his and Quita's plan as he prepared to put Laci's ass to sleep.

Laci observed the fierce look in Dame's eyes. "Quita!" she began yelling. "Quita!"

Dame grabbed Laci by her chin tightly.

"Get off me," Laci cried as she struggled. "Stop! Quita, help!"

Through the bathroom door, Quita heard the commotion and ran out to see what was happening. Dame had Laci on the floor and was trying to knock her head off. The Lord was on her side, because every time Dame tried to connect, he just skimmed her as Laci moved her head from side to side, dodging blows. Nothing solid connected.

"Dame?" Quita shouted. "What the fuck you doin'? Leave her alone!"

On one hand, Quita felt good about the ass kickin' Dame wanted to give Laci. She'd rather see Dame *bust* Laci upside the head than *give* her head. But on the other hand, she was afraid that Dame was going to kill Laci and that she would somehow be blamed for the death. Fearing a bid, Quita jumped on Dame's back and tried to calm him down.

Dame bucked, but Quita held fast. He tried to swat her off, but her grip was too tight. Quita didn't want to get into it with Dame, but she feared the worst. Murder was something she wasn't going to sit back and watch go down. She didn't want any part of that, so she maintained her grasp.

Laci held the side of her head and shot a murderous stare at Dame. In all her seventeen years, a man had never put his hands on her. Besides learning how to be a backstabbing broad, she had picked up from her girls that turnabout was fair play. Laci used the commotion of Dame trying to remove Quita from his back to get some revenge. She quickly gathered her clothes and what was left of Dame's drugs and slipped out the door.

Dame was heated that Laci had got away with his shit. Ordinarily, he would have arranged for her to be put six feet under, but with a little editing of that tape from the hidden camera that had rolled from the moment Laci and Quita walked in the door, he would still manage to make Laci wish that she were dead.

Chapter 13

The Apple Don't Fall Far

Laci searched hurriedly for a place to light up. She wouldn't dare smoke on the streets. If the police rolled on her, they might take her drugs. She had one other option, but she didn't like it. Not long ago a friend of an on-again, off-again friend had hipped her to a spot where she could get her mind right if she was ever in the area. Laci couldn't remember the building number, but she'd know the place if she saw it.

After walking up and down a few blocks, Laci found the building she was looking for. It was right off of 137th Street and Seventh Avenue. She hiked up the few stairs and headed for the door. Finally, Laci had somewhere to smoke in peace. Just when she thought she was home free, however, she ran into her uncle. Where in the fuck did he come from? She hadn't seen him in forever and a day. The only reason she even recognized him was that he was the spitting image of her own father.

"Laci?" he asked in shock.

"Uncle Sonny?" Laci replied.

"What the hell you doin' around here, baby?" he asked, and his eyes begged to know the answer. "Yo' mama know you hanging on a dope block?"

Laci smiled innocently. "Hey, Uncle Sonny. I was just coming from a friend's house. She lives in this building."

Sonny looked at Laci like she was crazy. She was standing in front of a dope spot, trying to match wits with a professional liar. Sonny had been a junkie for more years than she had been alive. He could tell by the way she was fidgeting that something was wrong. He looked into his niece's eyes and saw that all too familiar gaze, the same one that stared right back at him in the mirror.

"What's the real deal?" he asked. "I've been around for a long time. You think I don't know one of my own?"

"Uncle Sonny—" she began, but he interrupted her.

"Don't even go there, Laci. Okay?"

Laci thought for a few seconds. "Why would you think that? Do I look like a drug addict? I'm just tired. It's late. How do you expect me to look this late?"

Sonny stared at his niece, trying to get a line on her.

"What's your friend's apartment number?" he asked intuitively.

"Uncle Sonny," she said, then sucked her teeth. "I'm not going to tell you that so you can go bothering her, trying to check up on me. It's late, and people need their sleep. Speaking of which, I better get going myself."

"C'mon," he said, putting his arm around her. "I can't let you go off by yourself. I'll go with you."

"No, Uncle Sonny," she protested. "I'm okay. I'm good. No need for you to do that. You just go on."

"Why you gettin' all excited?" Sonny asked suspiciously.

"Like I said, I'm just tired. Can't wait to go home and get me some sleep." Laci let out a fake yawn and stretched.

Sonny knew damn well that Laci wasn't telling that truth and that she didn't have any friends in this area. He was looking around to see if there was anything that would give him an idea of what she was really doing in the neighborhood when a known local crackhead walked by and greeted her by name.

"Hey, Laci," the crackhead said.

"Hey, Angel," Laci replied as Angel strutted away, swishing her ass like she was the baddest broad on the block and always would be. Laci had heard that back in the day, she had been the finest girl around the way. But now she was a strawberry . . . a bum.

"I gotta go," Laci said, returning her attention to her uncle. She lowered her head and walked off.

Sonny called behind her, but Laci kept going. He ran after her.

"Hold up," Sonny said, catching up with Laci and grabbing her by the hand. He looked down, closed his eyes, and took a deep breath. He didn't even want to look in his niece's eyes again. He didn't want to see that look, but he had to.

"What is it, Uncle Sonny? I gotta get home."

Sonny lifted his head. "Looking in your eyes is like looking in a mirror, girl. That look in your eyes, I had it, too, back in the sixties, when I started using drugs," Sonny said in a deeply sincere tone.

Laci moved her lips in an attempt to respond, but Sonny shook his head to stop her from speaking.

"Don't talk. Just listen. I know what these streets can do to a girl like you, Laci. I've seen it. Hell, I'm a grown man, and I know what these streets done to me. Some things I'm too ashamed to even admit. Can't even face myself sometimes. No wonder your daddy won't have nothing to do with me."

"Uncle Sonny," Laci said, trying to interrupt.

"No, no, girl. Let me talk." Sonny paused, then continued. "I know I ain't been in your life enough to be telling you a damn thang. But I'm gonna tell you, anyway." Sonny shook his head and tightened his lips, almost as if he was fighting back his emotions. "Don't do it, Laci," he said, moving his hand up and down with each syllable while Laci's was still cupped inside it. "Don't become like your uncle Sonny here. You'll have nothing. You'll be nothing. You're far too pretty and smart. I know my brother ain't raised no fool. He's a strong man and proud. That's how I know you're strong too, Laci. You're strong enough to get out now."

"But, Uncle Sonny, I don't know what you're talking a— " Laci said before Sonny cut her off.

"You know, Laci. Look at me. I'm an old man. You think you can outslick a slicker? Battin' them pretty little eyes might work on ya mama, but not on me. I know these streets, and the streets don't lie."

Laci put her head down and pulled her hand away from Sonny's.

"Uh-uh," Sonny said, lifting Laci's head by her chin. "Don't go puttin' your head down now. It ain't too late to beat this thing. Go to your mama. She loves you, Laci. Your daddy is stubborn as a mule, but I'm sure he wouldn't turn his back on you."

"The same way he didn't turn his back on you?" Laci said sarcastically.

Sonny was silent for a moment, weighing Laci's point. "Your daddy and me is a different story. You are his heart. Ain't no man gon' love you like yo' daddy. And see, when a man loves you, even yo' daddy, he's got to appreciate you at your worst in order to appreciate you at your best. Remember that with any man, Laci. But you also need to re-member who *don't* love you, and that's the streets. They mean. And so are those who belong to the streets."

Laci had heard enough. She knew her uncle meant well, but getting high meant better. "I hear you, Uncle Sonny, but it ain't even like that with me. Look, I gotta get going." Laci gave her uncle a quick peck on the cheek, then ran off.

"Laci," he shouted. "Laci!"

She was gone.

Being an addict himself, he knew all the early signs of addiction. And he didn't like what he was seeing right now. It was bad enough that he had fucked his life up with drugs, but he couldn't bear to watch his niece go through the same thing. He had failed his mother and his brother, but the least he could do was save Laci.

As far as Jay was concerned, his brother, Sonny, no longer existed. He was dead. But that had never stopped his wife, Margaret, from staying in touch with Sonny to make sure he was still breathing. Whenever there was a problem that needed in-fluence or assistance from the streets, Sonny was always the first person Margaret contacted.

"Hello." Sonny answered the phone with a raspy voice.

"Hi. It's me, Margaret," she responded. It was always easy for her to sneak phone calls to Sonny, since her husband was seldom home.

"Hey now," Sonny said happily. "How's my sister-in-law doing? How long has it been?"

"Too long," Margaret said with a sigh.

Sonny laughed and then coughed. "I agree. Too damn long is right. How's that uptight little brother of mine?"

"Oh, you know Jay," Margaret said. "Still uptight, but he's coming around. It's your niece that I'm worried about." Margaret paused. But Sonny could hear her trying to bury her faint whine. He recognized it. It was the same whine his mother had tried to hide from his brother and him many nights behind her bedroom door.

"What do you mean?" Sonny asked, feeling her out. He didn't want to jump right in, not knowing fully what was going on.

"I don't know exactly," Margaret said, her voice trembling. "I don't want to jump to any conclusions, but something's not right with my baby, Sonny." Not being able to hold it in any longer, she began to weep.

Sonny took the phone from his ear and put it on his chest. Nothing sounded worse to his ears than a mother's cry. This was the cry he had tried to avoid hearing many years earlier, and now here it was, dead smack in his ear.

"Sonny, you still there?" Margaret asked after he hadn't responded for a few moments. Sonny put the phone back to his ear. "Sonny?" Margaret repeated.

"Yeah, sis. I'm here," he said, sniffling. "I, uh, saw her the other night. It was about two in the morning. She didn't look right. I mean, she still looked like my beautiful niece, but there was something in her eyes, Margaret. It was a look that I had seen before."

"Where?" she hated to ask.

"She was in a place she didn't need to be." Sonny sighed.

"No, I mean where had you seen the look before?"

Sonny was silent for a second. It killed him to say the words that were about to roll off his tongue, but he had to. "In the mirror. It was a look that I had seen before in my own eyes."

Margaret began to whimper even harder. Her cries cut like a knife. They were digging at old wounds in Sonny—very deep wounds. It seemed as if those wounds were bleeding afresh and would never stop. Sonny felt as though he was hemorrhaging.

"Oh, my God, Sonny," Margaret cried. "Oh, my God."

"Hey, hey," Sonny said, trying to soothe her. "C'mon now, sis. I'll take care of it. In fact, I'm already on it."

Sonny waited for Margaret to calm down a little, then asked, "What's Jay saying about all of this?"

"Nothing," Margaret said, wiping her nose with the back of her hand. "He's always at the hospital or something. He doesn't know, and I don't want him to know, either. You know how Jay feels about drugs."

"Yeah, I know," Sonny said, remembering all too clearly how his little brother had kicked his ass out of his own house.

"Sonny, you have to keep this quiet," Margaret said nervously. "You know what would happen if Jay thought Laci was doing drugs. He'd consider her dead, the same way he does y—" Margaret caught herself, but Sonny knew exactly what she was about to say.

"Promise me, Sonny," Margaret begged. "Promise me, please."

"You know me better than that, Margaret," Sonny said sincerely. He had no intentions of running to tell Daddy on his niece. The first thing he wanted to do was get a line on who was selling his peoples that shit.

"Thank you, Sonny," Margaret said, regaining her composure.

"No problem. That's my family. When I find out what's really going on, you best believe I'll handle it."

"You know she's supposed to go away to school this fall. I'm just so afraid that she's going to mess everything up for herself."

"Don't worry, Margaret," Sonny assured her. "I'm going to do everything I can."

"Thank you so much, Sonny. I'll get back with you soon, okay?"

"All right, Margaret. I'm on top of everything. You take care now. Kiss my brother and niece for me."

"Will do, Sonny. Bye-bye."

"Bye."

Sonny was almost in shock as he sat there with the phone to his ear, too stunned by the conversation he had just had with his sister-in-law to be able to move. How could this have happened? Hell, he knew firsthand how the shit could have happened. Perhaps it was his fault. Perhaps his niece knew how her uncle had chosen the monkey over family. If only he had been around more to show her all the damage this could do.

Sonny slowly removed the receiver from his ear. He had seen many young girls swept up by the current of the streets. Hurricane Ivan didn't have shit on those waves. But never in a million years had he imagined someone else from his family tree being caught up in its grips.

Rage took over Sonny's body. What he had feared the night he saw his niece out on the streets was coming to pass. He slammed the phone down so hard that he almost broke it. The thought of some nigga stringing his niece out made him mad . . . mad enough to kill.

Chapter 14

Forgive Me, Father, for I Have Sinned

Laci had just come from 145th Street and Eighth Avenue. She had been visiting a pusher named Tate. Tate was Laci's latest on-again, off-again thing. He had some bomb-ass powder, and his dick wasn't bad, either. He wasn't the ideal boo, but he served his purpose, just like the rest of them.

Laci had learned to turn her emotions on and off, thanks to her addiction. She couldn't have a heart and run the streets, and she regularly checked that shit at the door. She was now over her apprehension about drugs, as well. After what had happened with Dame, she didn't much give a fuck. All she wanted to do was get high.

Laci knew that her getting high had become a problem. She successfully hid it from her mother and father. Hiding it from her father was easy because he was hardly around. And she thanked

God for that. Laci had never truly believed she was hiding it from her mother. Her mother knew something was up, and she tried to stay hot on Laci's trail. Laci had become adept at maneuvering around her mother's suspicions, but it had gotten to the point where she was trying to avoid her mother altogether. Still, she felt that her mother didn't want to confront her suspicions, that she was partially in denial. The idea of seeing her daughter hopped up off crack was too much for her to face. Besides, things like this didn't happen to kids in their neighborhood—not to kids like Laci, anyway.

Still, Laci managed to graduate from high school. Up until recently, she had never missed a day of class or an assignment. And without studying, she had always passed her exams. Ordinarily, she would have gotten a perfect score. She didn't this time, but her grades still enabled her to graduate. Laci wasn't going to be able to pull off this type of thing in college. But no way was she going to run off to Boston and be that far from the streets she was growing so accustomed to.

Laci didn't see herself as an addict, which was the case with most addicts. She saw herself as being in love with getting high. She liked to think she could stop whenever she wanted to, but it went a little deeper than that.

As she walked along the street, Laci considered going home, but she couldn't get high there. She had two bags of weed and some powder that she had got from Tate. Her best bet was to find somewhere to get high and go home once she thought her mom was asleep.

When she got about four blocks away from Tate's, Laci sat on a curb behind a parked car and rolled her woo. The sensation from the high wasn't the only thing that was addictive to her. It was like every step of the process was an exotic ritual. The crackling of the burning rock, the dancing of the smoke. Laci was truly in love. Just hearing the rock catch fire made her feel relaxed.

Laci looked at the blunt and wept. She acted like she was cool with her lifestyle, but she really hated it. Thinking of what she used to be and what she had become made her want to vomit. It seemed like it was just yesterday that she was standing around with the girls, talking about going to Boston University. Then, with the same breath that she had used to speak so positively, she had inhaled crack. There was no way that Boston University was going to give a scholarship to a crackhead. She'd probably fail the first semester, anyway. She'd be too busy trying to find a connect to study.

"Fuck it," Laci said aloud to herself. "Just fuck it. Fuck everybody and everything. I don't even care anymore."

A loud truck drove by, snapping Laci out of the conversation that she was having with herself. She stood up, feeling weak from a lack of sleep, and caught her reflection in the rear window of the parked car she was hiding behind. Laci was just a shell of her former self, but not being able to accept the truth, she straightened her clothes and smiled, as if her reflection was telling her that she was the fairest of them all.

Fortunately, she made it home safely. Her goal right now was Rip van Winkle sleep. As she snuck through her house, trying to minimize the noise to keep her mother from waking up, she caught a glimpse of a picture hanging on the wall. It was her on her sixteenth birthday. This was the first time since she'd become addicted that she felt the painful sting of guilt.

Quita was the last of the girls to see Laci, and that had been over two weeks ago. And each of the girls, except Nay-Nay, was feeling guilty about what they had pulled on Laci. Quita tried to allow herself to feel for Laci and her situation, but that green-eyed monster had a tight hold on her.

When Laci had been around, the girls had had nothing but negative things to say, but they missed what she had added to the group, which was something that couldn't be replaced. Even if Laci were to forgive and forget and come roll with them tomorrow, it wouldn't be the same Laci.

"When was the last time you seen Laci?" Shaunna asked as the girls sat in Lisa's living room, watching television.

"Here we go with this shit again," Nay-Nay said, then sucked her teeth. "Y'all bitches is acting like the Save Laci Foundation. I know you're not going soft on me. I'm sure that wherever she is, she's livin' it up hood-style."

Monique snickered behind Nay-Nay's comment.

"Nay-Nay," Shaunna said, "you know that I always side with you, but you've heard the word on the street. Laci is fucked up. What all y'all did to her really fucked her up."

Monique twisted her face as she spoke. "What do you mean, *all y'all*? You was as much a part of the shit as the rest of us, Shaunna."

There was silence. Everyone knew that Monique was right. Even though Shaunna had been the last to know, she still knew.

"Have y'all seen her?" Nay-Nay asked.

"She hooked up with Quita and Dame," Lisa said.

Shaunna sighed and buried her face in her hands.

"Word?" Nay-Nay asked, surprised. "How you know? Have you seen her?"

"Yeah," Lisa said. "But she didn't see me. Actually, I've been seeing her around the spots and shit. I manage to keep clear. I must admit, though, seeing her like that do be making a bitch feel kinda bad."

"Quita and Dame?" Nay-Nay said in disbelief. "Shit. When was this?" Not giving Lisa a chance to answer, she continued. "Ain't this a bitch! How is it that Quita is running around, fucking my man, and you ain't said nothing before now?"

"I didn't say she was fucking him," Lisa replied, correcting Nay-Nay. "If she was fuckin' him, you'd know before me, right? I mean, he is your man to keep tabs on, not mine."

Shaunna stood up and paced. "This is bad, y'all. If she fuckin' with Quita and Dame, that bitch is blown. This could lead to some deep shit for us," Shaunna said nervously.

"Shaunna, just shut the fuck up," Nay-Nay snapped. "Stop acting like a fucking coward."

Shaunna sat back down, and without realizing it, Nay-Nay stood up and took her place in pacing the floor.

"Okay, let's say she *is* smoking," Nay-Nay said. "We can't be held accountable for that. We didn't tell her to smoke the shit."

"Uh, hello?" Lisa said. "Yes, we did."

"You know, not only did we tell her to smoke it, but we also laced that bitch," Monique said.

"Quita and Dame . . . ," Shaunna said under her breath.

"You act like my man is the fuckin' devil or something," Nay-Nay said.

Each of the girls looked up at Nay-Nay with twisted lips and looks that said, "Bitch, he is."

"Why did you have to go so far with it, Nay-Nay?" Monique said, starting to crumble. "Just getting her to blaze weed alone was a feat. Why did it have to be hard drugs?"

"I should have never been a part of this whole mess," Shaunna said, clutching her stomach. The stress had begun to give her abdominal pains. "She's really out there, y'all. She really is."

"You better stop that *y'all* shit," Nay-Nay said. "We was all down, and we gotta stick together on this. If anything happens, which it won't, we stick together."

"I sure hope she's going to be all right," Lisa said, looking off into the distance. "I mean, it wasn't like we was best friends or anything like that, but damn. When you really think about it, what did she ever do to us that was so wrong?"

"She tried to be our friend," Shaunna said sadly.

The girls all sat there as remorse started to set in. Monique's bottom lip was trembling as she tried to hold back the tears, and Shaunna started to bite her nails.

"Maybe we should call her house and talk to her. You know, just to see if she's okay," Monique suggested.

Lisa put her head down and prepared to confess. "I already have," she said.

"You spoke to her?" Shaunna said, anxious to find out more. "When? What did she say? Was she okay?"

Lisa shook her head. "I didn't get her. Her mother answered. She told me that Laci wasn't home and that she had been waiting by her phone for one of us to call. She wanted to know if I had seen her or noticed anything different about her behavior." Lisa paused and swallowed. "She told me that Laci had been sneaking out and staying out late. She asked me to talk to Laci if I did happen to see her to try to find out what was going on with her."

"That's the same thing that her mother told me," Monique confessed as well.

Nay-Nay looked at Monique. "You called her too? I thought you was gangsta. I guess I'm the only one that's true. A couple of weeks ago, all of you didn't have one good thing to say about Laci, now, all of a sudden, y'all in love with her. Y'all about some fake-ass bitches."

"It ain't got nothin' to do with being fake," Monique said. "We just concerned about her. I mean, you should have heard the sound in her mother's voice. If you had a heart in that fucked-up body of yours, you'd feel a little somethin' for her too."

"Yeah, I was down with the plan too, no doubt," Lisa said. "But the shit has gone too far. And I don't know about anyone else, but I'm ashamed. Laci didn't deserve no shit like that. Hookin' her on crack is some serious shit. That's not somethin' that you sit back and laugh about later. What the fuck were we thinking?"

"Too late for regrets now," Nay-Nay said in an uncaring tone.

"Fuck you," Lisa said. "It's never too late."

"You better watch your mouth," Nay-Nay said defensively.

"Why?" Lisa asked. "What you gon' do? Hook me on crack?" Lisa had never feared Nay-Nay like the other girls did.

"How about a left hook if you keep runnin' your muthafuckin' grill?" Nay-Nay said, flexing.

"Stop it, y'all," Shaunna ordered, holding her stomach. "Why we fightin'? Y'all act like y'all hate each other. We're supposed to be girls. What we need to do is relax and stop gettin' paranoid. We just need to pray that Laci will be all right."

The girls damn near choked on the suggestion.

"Pray?" Nay-Nay chuckled. "Since when do God give a shit about us?"

"Shaunna's right," Monique agreed. "We need to chill. We startin' to fall apart. And y'all all I got."

"Yeah, whatever," Nay-Nay said, maintaining her hard demeanor.

Shaunna looked around at the crew and wondered what was happening to them. It seemed as though they were all beginning to crack under the pressure. And their true colors were definitely starting to show. This was cause for Shaunna to distance herself from the group. She realized that not everyone was down for the crew. If they could hook Laci on drugs, she could only imagine what they would do to her.

Shaunna just prayed that God would forgive her for her part in what they all had done to Laci. She prayed for Nay-Nay too. Underneath that hard exterior, Nay-Nay had a heart. She had unknowingly revealed it to Shaunna on several occasions before. Shaunna had always looked up to Nay-Nay, who was the one she could go to whenever she was going through shit and needed advice. Nay-Nay was always right, but this time, Shaunna knew that she was wrong. If He never had before, Shaunna hoped that just this once God would give a shit and hear her prayers.

Chapter 15

Can't Fly With No Wings

Laci couldn't get that picture of herself on her sixteenth birthday out of her head. She had been so sweet, young, and innocent then. In that picture, on that day, she had been everything her parents could have ever dreamed of in a daughter. She had been their perfect child. Thank God they didn't have a picture of her now, strung out, with her mind on nothing but that next high.

How can I do this to them? Laci thought as she lay in her bed, tired and burnt out from the night before. She was even still wearing the same clothes from the night before. She looked down at herself. The dirt from the New York streets had settled on her clothes, her skin, her matted hair. *On second thought, how can I do this to myself?*

This was the first time in a long time that Laci thought about anything other than getting her high on. She hadn't thought twice about what she was doing to her parents. How she was living her life would destroy them and could perhaps destroy what she had grown up to know as a perfect family unit. Laci had never taken anything for granted. She had always acknowledged, respected, and appreciated the life her parents provided for her. In return, she had worked so hard to make them proud of her. She couldn't go out like that. She just couldn't. She refused to let her life thus far be in vain.

Laci jumped out of bed and went into the bathroom to start the shower. At that very moment, she decided that not only was she going to clean her body up, but she was also going to clean her act up altogether. Today was going to be a new day, the long overdue new beginning. It was time to let crack go, cold turkey. It was mind over matter, Laci thought. She didn't need some rehab center or some counselor telling her that she didn't need to do drugs. Hell, she already knew that. Laci told herself that it couldn't be as hard to give up crack as people made it out to be. After all, she had lived seventeen years without it. She didn't need it. She could live her life without it, the same as she had done before. Laci had come too far in life to fuck up now. College had always been a dream of hers, and she couldn't just up and let her dream die. She wasn't going to throw her life away in the name of an urge.

Laci was determined to make herself feel brand new. She cracked open a new Victoria Secret shower gel and lotion set that her mother had purchased for her. She took a long hot shower in hopes of washing the past few weeks down the drain. She washed and conditioned her hair as well. It had been a minute since she had done that. She had barely been running a comb through it much less washing it.

After stepping out of the shower and drying off, Laci wrapped a towel around her body and proceeded to comb out her hair. She stood at the bathroom mirror, watching the comb stroke her long locks of hair. From the roots the comb seemed to straighten Laci's hair, but once it reached her ends, her hair would bounce back into its curly form. As Laci watched the comb, with each stroke it seemed as though she could hear the sound of it running through her hair. For a minute it seemed so loud that it was going to make her eardrums burst. Laci's hand began to tremble as she continued combing her hair and listening to the aggravating sound.

Suddenly, Laci stopped, threw the comb down, and closed her eyes. "I know what it is," Laci said aloud to herself, having figured out why it seemed as though the comb was making such a loud noise. "It's too damn quiet in here. Yeah, that's what it is."

Laci exited the bathroom and entered her bedroom. She fumbled through her CDs and put in Whitney Houston. She turned the volume up, then snapped her fingers as she headed back into the bathroom, hoping Whitney's five octaves would be louder than the call of a crack rock.

After finishing up her hair, Laci went over to her drawer and picked out a white matching bra and panty set. She hummed along with Whitney as she slipped them on her body. She was purposely trying to keep herself distracted by humming and snapping and so forth. She then went over to her closet and grabbed a cute yellow and white romper to throw on. She put on some bobby socks and some Keds and then walked over to her jewelry box to find some matching accessories. Opening her jewelry box, with Whitney still blowing tunes, was almost like having reality slap Laci across the face. There were only a few pieces left to choose from. Before, she had had enough jewelry in her jewelry box to start her own boutique; before crack she did, anyway.

Laci had pretty much pawned, sold, or traded on the streets all her good pieces of jewelry that were worth anything. If she hadn't been selling and bartering pussy, she'd been selling and bartering her jewelry, all except for her Movado. After draining her bank account, Laci had had no other choice but to sell herself and her belongings. There was only

101 dollars left in her custodial account. The only reason why Laci hadn't smoked that up was that once her account fell under a hundred dollars, the custodian, who was her mother, would be made aware of the balance and she would need her to sign for any withdrawals. Laci didn't have the street smarts to figure out a way to get money.

In a sense, the Movado represented to Laci that she wasn't a crackhead. She was nothing like the ones she saw hanging out on the main streets in the hood, who had earned their titles. Crackheads didn't give a fuck about sentimental shit, but Laci saw herself as different from them. The Movado was one of the most special gifts given to her. She felt as though no high in the world was worth trading it.

The Movado sat in the jewelry box, where Laci had placed it after taking it off of her wrist. She didn't even want to tempt herself by wearing it out there on the streets when she was in search of a hit or a means to get a hit. She didn't want to tempt some crackhead out there, either, who might decide to knock her over the head and take the watch from her. The last thing she wanted was for somebody else to be out there getting high off the proceeds from her shit. Hell, if that was the case, she might as well smoke the watch her damn self.

The phone rang, startling Laci. She slammed the jewelry box shut without finding any decent accessories and then walked over to her bed and sat down as she picked up the phone.

"Hello," Laci said.

"Laci, darling," the voice on the other end said. "I finally caught you. Do you know how long and how hard I've been trying to reach you?"

"Daddy!" Laci exclaimed. "I swear, I was just thinking about you. I swear I was."

"Okay, dear. I believe you," her father said with a chuckle. "You okay? Where's Mom?"

"Probably at the hospital," Laci replied. "Yeah, I'm fine. I miss you, Daddy."

"I miss you too, darling."

Laci closed her eyes tight and squeezed her lips together. Hearing her father's voice wasn't enough. She needed him there.

"So, when you comin' home, Dad?" Laci asked, wiping the tear that fell from her eye.

"I'm really not sure. I was going to try to fly home this weekend, but it doesn't look like I'm going to be able to pull that off."

Laci could hear someone in the background talking to her father.

"Look, Laci. I'm needed, so I have to go, but I'll call you again soon. Okay, dear?"

"Okay," Laci said with a trembling voice, trying not to burst out crying.

You're right. You are needed. I need you, Daddy. Please come home. Just sit with me. Just stay with me. You have no idea what I'm going through. Please, Daddy, come home.

"I love you, little Laci," her father said. He said it to her the same way he had said it the first time he'd ever called her Laci. She had been five years old, starting kindergarten. Her mother had successfully taught her how to tie her shoes. She couldn't wait for her father to walk through the door so she could show him her latest accomplishment. "Good job. That's my little Laci," he'd said.

Ever since that day, she had insisted on being called Laci, but nobody said her name like her father.

"I love you too, Daddy." Laci hung up the phone and buried her head in her hands. She took a couple of deep breaths and then wiped away her tears. Hearing her father's voice had given Laci a burst of strength she didn't know she had. Uncle Sonny was right. Her father was strong, and so was she. She was going to fight to make sure she made her father proud.

Laci reached over to open up her nightstand drawer and pulled out a couple of brochures. They were brochures from Boston University. Laci flipped through them, comprehending nothing. It was just an attempt to keep busy. A failed attempt. Laci pushed the brochures aside and lay down on her bed. She grabbed her favorite teddy bear from the spot beside her and started stroking it. Laci soon found herself making silly goo-goo remarks to the teddy bear, as if it were a real baby or something. Once she realized how stupid she sounded, she threw the bear back down, then got up and walked over to her bedroom window. Laci lifted the blinds and opened the window. The birds were trying to upstage Whitney. Laci smiled at the innocent competition.

The sun was blazing. It was a nice, clear summer day. Perhaps it was too clear for Laci. As she gazed at the beautiful tall trees, the blue sky, and the green grass, Laci could see only one thing: smoke rising up over the city. The funnel of happiness. She envisioned herself hitting the pipe, blowing the smoke over the city so that everyone could experience the high. The feeling of the high was too good to keep to herself. The birds' serenade ceased, and she could hear them no more. All she could hear was the streets calling.

Snapping back to reality, Laci slammed the window shut and closed the blinds. She went back over to her bed and sat down. For a little while she tried to sleep, but she only tossed and turned. She then got up out of bed and began pacing back and forth, forth and back, until she started to wear a path in the carpet. Then, all of a sudden, she felt like she had to throw up. She started gagging, but nothing came up. Beads of sweat started to form on her body. She felt as though she was walking through fire.

Just a minute ago I was fine, Laci thought. *This shit is in my head. This shit is* all *in my head*, she thought repeatedly.

"Shit, it's hot," Laci said aloud as she quickly, and almost angrily, removed the romper she was wearing. She now paced with nothing on but a bra, panties, socks, and shoes. Still sweating profusely, Laci walked into her bathroom and ran cold water in the sink. She began splashing it on her face. She filled her hands with water and slapped it on her neck. Water dripped down to her chest, soaking her bra.

Laci walked over to the toilet and sat down on the seat. She began rocking back and forth while breathing heavily. She needed to get high. But she couldn't fly with no wings. She hadn't a dime to her name, and it was that time of the month. Finding a nigga grimy enough to want to fight the bloody battle would take a minute. She'd have to luck up on one of those kinds of triflin'-ass niggas, or getting high meant she'd have to do some other ole freaky shit, like sucking dick and balls, licking ass or another bitch's pussy, or some shit.

She continued rocking back and forth. One minute Laci would be telling herself that she was fine, that she could do this. She could fight the urge to want to smoke crack. She told herself that everything was going to be okay. She just had to get through this day, and then the days would get better. But the next minute Laci would be telling herself that one more hit wouldn't hurt. She could stop after one more hit. Just one last hit. The inner voices bickering back and forth with one another were starting to drive Laci insane. She put her hands over her ears, pulled her feet up onto the toilet seat, and sat there, rocking back and forth. Even if the part of Laci that wanted to answer the call of the streets prevailed, she would still find herself with a bad case of the shorts. Even if she wanted to smoke, with no money or means to cop, she couldn't . . . or could she?

"Hey, pretty lady," the owner of the pawnshop said to Laci. He spoke with an accent. He was Arabic or some nationality that Laci didn't much care to concern herself with. "You back to get your fancy CD Walkman player?"

Laci shot him a fake smile, which left her face just as quickly as it had come. "No. No, I, uh, got something else for you," Laci said with hesitation.

"Let's see what you got. I'm sure it will be pretty, like you."

Laci took a deep breath, then reached down in her purse. The pawnshop owner greedily waited for her to place the item on the counter.

"Oh, nice," he said, picking up the watch Laci had laid on the glass counter. He held it up and observed it. "A Movado, huh? Let me take to back of store and examine. I be right back. Don't go nowhere, pretty lady." He quickly dashed to the back of the store, admiring the watch the entire way.

Hell no, I ain't gon' nowhere, Laci thought. *Not as long as you got my shit, anyway.*

As Laci stood at the counter, waiting impatiently, she looked around the pawnshop.

I wonder how many hits the owner got off that, Laci thought as she looked at a pearly midnight-blue electric guitar. Her eyes moved on to a fairly new mountain bike. *Oh, I know they got plenty of hits off that,* Laci thought. It seemed as though everything amounted to hits on the crack pipe. Nothing had a value anymore.

"Not fake," the pawnshop owner said after coming from the back. "How much money you try borrow?"

"How much can you give me for it?" Laci asked in an anxious tone.

"To borrow, a couple hundred, but I give you good deal if you sell to me," he said, smiling.

Laci thought for a moment. "How much if I sell it to you?" she wanted to ask, but she didn't want to be tempted by the answer. Having every intention of coming back for the watch, Laci said, "Two hundred fifty dollars. I need to borrow two hundred fifty."

The owner eyeballed the watch a little longer. "I give you two hundred twenty-five. That's best I can do."

"Cool," Laci said, nodding her head.

Laci couldn't wait to get that money in her hand. She needed that high. With every intention of her soul, Laci intended to give up crack. Perhaps now she would realize that she couldn't do it alone.

After handling her business at the pawnshop and going to cop some rocks, Laci damn near burned her fingers while lighting up her shit. She was nervous and trembling in anticipation of getting high. After that first hit to the pipe, which felt like it had been forever for Laci, she closed her eyes and let her head fall back. She exhaled, then opened her eyes. When Laci raised her hand to her mouth in order to take that next hit, she looked at her vacant wrist, the one where the Movado had once been. Besides her body, she had given up something that meant a great deal to her. And now that it was all said and done, she really didn't feel so bad, given that the outcome was a good high. Laci had to give up the watch. It was the wings that would give her flight. At that moment she knew what she was no longer becoming and what she was now . . . a crackhead. A full-blown addict.

Chapter 16

I Solemnly Swear

Dink was posted up on the Ave, looking at his watch. He was supposed to meet Marco and Smurf at five o'clock. Smurf was on point, but Marco was late, as usual. Dink started to wonder about his friend's strange comings and goings. Sometimes Marco would disappear for days at a time, and no one would hear from him. Whenever Dink questioned him about it, he always had an excuse. This was just one more thing Dink would have to look into.

"Fuck is this nigga at?" Smurf asked, looking at his watch. "Fat muthafucka always late, man. This is some bullshit. For real."

"Calm yo' li'l ass down," Dink told him. "Why you always act so crazy when it come to my peoples?"

"Dink," Smurf said, looking him dead in the eye, "something ain't right with ya man. I can't put my finger on it, but something is just not right."

"How you figure?"

"It's kinda like when my moms was bringing them niggas through the crib. I used to be able to look at each and every one of them and tell what kinda nigga he was—a cheater, a liar, an abuser. I could smell it, yo."

"And what do you smell on Marco?" Dink genuinely wanted to know.

"Larceny," Smurf said with a dead set look in his eyes. "Larceny."

Lisa lay in the bed with her man, watching him sleep. He had treated her to a fifth of Hennessy and some mind-blowing sex. She thought about waking him and going at it again, but he was sleeping so peacefully that she couldn't bring herself to disturb him. It seemed as though lately she only got to see him so rarely that every moment was precious.

Dink was the best thing that ever happened to her. He might've spent a lot of time in the streets, but he was a good man. Dink talked shit more often than not, but he always made sure Lisa was good. She couldn't say the same thing, however.

Lisa was smart and knew how to get money, but she moved sideways. Dink was her main nigga, but she had a bench and an injured reserve. That's how her whole crew did it. They played the game the same way niggas did and thought nothing of it. To them it was whine or grind.

Lisa was glad that Dink was there, though. She hadn't been sleeping well. The shit that went down with Laci left a bad taste in her mouth. It was all fun and games, and then it had gotten out of hand.

Laci had become a totally different person. She was becoming familiar with all the hustlers and bagmen in the hood. Certain individuals knew that Laci was slippin', but it was still hard to believe in a sense, because Laci didn't carry herself like the average crackhead. She was learning to pimp her game just like the hustlers pimped their rock. She figured if all the Willies were going to be sniffing around her, then she might as well benefit from it. Laci would keep company with the hustlers if they could keep her secret and feed her habit. The girls couldn't believe that this was the same girl they used to clown for not knowing shit about the streets. Laci was slowly but surely learning everything about the streets that she needed to know.

Dink had been lenient in how he allowed Dame to run his business. He let him operate independently and wasn't constantly looking over his shoulder. He trusted Dame with a lot, and he wasn't handling his shit. It was high time that he put his affairs in order.

Driving around the turf for hours looking for his soldier turned out to be a bust, but it did produce Laci, and Dink wasn't mad at that at all. He ran into her in almost the exact same place as before, but this time it was clear to him why she was in the area.

Dink pulled up beside her. This time she acknowledged him immediately.

"What's the deal, baby? You following me?" Laci asked with a beautiful smile.

"Maybe," he said in a flirtatious tone. "Would it be a problem if I was?"

"Depends on what you're following me for," she replied with a wink.

"I'll make a note of that, Ma. Say, how come I don't see you over at the house anymore? Fuck you been up to?" he inquired.

Laci opened Dink's car door. She hopped in, wearing a big smile, and said, "Aren't you the inquisitive one?"

Dink could sit there counting her teeth all day if he could. Her smile was just magnetizing. But aside from the smile, Laci was starting to let herself go. The beautiful curly locks that he remembered were no more. She was repping the lazy-do—a pulled back ponytail that hadn't even been taken out to be redone in a minute. It was obvious that it had gotten the slick down hand job by the pieces that were out of place. Laci still wore the classy little name brand hook-ups, but it looked like she had been to a dozen sleep-over parties in them.

Dink's eyes scanned Laci, and his face clearly showed his disturbance by her condition.

For the most part, she was still cute. Shit, she looked better than most broads in the hood did on their best day. But seeing her again now only confirmed the rumors. However, that spark he felt the day he had met her at Lisa's house was still there.

"So, seriously, Laci," Dink said with sincerity, "what have you really been up to?"

"Do I look like a book to you?" Laci asked calmly.

"Huh?" Dink asked, slightly confused.

"Do I look like a book to you?" Laci changed her profile a couple of times for Dink to examine.

"No," he snickered.

Laci became serious. "Then stop trying to read me, baby. I'm good."

Dink smiled.

There was so much Dink wanted to say, but he couldn't seem to focus. He had so much on his plate that his feelings for Laci seemed secondary. He started to put it off for another time, but if he didn't do it now, he might never do it.

"Laci," he said, looking into her eyes. "I hope I don't make a fool of myself by saying this, but fuck it."

"What? Just say it."

"Ever since the time when I saw you at Lisa's house, I wondered what it would be like to have . . ." Dink started laughing. "Oh, this is some crazy shit. What the fuck am I doing, yo?" Dink paused and melted when Laci smiled. Then he manned up. "I'm feeling you, girl, and I can't help but wonder what it would be like to have you as my own."

"Your own what?" Laci asked, dumbfounded.

Dink snapped his head back and gave her a puzzled look.

"I'm just kidding," Laci said, smiling again. "I know what you mean." Laci hadn't smiled so much since she could remember. No one had ever made her smile like that before. But she snuck in that little joke because she really didn't know how to respond to Dink. His statement had thrown her off. She knew Dink looked at her in a more than friendly way, but she thought it was just a physical attraction. She could have easily gotten into him if he hadn't been Lisa's man. She wanted to tell him that, but she played it cool. She, too, had so much going on in her life.

"You probably say that to all the girls, Dink," Laci said, continuing to play around. "By the way, how's ya girl?"

"I haven't really been seeing a whole lot of Lisa," Dink said, hating that Laci spoiled the moment by mentioning her name. "She's probably got her hands full, anyway."

"Yeah, well, I don't see too much of her, either. I just haven't been in the mood to hang out with the girls these days. What's your excuse?"

"I'm not in the mood for her, either." Dink took a deep breath and stretched. "I'm thinking about moving on."

"Is that right?"

"Yeah. People grow apart, ya know?" Dink paused for a second. "Listen, I know that you and Lisa are friends or whatever, but I don't believe in wasted opportunities, so enough of talking about her. I'm trying to see about you, ma."

"So, what they say about you is right, huh?" Laci said in somewhat of a sensual tone. "You do run a good game." Laci looked down and started picking at her fingernails. "All guys like you do is scam on women. I know your kind." Laci sucked her teeth.

Dink was fully animated as he explained himself. "Look at me," he said, lifting Laci's face by the chin and turning it toward him so that they were eye to eye. "I put this on everything. You're like this perfect chick out of a movie or some shit. And I'm..." Dink searched for the right words. "I'm a hustler, baby. I ain't go to college or nothin' like that, and unlike yourself, I don't plan on going. I know you come from money, went to private schools and all that. I can't compete with that. Well, as far as the money part, I'm good. We wouldn't have to worry about finances."

"All your money is dirty, Dink," Laci said sincerely, still looking him in the eye. "And you and I both know what happens to dirty money." Laci paused to let him think on it. "It gets washed away. I mean, for real though. You can't buy a house with it. You can't even walk into a bank and get an account, so you can't even save it. Hell, you can't do shit with your kind of money but burn it on the streets."

"That's where you're wrong," Dink said.

"How so?"

Dink licked his lips and leaned in close to Laci. "Don't you worry your pretty head about that. I got that all figured out," he said before sitting back in position. "We won't even have to worry about that."

"What's this *we* stuff?" Laci asked.

"Because ain't no *I* in team, Laci. You and me—us. We could be a team."

Laci looked at Dink sideways, shook her head, then looked out the window. "Ain't no *I* in team, huh?"

"That's what I said."

Laci turned back to Dink. "Ain't no *we*, either." Laci let out a chuckle.

"You keep playing all you want, girl, but I'm for real."

"Dink, you have a girlfriend, so the fact that you are sitting here saying all of this, with me knowing you have a girlfriend, let's me know what type of man you really are. No offense, but if you're doing this type of stuff to Lisa, why should I believe that you ain't gonna do it to me?"

"Because I'm being real with you from the jump," Dink said.

"But I'm not the one you need to be real with right now. Lisa is," Laci said. "If you kept shit so real, then she would know how you supposedly feel about me."

Dink sighed. "It ain't no *supposed* feeling. I'm putting my shit on the line telling you this. And you know it must be real, considering—" Dink caught himself. He had almost slipped up and said something that might have hurt Laci's feelings. He truly didn't want to take it there. Besides, he wasn't one to go on rumor alone. He hadn't heard the shit from Laci, so a part of him still wanted to believe in something other than the obvious. Dink understood that sometimes people went through rough times. This could be one of those times for Laci. Dink would love to be there for her, to see her through—if she'd let him.

"Fuck it. I see I'm wasting my breath and have probably just made a complete fool out of myself," he said.

"Then that's a good thing," Laci said softly. "Means you got love in your heart."

"What?" Dink said.

"They say a person only makes a fool out of themselves for love," Laci said.

"Or for money," Dink said, looking deeply into her eyes.

Laci turned away and stared out the window. She felt as though Dink had her numbers and was just waiting for her to yell Bingo!

"I really dig the way you came at me and all, Dink. But the you and me and the we thing . . . It ain't a reality. I could never be with you."

"Why? Why not, Laci?"

Laci fought back tears. "Isn't it obvious, Dink. You deal drugs and I..." Laci paused. "I'm friends with your girlfriend." Laci's thoughts began to race. She wanted so badly to spill the beans to Dink. She needed help, but she bitched out. She just couldn't. Admitting who she really was to him would be admitting it to herself . . . again. And it already stung the first time. The second would just cut too deep.

"Laci, first of all, I told you that I'm cutting Lisa off. She's not what I'm looking for and if I'm going to have a woman in my life, it's gonna be the one I really want. And as far as the drug shit goes, I think I already know what time it is with you, Laci."

Laci looked at Dink in shock. She turned away in humiliation as tears flowed down her cheeks. "Guess I do look like a book after all," Laci sobbed.

Dink put his hand on her shoulder. He felt so sick inside that she was confirming that shit—just absolutely sick. He gritted his teeth hard to maintain his emotions. He wasn't tripping over Laci, but he had seen the best of them go down and he refused to watch the same thing happen to her.

"Did you think I wouldn't find out, Laci, doing what I do?" Dink asked. "I just can't figure out why and how you got into this."

Laci bowed her head in shame. In all her running and having fun, she never even considered how many people would find out, simply from word on the street. Dink was one of the biggest narcotics distributors in Queens. Laci tried to do her thing outside of her borough, but news always traveled from hood to hood.

Laci could feel Dink's eyes burning a hole through her as he waited on a response.

"Dink, don't look at me, please," Laci cried.

"It's cool, Ma," Dink said, running his hand over her hair.

"No, don't touch me." Laci jerked away. "You don't wanna touch me, trust me," Laci said, starting to feel sorry for herself. "It's not my fault," she sobbed.

Dink bit down on his lip and tried to maintain his composure, but what he really wanted to do was take her in his arms and hold her. He never wanted to let her go. He wanted to keep her from slippin' even deeper. "What do you mean it's not your fault? You gotta step up to bat before you can even think about changing the situation."

"No, you don't understand. It's really not my fault," Laci said emotionally.

"Somebody forced it on you or something? Talk to me," Dink insisted.

Laci scratched at her ponytail. "Not exactly," she sighed. "You just don't understand. I don't want to smoke, but shit just got so crazy. I tried to back away from it, but the shit just kept calling me back. I don't know what to do," Laci cried. "I don't know what to do, Dink. Oh, my God."

Laci felt as though a weight had been lifted off her shoulders. She had finally been able to just sit down and tell somebody. There was so much more she wanted to tell Dink, though, like how just the thought of getting high made her squirm. She thought about the rocks she had on her at that very moment and how much better she would feel if she smoked them. Talking to Dink made her forget about them at first, but that was only short-term. The stones were now humming in a low tone, but they would soon be singing in soprano.

Dink took Laci's hand into his. Even after hearing it from the horse's mouth, that Laci Casteneda was a crack addict, he still couldn't resist her. He simply saw her as a diamond in the rough. She just needed someone to shine her up a little bit. Dink had been in the game long enough to understand the addiction to crack. But with crack being a mental drug, each person had their own catalyst for getting hooked. He needed to understand Laci's before he could help her. He needed to know the driving force behind it. He'd heard the saying about not being able to turn a ho into a housewife. But here it was 1989, and the verdict was still out on crackheads.

Dink exhaled. "Tell me all about your addiction, Laci. What made you want to use crack for the very first time?"

Laci was compelled to shed all her bad skin in front of Dink. She began to air all her dirty laundry with little hesitation. Laci recounted the summer's events for Dink. She told him about the laced weed, what she did with Dame, and a host of other shit he wasn't aware of. On one hand, he felt like crying with her. On the other hand, he felt like killing everyone involved.

"Sons of bitches!" Dink roared as he beat down on his dashboard. "I could kill them dead, all of 'em."

"I've felt like that too," Laci said, not realizing that she had lifted her hand to Dink and was now running her fingers through his hair. "All I can do is pray that God takes care of them for what they did. That's all you can do too." Laci forced herself to smile.

Dink looked at her closely, and now he could see the hurt behind the smile. Now she wasn't fooling anybody.

He closed his eyes and took in the soft touch of Laci's hand touching him. He then looked over at her, grabbed her head, and rested it on his shoulder. She felt so much better talking to someone. She never thought in a million years that it would be Dink, especially the way she played him off the last time he tried to look out for her. He had every right to condemn her and push her away, but he was very understanding.

Laci and Dink exchanged long glances. He took his fingers and wiped Laci's tears away. He then kissed her softly on the lips and brushed her hair with his hand.

In those few hours Laci and Dink connected like they had never done with any other person in their lives. In just a matter of a few hours, they really did become a team.

Dink held on to Laci for dear life, it seemed. She basked in the attention he gave her, and her body language revealed that all her defenses were down. She wanted more, but she reluctantly showed restraint for the moment.

"I feel so much better," Laci said to Dink as she sat looking out of the car window, straightening out her clothes. "You're the first person I've been able to talk to about this. I used to talk to my mom about everything. She was like my best friend—

pillow-fights and all. But this . . . this would have killed her."

Dink nodded in agreement.

Laci stared at him and took in his silence for a moment. "Seems like now you know a lot about me, but I know nothing about you," she said. "Tell me about your family."

Dink became tense. "I don't have no family."

"Really? No mother? No father?"

"Nah. From what I was told when I was little, my mother was an addict and gave me to a pimp named Bruce Ward in exchange for drugs. I grew up crazy, and the only saving grace I had, even though it was short lived, was my cousin Fred. Fred was my stepfather's sister's son, and we instantly formed a bond like brothers. But he was an insecure dude, and deep down he hated me."

"Why did he hate you?"

"I don't even know, man," Dink said, shaking his head. "I guess he had a lot of reasons for hating me."

"That's sad, Dink. How did you deal with it?"

Dink smiled confidently. "By becoming somebody. No matter what, I wouldn't be broken. No matter what anybody did, they couldn't make me fall."

"You're a strong man. I guess that's why I feel so safe with you."

"You should," he said as he kissed her forehead. "I'd never let anything happen to you."

"You mean it?" she asked.

"Of course. I'm gonna look out for you if you let me."

"I, Laci Casteneda, do solemnly swear that . . . I will think about it," she teased. Laci suddenly paused and stared into Dink's eyes. For the first time she noticed how pretty they were. Her laughter faded as she melted in them.

"What's wrong?" he asked.

"Your eyes," she said, mesmerized. "You have very beautiful eyes." Laci gently touched the side of his face and ran her fingers across his eyelids, placing a soft kiss on each of them.

Dink slowly opened his eyes and looked at Laci. "Is it just me, girl, or does it seem like we've known each other forever."

"It's not just you," Laci said in a heavy whisper, as if she was trying to control her lustful breathing. "I feel it too, baby."

"Girl, you playin' with fire," Dink said.

"I can stand the pain of a burn," Laci assured him. "I've endured worse."

"I'm for real, Laci. This is not a game."

"So am I."

"So what are we gon' do, ma?"

"I don't, know, Dink," Laci said, settling back over on the passenger side. "There's still Lisa to deal with."

"That's a done deal. But you know if we gonna get down, your lifestyle has got to change."

Laci looked at Dink as if he was the pot calling the kettle black. "And your lifestyle, Dink?"

"Tell me what you need from me, ma, and it's done."

Laci sighed and tried to find the right words. "Even if I asked you to stop hustling, Dink—"

"I see where you're going with this," he said, cutting her off.

"I got a habit, you know," Laci continued. "I already admitted that to you. And how am I gonna roll with you if you're supplying? That's like putting a shark in a tank full of goldfish when he hasn't had dinner yet."

Dink laughed. "Girl, you crazy." He paused to look at Laci and saw that she was dead serious. "Look. I'll tell you what. We'll work on bettering both our lifestyles together. Deal?"

Laci didn't know how much of what Dink was saying was real and just how much of it was bullshit. But she did know that she liked what she was hearing. "You got a deal," she said.

"Let's make it official," Dink said, holding out his hand.

Laci looked at him as if she didn't know what he was talking about. The more she thought about it, parting with her rock didn't seem like much of an option. She wasn't ready—not yet. Her insecurity showed when she looked into his eyes, those eyes that revealed so much. They told her that it was okay to be weak, for he would be her strength. They told her that it was okay to crave, for he would be her fix. His eyes told her that it was okay to believe in him, and maybe someday, to even love him.

Dink shook his hand as if to ask Laci if she was going to leave him hanging.

Laci stared at Dink's hand for a few more seconds before pulling out her Zip-Loc baggie. She stared at the contents. She and her little torturers had been through quite a bit, but the road would have to end somewhere. Laci placed the bag of rocks in Dink's hand.

He looked at Laci with hope in his eyes. He looked around, opened the car door, emptied the rocks onto the ground and stomped every last one to nothingness.

Tears welled up in Laci's eyes, but it was for the better. Kicking her addiction was going to be a bitch, but she wouldn't do it alone.

Dink caught the tears that fell from her eyes with his fingertips. He hugged her tightly, and they prepared to face the future . . . together.

Chapter 17

A Long Time Comin'

After having their heart-to-heart, Dink and Laci decided to grab something to eat. She waited in the car as he went inside Crown Fried Chicken. While he was standing in line his pager went off. He recognized the number. Someone paged him from it a couple of times before. He stepped out of line to go to the pay phone.

"Yo, somebody page Dink from this number?"

"Nigga, it's Dame," Dame said from the other end.

"I've been lookin' for you for hours," Dink immediately dug into Dame.

"So I heard," Dame brushed it off.

"Where the fuck you been?" Dink said with authority.

"Oh, just chillin', nigga," Dame said, dismissing the tone Dink was using with him. "Me and Smurf been fuckin' with some bitches. And we was watchin' this tape of this li'l freak bitch I recorded a few weeks ago. Man, come to find out that bitch was a virgin. I'll let you check it out, but my man, Tee, making copies for distribution. No charge either. He said he recognized the ho and was willin' to do that shit on the house. You know, tapes in the hood make more money than at the box office. Bitches better recognize the next time they drop they drawers." Dame began laughing an evil laugh. "Yo, but I just dropped that cat, Smurf, off. Speaking of that little nigga. He don't take his strap off for nothin', huh? Homeboy was fuckin' this chick with his gun on. He crazy as hell."

"Nigga," Dink snapped, finally able to get a word in edgewise, "I ain't interested in that shit. We need to discuss how the fuck you've been conducting ya business, partner."

"Fuck is ya problem?" Dame asked, matching Dink's tone. "I told you, I got this over here, man."

"Yeah, just like you had that Titus thing, too. Dame, miss me with that shit. You fucking up, son."

"Dink, how you sound?" Dame asked offended. "You coming at me like I'm one of them okee-doke soldiers."

"You get what ya hand calls for."

"You bugging, Dink. I don't even like the way you're coming at me. You ain't got no right—"

"I got every right, cousin," Dink cut him off. "I was holding sway and put you down, remember?"

"You talking like I ain't bring nothing to the table, son? How many niggas I rocked for the team?"

"It ain't about that," Dink insisted. "It's about the way you're doing things now. Look, I'm sending some of my people down to Baisley to help you out. All you gotta do is tell 'em what you need, and everything will be cool."

"I don't need no help, yo. I got my own soldiers. We good."

"You know what? I'll take care of everything," Dink declared. "It's my hood. I got it."

"Why you buggin'?" Dame asked, defensively.

"Nah, I ain't buggin'." Dink chuckled. "You don't have to do shit."

"What you tryin' to say?"

"I ain't *tryin'* to say shit," Dink said, getting frustrated with going back and forth with Dame. "What I *am* sayin' is that you don't have to do shit, muthafucka!"

Dame was his own man. He was tired of taking orders, especially from an ole cocky, ego-trippin' nigga. Dink was talking some bullshit and he didn't like it. He felt that he was in a position to make things happen without the Queens cat. Fuck Dink and his whole faggot-ass crew. Dame felt that he was the real power.

"Let me put you on to something, my man," Dame said slyly. "You ain't no fucking body. Before I came into the fold, niggas was doing whatever the fuck they wanted around here. Now you talkin' 'bout respect the block. *I* brought the fear to this side, yo. My gun ring off! All that bullshit you poppin', you need to slow it up before you find yaself in a bad way. Word to mine, son."

"What?" Dink said, looking at the phone. *I know this nigga ain't trying to threaten me*, Dink thought. "A'ight. We gon' see about this shit." Dink slammed the phone down.

Dame was playing himself and he needed to be checked. Dink had long let all the little bullshit slide—the hoes, the slick-ass comments, etc. Well, now it was time to take action.

Dink immediately paged Smurf from the pay phone, but he put in his car phone number. He needed to put things in order within his camp. He couldn't focus on helping Laci if his own affairs weren't in order. That just wouldn't do.

He had almost forgotten all about the food, so he rushed back into Crown's and placed his order. Laci was switching the dials on the radio when Dink finally got back in the car. He handed her the food without saying a word. She immediately noticed that something was wrong. His body had become rigid, and he was flexing his jaw muscle.

"What's the matter, Dink?" she asked with a look of concern.

"Nothing I can't handle," he assured her. "I'm just waiting on a phone call. Did my phone ring?"

"No. Who you waiting on a call from?" Laci asked. She couldn't help but wonder if it was from Lisa. "Must be important if it's got you all uptight like this."

"It's just business."

Dink tried to hide his anger, but Laci picked up on it. He wanted to tell her what was wrong with him and be comforted, but he couldn't put his team at risk, especially his li'l man. Before Dink could think on it further, the car phone rang.

"What's up, D?" Smurf asked from the other end. "Your shit read nine-one-one. What's poppin'?"

"Ain't nothing," Dink huffed. "Got some shit that I need you to do, though."

"Just give me the basics," Smurf said, paying full attention.

"Ya man," Dink began. "The nigga you was wit a while ago. You know who I'm talking about?"

"Yeah," Smurf said, smiling and rubbing his dick. Just the thought of puttin' one in Dame gave him a hard on. "I know just who you mean, son."

"His time is up." The phone sounded as if it went dead. "You still there?"

"Yeah, I'm here," Smurf confirmed.

"You heard me?"

"Yeah, I heard."

Smurf and Dame were all right since they had been hangin' lately, but not like he and Dink were. They had fucked some bitches and gotten high

together, but that shit didn't count for much at the
moment. What mattered was that Dink wanted
him gone, and he called on Smurf to do it. The
teen knew that Dink had something brewing in his
heart, and he would be busy for the next few weeks.
Getting the go-ahead to do Dame was cake. But
if ever the day came when Dink asked him to do
Marco . . . that shit would be the icing.

"Time frame?" Smurf asked.

"Yesterday," Dink replied.

"A'ight. Consider it a done deal. What about his
business?"

"That nigga ain't gon' make or break my shit.
This has been a long time comin'."

"Yeah, I knew this was gon' happen. I knew that
if you weren't makin' plans to take care of him, the
business was going to eventually fall apart. That
nigga wants to shine more than he wants to grind.
He wanted your spotlight, boss. Even God had to
eventually throw Satin's ass out the gates."

"Yeah," Dink said with a sigh as he listened to the
li'l nigga make sense. "You can only give a nigga
a pass but so many times. He asked for it." Dink
paused. "I know you two was gettin' kind of cool
there for a minute. You got a problem wit it?"

"It's whatever you say," Smurf said, avoiding the
trap. "You my nigga, and I'ma rock wit you."

"Keep this quiet. I want to tell Marco about this
myself. I know that he ain't gon' have no problems

with it. He can't stand that nigga. If it wasn't for me, Marco would've tried to fire him on his own."

"I doubt that." Smurf chuckled. "But that's ya man. I'll get wit ya tomorrow, son." Smurf hung up the phone and went back to reading *The Devil's Tear Drop*. Dame was cool, but Dink was his employer. Smurf wasn't trying to bite the hand that was feeding him. Dame had to go.

Dink hung up the phone and took a deep breath. He hated that it had to go down this way, but fuck it. He figured he was getting ready to start a new life anyhow, so he needed to rework some things. He would eventually sever ties with the streets, but not just yet. Things needed to be put into perspective.

Dink scratched his chin and thought about what he was going to do next. He turned to say something to Laci, and she hopped into his lap. She grabbed Dink by the face and threw her tongue in his mouth. She kissed him long and passionately. He returned her affection, but the thought of unfinished business made him pull back.

"Laci, what are you doin'?" he asked.

"What does it look like I'm doin'? I can see you have a lot on your mind right now. Let me help you forget about some of it. Now stop fighting me, Dink."

"Laci . . ." Dink said, hesitating.

"Don't fight me, baby," Laci whispered, kissing him again. "Ain't you tired of fighting?"

Dink looked into Laci's eyes and felt sheer passion. Everything after that seemed to go in slow motion. They both exhaled when their lips touched this time. They shared a kiss that only soul mates share. Laci massaged the top of Dink's head, and he softly began caressing her breasts.

"Hold on," Dink said, pulling away again.

"What?" Laci whined.

"I can't do this, Laci."

"This?" Laci asked, puzzled. "What do you mean *this*?"

"I can't disrespect you like this." He looked around. "In a car? No, I won't allow you to go out like that."

"Please allow me to," Laci said, clawing at his pants and trying to kiss him again.

"Goddamn it, Laci, no," he said, grabbing her. "You deserve better than some dude fucking you in a car."

"But you're not just some dude, Dink," Laci said, panting like a puppy.

"You know what I mean, girl. Regardless of what you've been out here doing, you ain't some whore who drops her panties in the front seat of no man's car, and I'm not going to ever treat you like that. Don't ever allow yourself to be treated like that, either."

Dink paused as Laci climbed off him and sat back in the passenger seat.

Laci had never been with a man who wanted to stop when things got hot and heavy. Dink wanted to fuck her, because his dick was rock hard, but he showed restraint out of respect. She knew at this point that what came out of his mouth was legitimate and he meant business. She started to say something, but his pager went off again.

"Hold that thought," he told her as he looked at the number. "I'll be right back." Dink hopped out of his car and went to use the pay phone. It was Marco. He had to give him the rundown, and he didn't want to have to speak code in front of Laci again. He dialed the number and Marco picked up."

"Talk to me," Marco said into the phone."

"It's D. You just paged me, man?"

"What up, nigga?"

"Man, what *ain't* up," Dink replied, running his hand down his face. "I got lots of shit to holla at you about."

"Oh, yeah? What it look like?"

"Man, I'm thinking about making some changes."

"Changes like what?" Marco asked.

"First off, I'm' bout to cut Lisa off."

"Yeah, and?" Marco said, knowing that wasn't the meat of the changes.

Dink took a deep breath. "And I'm thinking about early retirement, fam."

"Get the fuck outta here!" Marco said in disbelief.

"Naw, man. I ain't playing," Dink assured him. "I've been runnin' the streets all my life, son. There's gotta be something better out here for me." Dink had a view of his car from where he stood. He looked through the car window at Laci, who just happened to be smiling at him. "As a matter of fact, I know there's something better out there for me."

"Well, when did all of this shit happen?" Marco said.

"Man, I've been thinkin' 'bout this for a grip now," Dink said. "I just see myself doin' something bigger and better. I can't see me doin' this shit at thirty-five, forty-years-old. I might want to have a wife and a family someday."

"A wife and family?" Marco gasped. "What kind of shit you smokin'?"

"My head has never been clearer," Dink told him. "I know what I want for my life."

"Man, you sound like a whole different dude. I hope you know what you're doin'. You know what they say about gettin' out the game, son."

"Yeah, but with a good woman by me, I can do this shit, man."

"But you just said you was 'bout to cut your woman off," Marco reminded him.

"I ain't talkin' 'bout Lisa," Dink said, looking over at Laci.

"Then who you talkin' 'bout?"

"You don't know her."

"Nigga, I know everybody you know," Marco said, sucking his teeth. "Who is she? Where is she from?"

Dink closed his eyes and took a deep breath. He might as well put it out there. In the hood, the shit was gon' get out there regardless. It might as well come from the horse's mouth.

"Laci. Her name is Laci."

"Laci? Who the fuck is Laci?"

Dink sighed a sigh of relief that Marco hadn't heard anything about a Laci on the streets. "I told you that you didn't know her, man, so just let it go."

"Whatever, man."

"You sound upset," Dink teased.

"How long have you known her?" Marco asked.

"Long enough," Dink said.

"How long is long enough?" Marco wasn't about to let Dink slide with that lame-ass answer.

"I don't know. About a month," Dink replied.

"What? A month? What kind of shit you on, nigga? You ready to give up the game for a girl you ain't known but a month?" Marco was too beside himself. "You playin' yourself, D. You playin' your crew." Marco had his own reasons for not wanting Dink to give up the life and run off with some broad.

"Nah, Marco, you wrong about that. I think I'm gon' marry this girl."

Marco started laughing out of frustration. "How the fuck you gon' marry somebody you've only known a month, dude? Do that sound smart to you?"

"Yo, I ain't talkin' 'bout gettin' married right away. We gonna establish a relationship and maybe get a place together in Boston or some shit. It'll be a while before I settle down and get married, but I'm gonna do it one day."

"Whatever you're using is what we need to be sellin', 'cause it's got you fucked up." Marco laughed.

Dink chuckled. "You crazy, yo."

"No, you the one that's crazy," Marco said. "I know one thing, though. If you leave, me and Dame gon' knock heads like a muthafucka."

Dink grinned. "Well, you ain't gon' have to worry about Dame much longer."

"What you talkin' 'bout?" Marco asked curiously.

"Like I said, you ain't gon' have to worry about that nigga."

"Why? Is he tryin' to run off and get married, too?"

"Nah. That nigga's time is up. He's done."

"Well, it's about fuckin' time," Marco said. "You know if it wasn't for you, I would've *been* cancelled the nigga. What made you finally pull the trigger on that fool?"

"He just don't listen," Dink half lied. "And he's been doin' a lot of shit that he needs to pay for. I don't really want to get into all of that, but he gon' pay."

"Man, if you could see the smile on my face."

"Yeah, I knew you were gon' like to hear that."

"You put you know who on him?"

"Yeah. He got that covered. And you need to stay away from Dame if you don't want to get caught in the crossfire."

"Bet," Marco said. "But back to this marriage shit. I still feel funny about that."

"Nigga, you act like I'm talking about tomorrow. It ain't like that. I just met somebody I click with. I want all my niggas to meet that special girl in their life one day. Then you'll see what I'm talkin' about."

"Fuck bitches, man," Marco said hatefully. "I ain't fuckin' with them like that."

"Damn, kid. You act like you hate women or something," Dink said suspiciously. "Don't nothin' feel as good as a warm pussy, nigga."

"Whatever," Marco said, sucking his teeth.

Laci had enough of Dink's phone calls. She honked his horn to get him to rush his conversation and get back in the car.

"Yo, let me get out of here," Dink said. "I'll speak to you first thing tomorrow. Better yet, as soon as I hear from Smurf, I'll call you."

"A'ight, peace."

"Peace," Dink said, hanging up the phone.

Dink strutted back to his car relieved. He had a new girl and his number one headache was about to get its medicine. Before he dropped Laci off at home, they went over their plan. Laci was to tell her mother everything, no matter how hard it was. Dink explained to her that she needed all the help and support she could get, and that her mother couldn't help her with a problem she didn't know about.

"Now page me if you need me, girl," Dink said as they pulled up to the front door of her house. "A'ight?" He looked directly into her eyes. Laci only smiled.

"What?"

"Nothing. It just feels like I've been with you all my life. You know how it is in the movies? You get to see someone's entire life in ninety minutes. Well, that's how this day has felt."

Dink smiled back at her. "Well, you definitely gon' get more than ninety minutes out of me, girl. But like I was saying, hit me up anytime tonight. I got some business I need to take care of in the morning, and then I'm going to come back through to check you out. Is that cool?"

Laci nodded. Dink wanted to get up first thing in the morning and get some info on rehabs so that he didn't show up empty-handed. He promised Laci he would help her, and that was exactly what he planned on doing. From here on out, any obstacle facing either one of them they'd tackle together.

Dink made sure Laci understood how serious he was about her kickin' that shit. He told
her that he intended to go as far as patting her ass
down if necessary. If they were going to try to do
the damn thang, she had to get her shit back in order. And college still had to be part of her future. If
it were up to Dink, she'd start on time with the rest
of the freshmen.

Dink warned Laci to stay away from Baisley
Projects too. And he told her that if she really
wanted help, then she would have to help herself
as well. He wasn't going to try to pull dead weight.

"I know all this might sound like I'm just trying
to step up in your life and take over, but this is
what I gotta do. Do you understand that?"

"Yes, I do," Laci said like an obedient child.

"Then you have to put all your energy into leavin'
that crack shit alone. You ain't been on it that long,
so maybe that counts for something. Right now
your mind is just caught up in it. It's got you thinking your body needs it, but it don't. It ain't gonna
be easy, but we'll get through it. Are you with me?"

"Sure, Dink," Laci said, trying to sound confident.

"Well, I'm gon' head out."

"Dink?" Laci said softy.

"Yeah."

"Where you headed? To Lisa's?" Laci couldn't
help but ask.

Dink sighed. "Don't even think like that. I'm takin' care of her. She's gon' get what she's got comin' to her. Don't worry about it. You have my word on that. So, are you truly with me?"

Laci paused. Life with Dink would be a gamble. She could try to make it work with him, but what if he turned out to be just like everybody else who tried to befriend her? Looking at her other options, which were somewhere between very few and none, Laci was willing to take a chance.

"Yes, of course I'm with you." She smiled.

"Good. Now head on in that house and handle your business with Moms."

"Okay," Laci said. She leaned in, kissed Dink goodnight, and opened the car door. Before getting out the car, she turned toward him.

"Don't hurt me," Laci said with desperate eyes. "Please don't hurt me, Dink."

"I'll never hurt you. We're going to grow old together and sit on our porch, drinkin' lemonade, watchin' our grandkids play."

Laci put her head down and smiled. "Do you promise?"

Dink looked warmly at her. There was nothing he wanted to do more at this moment than take her in his arms and ride away somewhere far—to get away from all the bullshit forever. But right now he couldn't offer her that. Right now all he could offer her was his word. "I promise."

Chapter 18

Backstabbin' Broads

Laci woke up the next day thinking that the night before was all a dream, that was until the grip showed up twice as strong. The desire to smoke wasn't the only thing that had Laci wide awake. Her phone kept ringing. Margaret must have already gotten up and headed out for the day or else she would have answered it by now. Laci tried to sleep through the annoying rings, but her craving wouldn't let her sleep.

The night before, Dink occupied her time and thoughts. Dink had been her rock. But now, all she had was a craving for that get-high.

"Hello," Laci said, frustrated with the caller.

"Hello? Can I speak to Laci?" the caller asked.

"This is she," she said, clearing her throat.

"Laci, it's Shaunna," she said with a pause. Shaunna figured two in the afternoon was enough time for anyone to sleep, so she rolled the dice and came up four-five-six.

"Shaunna?" Laci said, sounding both irritated and surprised.

"Yeah. Where you been, girl? Your mother didn't tell you that I called? I haven't seen or heard from you in weeks."

Laci remained silent, trying to focus her eyes. Hell, it might have been two in the afternoon, but it felt like the middle of the night for her.

"I know that you haven't heard from me in a while, but I did try to call you."

"What do you want?" Laci asked dryly. She wasn't interested in anything Shaunna had to say.

"What do I want?" Shaunna asked, as if she was surprised by the response.

"Yeah, you heard me," Laci snapped. "I know you're not my friend. Only friends call each other just to say hey. So why are you calling me? You feel guilty?"

"Guilty?"

"Yeah, guilty. Why are you trying to act stupid? You were a part of the whole thing too."

"I didn't want to do it, Laci, I swear," Shaunna confessed. "I even got into an argument with the girls after the fact."

"Yeah, whatever, Shaunna. You just trying to clear your conscience. You don't give a fuck about what happens to me."

"You're wrong, Laci," Shaunna said in a sincere tone.

"The only thing I was wrong about was fuckin' with you and your clique."

"I understand that, but I'm tryin' to apologize for my part."

"I don't want an apology from you. What the fuck is an apology gonna do for me now?" Laci sobbed. "What you did to my life . . . oh, man . . . there aren't any words. But I'm not gon' let y'all bitches break me. I'm gon' clean myself up and go off to college as planned. Just watch and see."

"That's good," Shaunna said, genuinely happy for her. "I know you ain't tryin' to hear it, but all I can do is tell you that I'm sorry. I realize I was wrong and wouldn't wish on anyone what we did to you."

Laci paused; then her other phone line clicked. Before clicking over to answer it she said to Shaunna, "You're right. I ain't trying to hear it."

Laci disconnected Shaunna and answered the other line.

"Hello?" Laci said.

"Laci?" asked another familiar voice.

"Quita?" Laci said, shocked to hear her voice on the other end. Nobody had ever given two shits about her. Why were folks calling out of the blue now?"

"Laci, you know that I've been tryin' to get into contact with you forever? What's up? Where have you been?"

Laci began to laugh. "What is it with you bitches all of a sudden coming out of the woodworks to try to get at me?"

"Damn," Quita said in a stink-ass voice. "Why you tripping?"

"Why am I tripping?" Laci exclaimed. "Bitch, you gave me crack! For the past few weeks my life has been fucked up. Instead of helping, you fed me more of the poison. I shouldn't even have to go into what happened at your man's house. As you all say, you violated big-time."

"Laci, you came to me," Quita said. "What do you think we were going to do? Go shopping, to lunch, and a movie? I know you mad about everything, but-"

"Mad?" Laci interrupted. "Quita, you tried to kill me."

"Bitch, I saved your life," Quita snapped, catching herself, then calming down. "Look Laci. Anyway, you being extreme. It wasn't that serious."

"It wasn't that serious?" Laci huffed. I was a virgin, Quita. If I ever have kids one day and just happen to have a daughter, what am I supposed to tell her about my first time? How am I supposed to sit down and have the talk with my daughter knowing how something so precious was taken from me?"

Quita had no comment.

"Nothing to say, huh?" Laci said. "I'm not going to lie. I wanted to see you dead. But that ain't my place. I just hope that karma kicks your ass. Goodbye, Quita."

Laci slammed her phone down as hard as she could. A few seconds passed and it rang again.

"What the fuck!" Laci screamed. Thinking it was Quita calling her right back she quickly picked up the phone enraged.

"What the fuck do you want now?" Laci shouted into the phone.

"Damn, what did I do?" the caller asked.

"Who is this?" Laci said to yet another female voice on the other end of her phone.

"It's Monique, Laci," Monique said, surprised that Laci was even home. "Where have you been? We've been worried sick."

"What, did all of y'all have a meeting and decide to call me today? This shit is starting to make me nervous."

"What are you talking about?" Monique asked, confused. "I'm just callin' to see if you are all right. I can't even lie. You been heavy on my mind."

"Please." Laci sucked her teeth. "Guilt has gotten to you, too, huh?"

"Laci, what are you talking about?" Monique played stupid. "What's wrong with you?"

"What's wrong with me? How about that fuckin' crack that you had me smoke? Does that sound about right?"

"Aw, girl, that was just a joke. It wasn't nothin' serious."

Laci growled in frustration. If only they knew what she was going through. If only they knew the battle between her brain and her body.

"Why does everybody keep saying the same thing? 'Oh, Laci, it's nothing serious.' I'd hate to see what y'all consider serious."

Just then Monique's other phone line beeped.

"Hold on, Laci," Monique said. "That's my other line. Please don't hang up. Just hold on for a second."

Monique clicked over to her other line. "Hello," she said.

"What choo doin', girl?" the caller asked.

"Who is this? Lisa?" Monique asked.

"Yeah, bitch," Lisa snapped. "Who the hell else it gon' be?"

"What up, girl? I ain't doing nothing but talking to Laci on the other line," Monique said.

"What the fuck you talkin' to her ass for? Are you crazy? Hang up on that bitch."

"Relax. I was just checkin' on her since we hadn't heard from her in a while."

"Fuck that," Lisa said, becoming more enraged. "Hang up on her now!"

"Lisa, you not the least bit worried about what we did?"

"Right about now, Monique, that bitch had it coming, and I'd do the shit all over again if I could. Only this time I'd make sure the bitch OD'd."

Monique could tell that some shit must have gone down to make Lisa be on the rampage like she was.

"What's up?" Monique asked, concerned. "What happened?"

"That bitch and Dink rode around all day yesterday like they were the fuckin' Dukes of Hazard."

"What?" Monique said shocked.

"Hell, yeah."

Hmmm, Monique thought. "Dink know Laci out there like that. She had to be trying to cop. He ain't gon' fuck up what y'all have for no crackhead. But then again, he was pushing up hard on her that day at your house. But on the same token, she wasn't showin' him no kinda love. That was all on your man."

"What?" Lisa asked defensively.

"I'm just tellin' you what I saw."

"Whatever, Monique. Listen, I'm tired of this sometimey shit. I'm with Nay-Nay now. Either y'all bitches rollin' wit us or not. And if you rolling wit us, then you ain't in contact with her. Feel me?"

"Yeah," Monique said in a low pitch.

"So, you know what you gotta do, then, right?"

"Yeah," Monique said reluctantly. "I know what I gotta do."

***

Quita lay on her couch, sweating and clutching her stomach. The cramps that she was having made her feel like she was going into labor. She needed to get high and didn't have any way to do so at the time. Her pussy was old pussy on the block. Niggas wanted some new shit, but her pretty little pawn wasn't with it.

Ever since the situation with Laci, Dame hadn't been fucking with Quita at all. He blamed her for the whole thing going to shit. Being that he wasn't fucking with her, she didn't have an unlimited supply of powder. It wasn't until she had to go without her high that Quita realized that she wasn't any better off than Laci when it came to the addiction. She thought of all those times she laughed at Laci and called her a base head. Karma was a muthafucka.

Quita was finally able to pull herself off the couch and hit the streets. Her clothes had been slept in for the past few nights and her hair hadn't been done in a minute. Quita was looking crazy, but she didn't care. All she wanted to do was make the pain go away.

Quita tried to holla at a few of the older hustlers on the block, but nobody was fucking with her. It had gotten to the point where Quita was going from corner to corner trying to get some crack or powder on credit. She finally broke luck on

Jamaica Avenue when she ran into a young coke dealer named Sammy. Sammy came up with a solution to her problem. Quita got her rock and Sammy got to watch his crew, plus their pit bull, freak off with her.

Chapter 19

Confessions of an Addict

Margaret got home at about three in the afternoon. By now Laci was fully awake, but not fully functioning. The phone had fucked up her rest with its ringing off the hook. The fucked up part about it was that not one of the callers was Dink. Perhaps last night *was* just a dream.

Laci heard her mother enter the house. She took a deep breath and braced for the blow. It would only be a matter of minutes before she'd come up to her room and begin her usual interrogation. Laci had succeeded in brushing her mother off, but this time she had to come clean. She promised Dink that she would. Still, she reconsidered telling her mother everything about a thousand times as she lie in bed waiting for her to come and check on her. Fuck what she promised Dink. He promised that he would call and he hadn't. Besides, her body still wanted to get high. And if she told her mother, it would only make it more difficult to score and get what she needed.

Several minutes had gone by, and Laci's mother didn't come knocking at her door like she expected her to. Perhaps she had already given up on her before she even asked to be saved.

Laci managed to go to the bathroom and make herself look half presentable. She threw on a jogging suit that she had forgotten she even had. She hadn't been the least bit concerned about making a fashion statement lately. Laci stopped in front of the full-length, freestanding mirror beside her chest. She looked at her reflection for a few seconds until she couldn't stand the sight of herself. She flipped the mirror so that it was facing the wall. Laci told herself that it would remain in that position until she changed and made herself worth looking at again. She exited her bedroom and began to search for her mother.

"Ma," Laci called as she pushed her parent's bedroom door open. She stuck her head in, but her mother wasn't there. She then proceeded downstairs. "Ma," Laci called again as she entered the kitchen. Still, she got no answer. She knew damn well that she had heard her mother come in the house. She had to be there somewhere. Why hadn't she come upstairs to check on her? Why wasn't she answering her call?

Laci proceeded to the living room. When she got there, she stopped in her tracks. "Ma," she said in a confused tone. "Ma, what's wrong?"

Margaret was flopped down on the couch in a zombie-like state. She didn't respond to Laci. She didn't move. She didn't even look up at her.

"Ma, are you okay?" Laci said, slowly walking over to her mother. When she approached her mother, she noticed an envelope and some pictures laying face down on the couch next to her. There were also a couple of pictures in her hand. "Ma, talk to me. What do you have here?"

"You left me no choice, Laci," Margaret said in a faint voice. "I tried to talk to you. That's what I told him. I said 'I tried to talk to my baby, but she wouldn't be honest and tell me what was going on'." Margaret's eyes began to fill up with tears.

"Who, Ma?" Laci asked, sitting down next to her mother. She took the pictures from her hand, looked at them and turned pale as a ghost.

"Detective Logan," Margaret said. "That's what I told private detective Logan, the private eye I hired to see what was going on with you." She finally looked up at Laci.

Detective Logan was the same investigator Margaret used to follow her husband. Jay was a hard-working man and strongly dedicated to his profession, but she just wanted peace of mind. She had gotten tired of worrying about whether or not her husband was really performing a six-hour surgery or out of town at medical conventions and speaking engagements. When she married Jay, she knew how dedicated he was to his work. She had initially served as a nurse under him. But once he gained such respect and notoriety within the medical community, he insisted she give up her full-time career as a nurse and spend the majority of her time raising their only child.

Jay constantly recalled what happened with his brother and told himself that he'd do whatever it took to make sure that it never happened to anyone else in his family. He knew that a child needed full-time support and nourishing. That was to be Margaret's sole responsibility. At the same time, he also knew that a child needed financial stability. That was his responsibility. Margaret gave up her career, with the exception of the volunteer hours she dedicated to the hospital, and Jay buried himself in his. For Jay, it would be a double-edge sword. He wouldn't be in the home long enough to see the road in which his daughter was heading. Although he felt that it was a sacrifice, he was certain that, for the sake of the child, it would all pay off in the end. And this is what they got in return.

Laci couldn't even look at her mother in the eyes. Her hand was over her mouth and tears were falling from her eyes. She began to sniff and snort, as she couldn't hold back the pain of what she saw in those pictures. It wasn't even just the fact that it was pictures of her copping crack, smoking crack, even giving head in parked cars for crack, it was the fact that her mother had seen the pictures.

Laci began to wail as if she were in pain. Margaret was too done to even hold her daughter. She was all cried out. All she could do was sit there and listen to the wails of her child.

"Ma," Laci managed to get out of her mouth in-between the wailing. "Don't tell Daddy. Please don't tell Daddy."

Chapter 20

Breakin' Up Is Hard to Do

Dame must've felt the vibe because he called in a little extra insurance. After placing a quick call to Brooklyn, he had some of his goons come out to Queens. The first call he placed was to his man, Malice. Malice was a freelance hitter that Dame had known since childhood and was his best-kept secret. Anytime murder was the case, Dame enlisted his franchise player to silence the competition.

Meanwhile, Smurf called Dink to tell him that he was on Dame.

"Yeah, I'm on the nigga right now," Smurf said. "He gon' be out in a minute."

"Wait, how you gon' do it?" Dink asked.

"Depends on the opportunities available," Smurf said. "But don't you worry about that. You never have before. This time ain't no different. Let me do my job."

"You right. Cool, cool," Dink said, rubbing his hands together.

"The wheels are in motion," Smurf said. "Just let them roll."

"So, page me when everything is done, a'ight?"

"Done."

"Peace."

Dink was pleased with the way things were going. Smurf was gonna dust Dame, and Marco could take over his territory. Soon he would leave the business to Smurf and Marco. Them niggas couldn't fuck it up too bad. Since he was on a roll at handling shit on his to-do-list, Dink decided to call up his soon-to-be ex, Lisa.

Lisa's phone rang twice; then her answering machine picked up. Dink hated to leave her a message, but at the same time he didn't have time to keep trying to get at her to say the simple shit he needed to say.

"Hey, Lisa. It's me," Dink said.

"Hello," Lisa said out of breath. "Dink?"

"Yeah, what you doin'?"

"I was in the bathroom. Where you been? I see less and less of you these days."

"Yeah, you know how things are. I'm busy as hell. If I don't make the money, someone else will."

"I hear that. Speakin' of money, I need some. When do you think you'll be able to stop by?"

"I don't know."

"How about tonight?" Lisa suggested.

"I don't think that's gon' happen. I got a lot of shit I need to do. Maybe tomorrow. As a matter of fact, I'll see you tomorrow. I'll call you as soon as I can make a move."

Dink could see Lisa's pout through the phone.

"All right," Lisa whispered.

"What's the matter?" he asked.

I just want to see you. It almost seems like you don't want to be with me anymore. You don't want to be with me, Dink?"

"Lisa," he started. "Never mind. I'll just talk to you tomorrow." Dink couldn't bring himself to tell her over the phone. He thought a face-to-face might be in order. That way he could give her an opportunity to explain herself.

"I just miss you, Dink," Lisa said, meaning every word of it.

"Yeah, I know."

"You know?" Lisa said with a faint chuckle. "No, Dink, I don't think you *do* know."

"Yes, I do. Believe me, I do. Like I said, you'll see me, trust me. How are your girls?" Dink fished.

"They all right." Lisa played into it.

"What about ole girl with the baby? What's her name?" he asked.

"Shaunna?"

"Yeah, Shaunna. How's she doin'?"

"She cool," Lisa said nonchalantly.

"That's good. What about Dame's girl, Nay-Nay?" Dink said, working his way down the list.

"She crazy, but she a'ight," Lisa said, allowing him to carry the conversation.

"What about the college girl?" Dink asked, finally getting to the point.

"Who? Laci? I haven't heard from her," she lied.

"Seriously? Why?" Dink asked, giving Lisa the opportunity to tell him the truth.

"She's a stuck-up bitch. That's why," Lisa said, then sucked her teeth.

"I thought that was your girl."

"Hell no!" Lisa said without hesitation.

"Why you say it like that?" Dink said, still fishing.

"'Cause stuck-up bitches make me sick. Laci's a stuck-up bitch, so she made me sick," Lisa said with pure hatred in her voice.

"You sound like you have a personal problem with her."

"She was the kind of girl who bragged about what she had, tryin' to make the rest of us feel bad. We just got sick of her shit and got even. That's all."

"Got even?" Dink inquired, getting angrier and angrier with each word Lisa spoke.

"That's right," Lisa said, not feeling the way he seemed to be so interested in Laci.

"How?" he asked.

"I don't want to talk about it," Lisa said, deliberately leaving Dink on the edge of his seat.

"What? Tell me what you did, Lisa!" he demanded, no longer able to hide his emotions.

"Damn. Why you gettin' all mad and shit?"

"You know, I don't like it when you start that 'I don't wanna talk about it' shit, Lisa."

"Fuck it, then," Lisa said, ready to get a rise out of Dink. "We hated her conceited ass, so we gave her something special. She was thinking she was smoking weed when her dumb ass was really smoking crack," Lisa blurted out.

Dink was silent. He didn't think Laci was lying about how she had started smoking, but to hear the story come out of Lisa's own mouth made any thoughts of empathy for her go out the window.

"Now I hear that bitch is a strawberry." Lisa laughed. "You wouldn't believe some of the nasty-ass niggas she done let run up in her for a hit of that pipe. You wouldn't believe some of the nasty shit that bitch has done. She'll never get a man now. Her rep is tainted. Anybody would be stupid to fuck with her."

Lisa felt good twisting the knife into the pit of Dink's stomach. If he *was* thinking about fucking with Laci, she hoped that she had just made him reconsider.

Dink allowed his anger to boil on the inside, and he continued his conversation with Lisa.

"You gave her crack?" Dink asked. "What kind of shit is that? Where the fuck did you get crack from?"

"Nay-Nay got it from Dame," Lisa said and giggled.

"From Dame! He gave her crack for that shit y'all pulled?"

"He didn't give it to her. She snuck it from his stash."

"What?" Dink said. When one of the links in Dink's chain was weak, it burned him like gonorrhea. If Nay-Nay could take Dame's shit from right up under his nose, then anyone could.

"Yeah. That's how we got the crack. We got it from Nay-Nay, and Nay-Nay got it from Dame."

"You a cold-blooded bitch," Dink spat. "To do the shit you did, you can't possibly have a heart. You also put all your cronies in danger."

"What? How?" Lisa said as a stroke of fear brushed over her.

"Laci could press charges on y'all. Did you ever think of that?"

"What are you flappin' about?" Lisa tried to brush it off.

"You do know that crack is illegal?"

"So is weed," Lisa said, like she was telling Dink something new. "Laci ain't gonna say nothin', 'cause them muthafuckas is gonna know she was trying to get high regardless."

"You crazy," Dink said. "Let me paint a picture for you, Lisa. Let's say Laci's mother catches on that her daughter's got the itch and decides to get the authorities involved. They're gonna wanna know where she got the crack, and she's gonna point them to all y'all stupid bitches," Dink said in an attempt to scare Lisa. "Then the police would come after y'all, and of course, y'all would break. But it doesn't stop there," Dink continued. "They'd go after Dame, which would fuck up my money. You see how your little bullshit act of jealousy had the potential of fuckin' me!"

The cat had Lisa's tongue.

"You see where I'm going with this?" he asked. "You always do dumb shit that can come back to bite me!"

"I'm sorry," Lisa cried. She forgot all about her initial intention—to steer Dink away from Laci. "I didn't know that it could hurt you. Please believe that I wouldn't have done it if I knew that it would."

"I don't know, Lisa," Dink continued, sounding like he was her father. "Every time I turn around, there's something new with your ass."

"C'mon, baby. You know I'd never do anything to hurt you. I'll make it up to you. I promise!"

"Make it up to me? How you gon' do that?" Dink asked. "And I don't know if I can trust you anymore. That was some stupid-ass shit y'all did."

"Don't act like that, Daddy," she pleaded.

"I don't know," he sighed.

"Please, Dink. Give me one more chance."

Dink paused as if he was deep in thought before replying. "All right, all right. I may have something that you can do to make it up to me."

"Just name it, Dink," Lisa said desperately.

"I might need you to deliver a piece to one of my partners."

"Is that all, Daddy?" Lisa said, happy to do it. "Consider it done already."

"I shouldn't even be talking to your ass, let alone giving you a job. But we just gon' start off with something small till I'm sure I can trust you."

"A'ight, well, I'll be able to do that with my eyes closed," Lisa assured him.

"We'll see," Dink said. "Page me first thing in the morning so I can tell you everything you need to know."

"Yes, Dink," Lisa said, eager to please her man.

"Peace."

"I love you, baby," Lisa said, but Dink had already hung up the phone.

He had ended his call with Lisa, but he wasn't finished with her by far. Now he was certain that cutting her off on the phone would even be too good for her. She deserved more than that. Oh, hell, yeah. She deserved much more indeed.

Chapter 21

When One Door Closes

Smurf hadn't known Dame long, but he knew his style. He had arranged for some fresh-faced PYT (Pretty Young Thing) named Tammi to get at him. He knew exactly how Dame fell prey to new pussy. That nigga would be all over her, trying to play the cool-ass pimp role. And Smurf was absolutely correct in his assumption, because it wasn't long before Dame began to front and offer to take Tammi into the city. He had a night of dinner and a little fun at an expensive hotel in mind. Tammi agreed, as she had planned to. She would get Dame drunk and then make her move.

Tammi was a fine yellow chick from the Bronx. She was about five foot nine and was built like a stallion. Tammi was a girl that Smurf knew from going to the strip clubs. And she was a bitch that was always down to get money.

During their bar hopping, Tammi noticed that Dame was carrying a huge knot of money. He kept flashing it, hoping that it would impress her enough to give him some pussy, but all it really did was motivate her to complete what she'd been hired to do. After tasting alcohol from several different establishments, the two ate and then headed for the Marriott.

Smurf strolled the streets of Manhattan, trying to kill time. It would be a while before Tammi was to contact him, so he tried to find something to do. He heard that the village always held an assortment of females, so he headed down that way.

The West Village was like nothing Smurf had ever experienced. It was colorful and wide open. Same sex couples walked the streets holding hands and kissing. It repulsed Smurf to see such displays of homosexuality. That was something his mother always taught him was a sin. But then again, who was she to judge anybody? He blocked her from his mind and kept it moving.

Smurf was cutting across a back street when he thought he saw a familiar car in an alley. As he looked more closely at it, he confirmed that it was Marco's. He wondered what his fat ass was doing in that neck of the woods. He was just about to approach Marco's car when an unmarked Lumina pulled up behind him. The car didn't bare the markings, but Smurf knew pig when he smelled it. He just laid in the cut and watched.

The cop car flicked its high beams twice, then killed the lights. Marco got out of his car holding an envelope. He walked over to the Lumina and climbed into the front. Smurf's mind began to spin. Smurf scratched his head, trying to figure out what the hell was going on. The only time a nigga was supposed to get into a police car was if he was under arrest. Even then, his ass was supposed to get into the back seat. Marco had to be a snitch like Smurf had suspected all along. He knew there was something shady about that nigga. Smurf making his move would be dangerous, but fuck it. He lived a dangerous life. As Marco and the officer conversed, Smurf moved in closer.

Inside the car the unthinkable was going on. Marco handed the officer the dossier containing information on Dink and his drug operations. He didn't like what he was doing, but the police had him by the balls. Dink told him time and again about riding dirty, but he was a know-it-all. He knew everything except what to tell the police when he got caught with two ounces of coke. Hence, his predicament. He sacrificed his lifelong friend to save his own skin.

"Is this everything?" the officer asked.

"Yep," Marco said. "Account numbers and how much he clocked this month. It's all there. Can I go now?"

"Not just yet," the officer said with a mischievous look in his eye. Where are your manners? You haven't even greeted me properly."

"My bad," Marco said. He leaned in, kissing the officer on his lips.

"That's better," the officer said, unbuckling his belt. "Now hook me up before you go."

Marco smiled wickedly as he went down on the officer.

Smurf watched as Marco leaned over into the officer's lap. The officer threw his head back in ecstasy as Marco's head bobbed up and down.

If Dink could see him now, he would shit a brick. The secret that Marco kept from all his street cronies was that he was a down low faggot. Another secret no one knew was that he had been molested by an uncle as a child, which left him with permanent emotional scars. He even participated in homosexual activity while he was locked up. But the biggest secret of all that pained Marco to keep from Dink was the fact that he was his heart. The thought of him falling for some chick and going away with her didn't sit well with him at all.

It took all Smurf's self-control to keep him from emptying his gun into the Lumina's windshield.

It was bad enough that Marco was dealing from the bottom, but he was a homo too! That shit was crazy. Dink had been good to Smurf. He had been good to all of them. He made them a family and that muthafucka Marco turned out to be rotten.

He wanted to call Dink and tell him what was up. He wanted Dink to give him the go-ahead to blast that nigga on the spot. But he knew Dink all too well. He would have wanted Smurf to fall back and let him handle things himself. Smurf couldn't see walking away from the scene before him, so he made a judgment call. He disappeared into the shadows and waited.

When it came to sex, Dame enjoyed being aggressive. He never met a female that was confident enough to flip the script, but there was a first time for everything. Tammi loved sex and being in control. She was a vet and extremely conscious of how the thought of sex made all men, at some point, fall victim. But right now she had a job to do and intended on keeping it street.

From the moment they walked through the door of their hotel room, Tammi took charge. She wouldn't let Dame touch her unless she gave him permission. Dame was thrown off balance. He was a man who liked being in control. He wasn't used to a female taking the lead. Normally, he would have been pissed off, but strangely enough, he was turned on by it.

"Turn your ass around, nigga!" Tammi commanded. Dame reached out to feel her breasts, but she wanted her ass felt. "Feel this ass, nigga," she said as she grabbed his hand.

"What the fuck you doing?" Dame said, jerking his hand away.

"Nothin', baby. You scared of me?" she purred. "You afraid of a woman that takes the lead?"

"Shit!" Dame stepped back toward Tammi, attempting to seduce her with his kisses. Tammi still wanted her way, and she grabbed his hands and placed them on her ripe ass.

"Here, you feel that?" she asked. "Doesn't it make your dick hard?"

Dame figured he'd play Tammi's game, just as long as intercourse was at the end of the tunnel.

"Yeah, ya shit is crazy soft. Damn, girl. You got my ear. I'm listenin' like a muthafucka."

Tammi unbuttoned Dame's pants and pulled out his penis. His organ impressed her, but this was business, not pleasure. She put Dame's penis in her mouth and began to suck him. He began to quiver.

"Damn, baby," he moaned.

"You like that?" she asked, looking up at him. "Tell me you like that." She continued to suck.

"I like it," he groaned. "Yeah, baby. Do that shit."

Dame closed his eyes and tilted his head back as Tammi pleasured him. He was so into it that he never saw her slide the switchblade from the tote she was carrying. Tammi worked Dame's dick with one hand and opened the switchblade with the other. She took her mouth off of him and with a sweep of her arm, she cut his dick completely off. Dame tried to scream as he leaned over in pain, but Tammi was quick to cut his throat.

As Dame lay there dying, Tammi relieved him of all his goods. All his jewelry and every dime in his pocket went into her tote. As the life fled his body, his anger grew. Dame hated and abused women all his life, only to have karma catch up with him. It was a woman who brought him into the world and a woman who took him out.

Tammi looked at herself one last time in the mirror to make sure she looked okay. Everything was straight. She glanced at Dame. "You were a big one, too. Too bad, baby. I'll bet you could fuck the shit out of a bitch, huh?" She blew him a kiss and exited the room.

Once Tammi left the hotel building, she walked a couple of blocks and hailed a taxi. In addition to nice jewelry, she had a total of twelve thousand dollars in her tote. She would report five to Smurf and cuff the seven. Hell, she had to eat, too. After giving the driver instructions on where to take her, she settled into the back seat and enjoyed the ride.

***

Smurf waited nearly a half hour for Marco to get out of the Lumina and for the officer to drive off. Finally, Marco was in the alley alone. When the officer's car was out of sight, Smurf slid up behind Marco as he was getting back into his car.

"Yo!" Smurf said.

"What the fuck." Marco jumped. "You scared me, kid."

"My bad," Smurf said with his arms folded. "I was walking by and I saw your car. What you doing down this way, fam?"

"Minding my business, li'l nigga." Marco didn't like Smurf's demeanor. "Fuck you doing questioning me?'

"Nah," Smurf said, moving a little closer to Marco. "Seeing your car parked in an alley down in the village just seemed a little funny, that's all. I mean, I know we ain't got no business down here."

Marco could've kicked himself for not strapping his pistol. He took it off and put it in his glove box before meeting up with the officer. He knew Smurf's MO. If he dared reach for it, Smurf would surely kill him. He had to play it cool and see what the kid knew.

"Ain't nothing. I was down here wit a bitch," Marco lied.

"Where she at?" Smurf asked, looking around.

"Uh . . . around the corner using the bathroom. She should be done by now, so let me pull the car around to meet her."

"I'll ride with you," Smurf volunteered.

"No," Marco said a little too quickly. "I mean . . . come on. Why you wanna be a third wheel?"

"Same reason you wanna be a snitch!" Smurf said, unfolding his arms and exposing the Glock he had been concealing in his right hand. "I seen the whole thing, Marco. As good as Dink was to you, why?"

Marco stood there staring at Smurf. Then something came to mind. If Smurf saw him in the car with the officer, then nine times out of ten he saw *everything*. First it was Dame who caught Marco with a man almost in that very same spot. He lied his way out of it, telling Dame that he didn't see what he thought he had seen, but Dame knew better. Marco wasn't 100 percent certain whether Dame truly believed him. So, with no words at all, Dame held that incident over Marco's head. Finding out that Dame's lights were getting put out lifted a huge weight off of Marco's shoulders. As the saying goes: when one door closes, another one opens. He supposed that Smurf was that new open door.

Marco knew that there was no way out this time. He knew what his destiny was with this li'l nigga. No need being a punk now. "Fuck you, li'l nigga,"

Marco spat. "I did what I had to do. It was me or Dink, fam. That's the way shit is out here—survival of the fittest. A lot of shit you wouldn't understand, son."

"You know what?" Smurf said after spitting on the ground. "I might not understand a lot of shit, but I understand loyalty." Smurf fired two shots into Marco's heart. He raised his left hand and put the cell phone to his ear. "You hear all that, Dink?"

"Yeah," Dink replied on the other line. "I heard it all."

Smurf ended the call and kept moving.

Dink sat in his car as a lone tear ran down his cheek. When his car phone rang minutes earlier, he had picked it up to say hello but hadn't heard anything. Then he'd heard what sounded like Smurf and Marco having an argument. As he listened in, he'd understood what was going down. Marco was a snitch.

He and Marco had grown up together. When Marco got locked up, Dink took care of him. When he came home, Dink put him on. Marco rewarded Dink's kindness with treachery. He wiped his eyes and tried to gather his wits. He would miss the Marco he thought he knew, but that was how the game went.

Dink hung the car phone up and got out of the car to continue his destination. He walked up to the most beautiful house on the street, knocked on the front door twice and waited. After a few moments, a woman came to the door and eyed him suspiciously. The woman had to be Laci's mother, as they looked so much alike.

"Mrs. Casteneda." Dink spoke in a clear voice. "My name is Din . . . I mean Daryl. I'm here to talk to you about Laci."

Tammi called Smurf as soon as she got out of the cab. It took him about five minutes to walk from West Eighth Street to where she was. When he spotted her standing in front of the train station, she didn't even look nervous. Tammi had just caught a body, but she was calm and collected. Smurf almost felt sorry for what he was about to do to her.

"Hey, baby," she said with a smile.

"Did you take care of business?" Smurf cut to the point.

"Of course, I did. Shit. I told you that it was a piece of cake. That nigga was easy. All I had to do was give him some head and it was a wrap."

"Whatever. Did you get any money from him?"

"A little something. Not much," she lied.

"What's not much?" he questioned.

"A couple of grand or so."

"A couple grand?" Smurf asked in disbelief. Dame was a baller. That nigga was a pimp. That nigga had to be holding more than that. "You sure? That nigga Dame wouldn't be caught dead with less than five grand in his pocket."

"I beg to differ," Tammi said with a devilish grin. "But seriously, that's all he had. I was just as surprised as you. I thought that I was gon' have a grip and all I ended up with was a pinch."

"I hear you," Smurf said, sizing her up. "Don't worry about it. You keep that for your trouble. Come on, so I can give you the rest of your money." Smurf walked down a side street. Tammi followed behind.

"You giving it to me now?" she asked. "Niggas usually have this twenty-four-hour waiting period until they could confirm the shit."

"Yeah?" Smurf said. "Would you rather get it tomorrow?"

"No!" she said greedily, running behind him.

"What you been up to lately?" he asked, making small talk.

"On the grind," she responded. "Stripping ain't paying like it used to. Niggas is getting cheaper by the day."

"I hear that, Ma. Yo, let me ask you something. Was you born stupid, or did you have to work on it?"

Tammi was still pondering the question when Smurf hit her with the Glock. He fired two bullets into Tammi's chest, monkey flipping her to the concrete. He dug through her tote and found the twelve grand she had been trying to cuff. Smurf took off his jacket and wrapped it around the tote. He then placed it under his arm and got off the block.

Chapter 22

Sonny Days

It didn't take long for Sonny to get the rundown on what had been going on with Laci. From what he gathered from the streets, his niece had been quite busy. She was known to just about everyone on the underground circuit. Some people had good things to say about her, while others didn't. None of it mattered to Sonny. He just wanted to know who caused her downfall.

As Sonny made his way through Baisley, he noticed a young head slinking around trying to get a fix. Sonny couldn't be sure, but he could've sworn she fit the description of the person a couple of folks said they had seen Laci hanging out with. Sonny decided to approach her.

"Hey," Sonny called to her, "c'mere for a minute."

The girl stopped and looked at Sonny, trying to figure out who he was.

"Yeah, you," Sonny said. "C'mere."

"What they call you?" Sonny asked the girl as she made her way over to him.

"Quita," she replied scratching her arm. "You need a date, baby?"

"Nah, sugar," Sonny said, thinking about it. Quita was a little dusty, but she was still kinda cute. "Maybe later. Right now I need to ask you something."

"Please," she said, looking him up and down. "I don't give out information. If you want information, call four-one-one." Quita started to walk away, but he stopped her.

"Not even for this?" Sonny asked, waving a twenty-dollar bill in front of her.

"Now you're speaking my language," she said, snatching the bill. "What's up?"

"You know some chick named Laci?" Sonny asked.

"Yeah, I know that bitch," Quita said, snaking her neck. She robbed my old man for his stash. The nigga had the nerve to kick my ass for it. What about her crack smoking ass?"

"That's what I wanted to ask you about. How long she been out here like that? I mean, how did she even get strung out in the first place? Who she smoke with?" Sonny rambled on, anxious for answers.

Quita flashed a yellow-toothed smile. "Shit, that's an easy one. Her stinking-ass friend Nay-

Nay and her no good man, Dame. Those two done it not too long ago," Quita half told the truth.

"Muthafucka!" Sonny cursed. He knew who Dame was, and wasn't surprised that he fed Laci's habit. He was a snake like that.

"Where the fuck are they now?" Sonny growled.

"Damned if I know." Quita shrugged. "I ain't seen Dame in a week. But that bitch Nay-Nay hang around anybody with some money. That hood rat bitch'll pop up sooner or later."

"All right," Sonny said, then walked off. Rage flooded every fiber of his being. That snake muthafucka Dame and his bitch would pay. Sonny really had nothing left to live for, so if he gave his life for his niece, then so be it.

Sonny had been searching the streets for any sign of Dame. He checked all the hot spots in the hood but came up with nothing. Scores had to be settled.

Sonny had just about given up his search when he spotted a group of young ladies standing outside a liquor store. *One of those bitches gotta know Nay-Nay*, he thought.

"Hey, ladies," Sonny said, approaching the girls.

"Hey," one of the girls said. "You goin' in there, Pops?" Not waiting for Sonny to respond, she continued. "Can you cop some brew for us?"

"Damn, Nay-Nay," Sonny heard another one of the girls say. "You just jumped right on him. He could be the man for all you know."

"He ain't the man," Nay-Nay said. "Are you, Pops?" Nay-Nay moved in closer to Sonny, almost brushing up against him. "So, you gon' do that for me? Huh, Pops?"

"Sure," Sonny said, almost in a daze.

"All right, bitches. Chip in," Nay-Nay said, turning her back to Sonny so that she could collect money. The girls she was with were named Tasha and Shelly. They were the first members of the new clique Nay-Nay was putting together.

Nay-Nay was so busy collecting for the pot that she didn't even notice Sonny slide out his army knife from the pocket of his dingy fatigue jacket. When Nay-Nay turned around, he hit her in the gut three times with the knife.

The girls began screaming and broke out immediately. As Nay-Nay slumped to the ground, Sonny stood there looking at her body in amazement. It was tragic that he had to kill the girl, but fuck it. He had failed his family years ago and had no intentions on doing it again. Once he found Dame, the scales would be balanced.

Chapter 23

Two Birds With One Stone

Dink, Margaret, and Laci all sat around the coffee table. Margaret's and Laci's eyes were red from crying. Everything that Laci had gone through had finally been laid on the table. The drugs, the sex, everything. Laci had painted a much more descriptive picture than the private eye's snap shots ever could have. Margaret almost fainted twice, but Dink managed to keep her on her feet.

Margaret was amazed at Dink's courage and honesty. He kept it totally funky with Margaret. He told her about his sordid past, his career choice, and his plan to retire so he could be there for Laci. Margaret was a little thrown by the man at first, but she respected his strength. She could tell by looking in his eyes that he really cared for Laci. Most young men won't even take the time to come in and meet a girl's parents. Here Dink was demanding an encounter. Dink asked if Margaret would arrange a meeting between him and Laci's father too, but Margaret shared a little bit about his past dealings with addicted family members, and they decided that the two of them together would help Laci.

How did you hide a drug addiction from a parent?

People did it every day.

Margaret and Dink stayed on the phone for hours, trying to find a treatment program for Laci. They finally found one that sounded like it had the perfect twelve-step program for Laci. It was also the only one of a few that actually had a bed available, but it was all the way in North Carolina. While Laci was there, they decided they would tell Laci's father that she was going on her trip to Puerto Rico.

Margaret hated the thought of sending her daughter away, but the girl needed help. Dink promised Margaret that he would make sure she got to the facility safely and would fly back and forth to check on her as much as possible. When and if she made it through the few weeks of the program, they had even managed to find some outpatient programs that Laci could attend in Boston.

Margaret breathed a sigh of relief that things were out in the open and steps were being taken to help her daughter. She had kept her husband in the dark, and she felt bad about it. But she didn't want to see what happened between him and his brother repeat itself with him and Laci.

While Margaret and Dink took care of business, Laci lay in her bed in a fetal position, cramping. Her forehead was clammy, and she was continuously sweating. Dink hated to leave her, but Margaret was a nurse and wouldn't let anything happen to her.

"Hey," Dink said as he sat down on Laci's bed to tell her good-bye.

"Hey," Laci said, weakly, but trying to be strong for Dink. She smiled. He wanted to cry seeing Laci in so much pain, but he, too, tried to be strong for her.

"I'll be back to check on you later on. Okay?" Dink said, kissing Laci on the forehead, his lips now moist with her perspiration. He didn't care though.

"Promise?" Laci asked.

"Now you know you don't even have to ask me that." Dink kissed her again and started to rise from the bed.

"No," Laci said, grabbing his hand. "Promise me, Dink. Promise me you'll come back."

Dink swallowed back his tears. He then looked up at the ceiling and squeezed his eyelids shut. He couldn't let Laci see him weak. Then what possible reason would she have to be strong?

"Promise," Dink said. "I promise. But you promise to be strong."

"I promise," Laci said, forcing a smile as she was having a severe cramp.

Dink rubbed his hand down Laci's hair. "That's my little Laci." He kissed her once again on the forehead.

Dink left Laci's room and headed for the living room door. Margaret was in the kitchen, preparing some soup and tea for Laci.

"Mrs. Casteneda," Dink said to her. "I'm leaving now, but I'll be back later."

Margaret quickly walked over to him with her arms out. "Thank you, Daryl," she said, hugging him. "When you come back, make sure you have an appetite. I'm going to cook Laci's favorite dinner tonight."

"Yes, ma'am," Dink said. Just then, the phone rang. "I'll let myself out," Dink said before he exited the home.

Margaret quickly answered the phone.

"Hello," she said.

"Is Jay there?" the voice asked.

"No, he isn't. May I . . ." Margaret paused, catching on to the voice. "Sonny, is that you?"

"Yes, it's me," he replied. "I just wanted to make sure Jay wasn't around."

"Oh, no," she assured him. "He's out of town. I'm glad you called, Sonny. I was going to call you tonight, but I've been so busy with finding treatment programs for Laci."

"That's great," Sonny said, looking around. "Good luck with that. But, hey, listen, I can't talk long. I just called to tell you that one part of the equation is solved."

"Sonny, what're you talking about?" Margaret asked confused.

"That girl, the one responsible for turning Laci onto crack in the first place. Let's just say she won't be ruining any other girls' lives."

"Sonny," Margaret gasped. "I hope you're not trying to tell me what I think you are."

"This shit wouldn't let me sleep, Margaret. Just the thought of my niece strung out . . ."

"Were you involved, Sonny? Did anybody see you? Listen to me. Just come over before the police get involved," she pleaded.

"Can't do that," he told her. "There's still another piece to the puzzle that needs to be handled. There's this guy, the so-called supplier. He's next. After that, I'll be able to sleep. But you know what, Margaret? After this, I'm getting some help for my damn self. It's a whole different ballgame when you out in the stand, watching the game, instead of playing it. It's time for me to turn in my mitt before I strike the fuck out."

"Please, just come to me, Sonny. Please," Margaret begged. Now she wished she had never involved Sonny.

"I'll be okay, Mar. Sometimes we gotta battle the demons on our own. Tell Laci I love her, and tell my brother I'm sorry I wasn't strong enough."

Margaret tried to plead with Sonny but got the dial tone. She said a silent prayer for Sonny. She hoped that Laci's situation really would inspire him to get himself cleaned up. He was her husband's family, and she wanted him to be a part of their lives. Margaret's hopes would go unfulfilled, as in the days to come, Sonny would be found in a hotel room with Quita, both of them dead from an overdose.

When Dink exited Laci's house, Smurf was sitting on his car. Dink had paged him and told him where to hook up with him.

"So, whose nice-ass crib do this belong to?" Smurf asked, hopping off the car and walking toward Dink to give him some dap.

"It belongs to my future, Smurf," Dink said, walking past Smurf as he stood at the walkway, admiring the outside of Laci's home.

Just as Dink walked past Smurf to head for the car, Laci managed to get out of bed and go to her window so that she could watch Dink. When Smurf saw her in the window, a peculiar feeling came over him. It was as if he had seen her somewhere before.

"Is that yo' chick," Smurf asked Dink, pointing up at the window.

Right before Dink got into the car, he looked up and saw Laci standing in the window. She waved at him and smiled. A huge grin covered Dink's face. Laci couldn't believe she could put a smile like that on any man's face with the way she was looking. She was in the worst possible state she had ever been in, in her life. If she was still able to put a smile on Dink's face now, she could only imagine how good things were going to be once she got herself back right.

Uncle Sonny must have been right, Laci thought. *A man can't appreciate a woman at her best until he's appreciated her at her worst.* Looks like her and Dink's relationship didn't have anywhere to go but up.

Smurf had never seen his man caught up in no broad like that. No chick had put a smile on his face like that before for as long as he had known him.

"Yep, that's my girl," Dink said, waving back at Laci. "That's my future."

Dink got in the car just as Smurf suddenly recalled where he had seen Laci before.

"That's that ho in the tape," Smurf said under his breath. "Hell no."

Smurf was in shock. No way did his boy know everything there was needed to know about this chick. Every nigga in almost every borough had hit that. And if they hadn't hit it, they surely had jacked off to it with as many times as Dame's ass had shown that tape around. Smurf couldn't let his boy go out like that. He had to tell him about the tape.

"You coming or what, man?" Dink yelled to Smurf.

"Yeah, man," Smurf said, getting in the car. "So how long you been kickin' it with ole girl?"

"Not long, but long enough," Dink said as he smiled.

There was that smile again.

"Word?" Smurf said, nodding his head. "You like her?"

Dink tilted his head and smiled. He bit down on his bottom lip after contemplating his answer. "Yeah, man. I like her a lot."

Seeing his partna wrapped up into this broad, with a smile on his face that could stretch across the tri-states, he did what he knew was right.

"Is that so?" Smurf asked, nodding.

"Yep, Smurf. That's so."

Smurf stuck out his hand to shake Dink's. "Then I'm happy for you, man. Best of luck to y'all."

Dink looked down at Smurf's hand and shook it. "Thanks, man."

Smurf cleared his throat. "So, what up, boss?" Smurf asked, quickly changing the mood.

"Shit," Dink said. "Did that shit get handled?"

"If it hadn't, I wouldn't even be here right now, boss," Smurf said. "I even got a li'l somethin' for you." Smurf laid his jacket on the floor and unwrapped it from around the tote. He then held up both hands full of money.

"Damn, how much was he holdin' on him?" Dink asked, taking a stack of money from Smurf's hand, sniffing it, then placing it back."

"Twelve grand," Smurf said proudly, as he began to stuff money into Dink's glove box.

"Take six for you and leave me six," Dink told him. "You still got the pistol you whacked Marco wit?"

"Yeah," Smurf said, pulling out the Glock. "I'ma toss it tonight. Marco was the third body I caught with this hammer. Three strikes and you're out. Time to let it go."

"Nah, give it to me," Dink said with a wicked grin.

"Fuck you gonna do wit this hot-ass gun?" Smurf asked.

"Settle a long overdue score."

"Dink," Smurf began, "I can tell by that look on your face that you're scheming. What the deal, son?"

"Don't even worry about it," Dink said, placing the gun in a shopping bag that was under his seat. "I got a special plan for you. Over the next few weeks, we're gonna start looking for your replacement."

"You firing me, son?" Smurf asked, a little hurt.

"Never, yo," Dink assured him. "You're the only nigga in this game that I can trust. I'm promoting you, dawg. I'm planning an early retirement and I gotta know that my business is in good hands. I worked hard to get shit to this point. You think you could handle being the boss one day?"

"Muthafuckin' right," Smurf said, beating his chest. "I'm ready to do whatever is asked of me for the team."

"That's why I fuck with you, Smurf," Dink said, with a sly smile.

Dink dropped Smurf off at his crib and got back into traffic. He picked up his car phone and called Lisa. It was time for her to answer for what she had done to Laci.

"Lisa?" he said into the phone.

"Hey, baby," she greeted him. "What you doin'?"

"Ain't nothin'," Dink said nonchalantly. "I'm ready for you to put in some work."

"That's what I've been waiting to hear," Lisa said, ready to make things right with Dink.

"Remember when I told you that I needed you to give my man a piece?"

"Yeah."

"It's time."

"Okay. So how we gon' do this?" Lisa asked anxiously. "You comin' over here to give it to me or what?"

"Nah," Dink replied. "You come over here to my spot."

Lisa paused.

"Somethin' wrong with that?"

Lisa hesitated. "No. Not really. It's just that I got Monique with me."

"So," Dink said, with his smile getting broader. "It's all right. Bring her along, too. Just bring yo' ass."

Dink hung up the phone and waited patiently. It wouldn't be long now. All the pieces of the plan were beginning to come together. Dame was six feet under and soon everyone else who had wronged Laci would pay as well.

It only took Lisa and Monique about a half hour to get to Dink's crib. Lisa couldn't wait to put in some work for her boo in order to get back in good with him. She saw her hold slipping on Dink and had to get it tight again. She would've been a fool to let Dink slip away. He had money and power. What more could a girl want in a man?

When Lisa and Monique showed up at his house, Dink got right down to business.

"Look," he said, handing her the bag with the gun Smurf had given him. "Take this shit to my man, Stoney, up the way. Just hand my man the bag and break out. That's all you gotta do. He ain't gon' ask you no questions, so don't ask him none, either."

"I got you, boo," Lisa said, winking at Monique. "When I get finished with this, maybe we can spend some time together? It's been a while since I've gotten any." Lisa moved in close to Dink.

"Lisa," he said, kissing her once on each cheek. "You pull this off and you're gonna get more time than you can handle."

"That's a bet. Come on, Mo." Lisa led Monique out Dink's front door. What Dink didn't know was that Lisa had fucked Stoney once or twice. She figured that once she dropped the gun off, she could crack on Stoney for some dick and a little pocket money, then do the same to Dink. Little did she know, the shit was about to hit the fan.

Once Lisa had the tainted burner in hand and was on her way to meet Stoney, Dink wasted no time calling the authorities. He made himself sound as dramatic as possible when he told the police that there was a crazy girl in a red jacket shooting a gun outside. He gave them Lisa's description, the address where she was going, and hung up. All he had to do was sit and wait.

Just as Dink was hoping, a police unit was dispatched. A description of the supposed shooter was put out with the added "armed and dangerous." Everything had been timed to perfection. Just as soon as Lisa reached her destination, the police would be there waiting for her.

By Lisa bringing Monique along, the plan was working out better than Dink had expected. He couldn't help but laugh when he thought about how he could possibly have killed two birds with one Stoney.

As soon as Lisa and Monique reached Baisley Park Houses, the police were rolling through. Spotting Lisa's red jacket and the bag she held, this told them that they had their suspect.

"Police. Hold it right there!" the officer in the passenger's seat yelled.

The two girls didn't think the police were talking to them, so they kept walking.

"I said, 'Freeze, goddamn it!'" the officer repeated "You in the red jacket, drop the bag, put your hands up, and back away from it!"

Neither Lisa nor Monique knew what to do. The two were frozen in place.

"Oh, shit, Lisa!" Monique said in panic. "They're fuckin' talking to us. What the fuck we gon' do?"

The entire neighborhood began to spin as Lisa stood in place. She was freaked out. If the police checked that bag, she was going to jail. Monique didn't have a record, so she was good. Lisa, on the other hand, had an open case for receiving stolen property. Monique boosted a leather coat with fox fur trim, but when it didn't fit her, she gave it to Lisa. Lisa's greedy ass tried to take it back to get the money for it, and the son of a bitch still had the security sensor buried in the inside seam. The store had only received five pieces of that particular designer style. They could account for the sales of all but one . . . the one Lisa just happened to have been returning.

Lisa tried to argue the clerks down, but the dead giveaway was the price tag on it. It had been that store's policy to tear the bottom of the tags off upon purchase. The coat Lisa was returning still had the full tag on it. Lisa caved in and began insisting that she wasn't the one who stole it, but when she wouldn't give the name of the person she received it from, they charged her with receiving stolen property. Dink told Lisa that she would be straight, that they were just fuckin' with her because she wouldn't give up any names. He knew the case would be thrown out, but for added security, he gave Lisa two grand to retain an attorney. Instead of using the money for what she was supposed to, her and the girls went shopping and drinking. Needless to say, the court date had come and gone without Lisa making an appearance.

"Lisa, they gon' shoot us," Monique said in a panicked voice.

"Get on the fucking ground," the cop who had been driving said, now with his gun drawn. By then, two other police units had arrived on the scene, all jumping out of their squads and drawing their guns.

Monique hit the ground with her arms stretched, but Lisa's legs wouldn't budge. Lisa was sweating so bad that the paper bag she carried under her arm was soaked. It looked as though she was carrying a bag of fried chicken straight from the grease. The bag began to tear, exposing part of the gun barrel.

"Drop the fucking gun, goddamn it!" a cop screamed.

"Wait," Lisa screamed. "I'll give it to you!"

"Lisa," Monique cried. "Please just drop the bag! Stop talkin' to them and just drop the bag."

Lisa had never been so scared in her life. She had never had this type of dealing with the law. All she wanted to do was give them the gun, go home, and pretend none of this ever happened. Fuck Dink. Fuck pleasing him. She just wanted to go home. Lisa ripped the gun completely from the bag in an attempt to surrender it to the police. But then the unthinkable happened.

Fearing that she was trying to draw the weapon, the police opened fire on Lisa. Her chest and knees exploded as she shook from side to side. When the shooting was over, what was left of Lisa was stretched out on the ground.

"Nooo!" Monique screeched as she went into shock. She completely bugged out at the sight of her friend lying out on the ground like that. She jumped up from the ground and looked around wild-eyed. No one knew if it was fear or stupidity, but something made Monique take off running.

The police yelled for her to stop, but she kept going. Monique was so busy looking at the police to make sure they didn't shoot her in the back that she didn't see the bus coming when she went running out into the street. Monique's body sailed about twenty feet in the air. She was dead before she hit the ground.

Chapter 24

Every Big Dawg Has His Day

The next few days were good for Dink. For the most part, his problems were just about settled. His enemies were being put to death one by one. His block was clicking and his peoples were eating. Laci was having a tough time kicking her crack habit, but the worst was just about over. Before they knew it, they would be on their way to a different world together. Their pasts would soon be behind them.

But would it be soon enough?

The sun was shining and everyone was out on the block. Dink was standing on the corner waiting for Smurf when a kid approached him.

"Sup, yo?" the kid asked. He stood about five feet, five inches tall and was black as night with tiny boxed braids.

"Chilling, li'l man," Dink said, half-ass paying attention to him as he looked off in search of

Smurf. He expected the kid to just move on since he didn't know him like that, but instead he stayed put. Realizing that the kid was still standing there, Dink looked at him.

The kid stood there glaring at Dink. He had hunger in his eyes. He wanted something. It was almost like déjà vu, like back when he first encountered Smurf. But Dink's days of running the block was numbered. His addiction to that street money would be behind him, much like Laci's addiction to crack. Funny how the drug money became his drug and kept him bound to the streets, while it was the drug itself that had Laci bound.

"Not for long, though," Dink subconsciously thought aloud.

"'Scuse me?" the kid said, bringing Dink's thoughts from the clouds and back to the streets.

"What you doing sniffing round these streets all by yaself?" Dink asked with an attitude, salty that he'd been kicked off his cloud nine. He looked off into the distance, in search of Smurf again, as he waited on a response, but the kid ignored Dink's question.

Dink turned his attention back to the kid. "Yo, can I help you with something?"

The kid looked Dink up and down. He then peeped out at his surroundings, as if he was afraid his mother was going to run up on him and catch him being up to no good. "As a matter of fact, yeah, you can."

Dink's first instinct was to serve the kid so that he would keep it moving. After all, what was one last transaction before throwing in the towel? He had to laugh within at that one. What if Laci was saying the same thing about smoking crack that he was saying about selling it? Besides, this kid looked as if he was still in junior high or something.

"Damn, addicts getting younger and younger." He shook his head.

In that moment, he thought of Laci. An addict. Just then a montage of his and Laci's whirlwind relationship swirled through his head. The corners of his mouth rose into a slight smile. But his lips leveled out when he couldn't help but replay the parts where she wasn't at her best. The parts where she couldn't hide that she was a stone-cold geeker. And there was a piercing sting in his heart when he thought of how the very drugs he had pushed—that he had put in the hands of his workers—Lacie had pushed into her precious body.

Dink once again spoke his thoughts aloud under his breath. "Cold turkey." If he expected Laci to just stop her habit, then he would have to do the same.

"Huh?" the kid asked with a puzzled look.

Dink was pulled out of his thoughts like a weed head pulls smoke out of a blunt . . . and then exhales. He exhaled. His mind was made up.

"I said cold turkey," Dink replied. "Either you gon' have to give up that shit cold turkey, or you gon' have to get it from somewhere else, 'cause I ain't giving yo' little ass shit." There, Dink had done it. He'd stopped cold turkey too. Now only if Smurf would bring his ass on before the turkey warmed up and tempted him.

"Man, yo, what the fuck you talkin' about?" The kid placed a balled fist over his mouth and chuckled into it. "Sounds like you da one that needs to stop smoking that shit." He stood there, laughing in Dink's face.

The more the kid laughed, the more Dink wanted to give him some crack. Overdose his little ass. But the more Dink looked at him, the more Dink realized that there was something familiar about this kid. "I know you?" Dink said, taking a defensive position.

The kid stopped laughing and stared Dink straight in the eyes. "Of course you do," the kid said, throwing his hands up and striking a pose. "Man, you don't remember me?"

Dink simultaneously scanned his mind and the kid's eyes, trying to figure out where he knew this kid from. "Nah, fam." Dink said, backing up, both to give the kid a full once-over plus to put some distance between the two of them.

"Come on, dawg," the kid said, smiling. "You used to give me dollars back in the day and shit.

It's me, little Rich." He raised his hands higher and spread his arms out wide as if giving Dink a full body Kodak picture instead of a headshot would jog his memory.

"Naw," Dink backed up, putting even more space between him and the kid as his instincts kicked in. "I'm sorry, but I don't know you, son." Dink headed for his car.

With each backward step Dink took toward his car, the kid took a forward step toward Dink. "Well, maybe you remember my man, Dame?" The kid stopped smiling. Cold turkey. Dink went to turn around so that he could get to his car faster by walking forward, but ended up slipping on a crack pipe, falling to the ground. Before he could get up, he was staring down the barrel of two nines. "Who the fuck are you, for real, man?" Dink asked.

"Oh, now I'm a man." He let out a tsk. "Funny how the tables have turned. Now I'm the man. You the kid, down there on the floor, like a clumsy-ass toddler." He laughed. "I guess one nigga with two nines will turn any grown man into a bitch."

"I said, who the fuck are you?"

"I'm Dame's insurance policy, motherfucker." His lips tightened as his next words fought to sliver from between them. "Little Rich, nigga." He cranked his head from side to side.

"Malice." The face had escaped Dink's mind, but not Little Rich's street name.

"My boy Dame knew you was coming for him," Little Rich said. "I knew if anything happened to him . . ." His words trailed off as he gave Dink's thoughts the honor of finishing his sentence for him. He simply stood there, that look once again entering his eyes. That look that Dink had recognized before. Only it wasn't the look he'd seen in Laci's eyes and so many other addicts. It was the look he'd seen years ago in Smurf's eyes. A look of hunger that wasn't going away until it was fed. No matter what anyone said.

Not even attempting to waste his words, Dink tried to get up and scurry to his car, but the bullets were quicker. Malice hit Dink ten times before he fled like a thief in the night. Only he wasn't a thief in the night. He was a thief in the day. He'd just stolen Dink's life.

On that day, in the summer of 1989, Daryl "Dink" Highsmith was murdered on the very street where he grew up.

The news of Dink being murdered rocked Laci. For three days she never left her room. By now her father had returned home from his business trip and Margaret had talked him into taking a few days' vacation from the hospital. But what she didn't talk to him about was Laci. At least not her addiction. She did, though, tell him about Laci's "summer fling." Now Dink had passed, and Laci wasn't taking the loss of her first love so well. Jay easily mistook Laci's condition as grief.

Both her parents tried to comfort her, but it was no use. Someone who was just becoming very special to her had died. Margaret thought that Laci was going to dive headfirst back into her old ways and start smoking again, but she did everything within her power to make sure that didn't happen, which meant that she stayed in Laci's room three days as well. Laci did manage to sneak out of the house late one night. But after that, Margaret never allowed Laci to leave her sight. There were times when Laci was in so much pain from the unbearable stomach cramping that Margaret herself wanted to go out and cop some crack for her to smoke, but she stayed strong and stayed by Laci's side.

Even though Margaret was Laci's backbone to recovery, they still needed outside help. Laci never went all the way to North Carolina, but instead, she and Margaret sought out other rehab centers and support groups. They weren't ignorant to the fact that they had a hard road ahead of them, but one that Laci needed to travel if she was going to live out her dreams of going to college.

Perhaps she would fall off again, like the time when she had tried to stop on her own. Perhaps she wouldn't. But she wasn't going out without a fight. There was no way she wanted to end up like her uncle Sonny.

Shaunna continued her attempts to call Laci and apologize, but Laci refused her calls. That was a part of her life she wanted behind her. Besides, Shaunna had hers coming, too, and Laci didn't want to be anywhere near her when she got it. Indeed, Karma did manage to track Shaunna down and punish her for her part in what happened with Laci. In the hospital, after Shaunna gave birth to her baby, she tested positive for marijuana. After three days in the hospital, Shaunna was released, but the system kept her new baby daughter.

It would be through several hard months of rehab and parenting courses before Shaunna would get her baby back. Her friend at housing did manage to get her a place and she even landed a nickel and dime job. It wasn't much, but it beat trickin' with niggas for dough. She had a daughter herself now. The thought of seeing her baby girl living how she was living made her stomach turn. It was time for her to set an example for her children. She realized that she was getting a second chance that Nay-Nay, Monique, or Lisa would never get. Shaunna even started attending church on the regular, praying to God that she would have better days for her and her children. If He never had before, Shaunna hoped that just this once God was listening.

***

With Dink and the rest of the crew gone, Smurf figured that he'd be able to take over the hustle. For a while he did his thing, but the murder of a little boy named Edward Byrne dried the block up for a while. Smurf was forced to go back to live with his mother, who hadn't really changed her lifestyle much. The difference now was that Smurf was a seasoned killer and wasn't going to take any shorts from anyone.

On his eighteenth birthday, Smurf's mother threw him a party. At the party his mother's latest boyfriend got drunk and started slapping her around. Smurf murdered the man in front of everybody at the party. Smurf always wanted to be treated like a man and make his own decisions. Now he had to hold the time that came with it.

Margaret managed to keep Jay in the dark about of lot of the ongoings with Laci. But in all reality, Jay managed to keep himself in the dark. He had been so focused on not becoming like his brother, not letting down his family the way Sonny had let down theirs, that he almost lost his family. Spending those few days with his wife and daughter was rejuvenating for all three of them. It was then when Jay made up his mind to be more involved in the lives of his family.

Jay, who had never really been outspoken, started communicating with Margaret and Laci more. When he learned of his brother's death it devastated him, sending him into a brief depression. His own state was just one more reason why he was blind to what Laci was going through. Finding out that Laci had been traveling down the same path as his brother would have killed him. He knew how hard it was to get back on the right path, as Sonny never did.

Jay had always dreamed about the day Sonny would trade in drugs and come back to his family, but of course, it never happened. But as quiet as it was kept, Jay still never stopped loving his big brother, Sonny, the man who growing up he wanted to look like, talk like, and walk like. Unfortunately, though, he never got the chance to tell Sonny. All the years he spent avoiding Sonny and hating him, he could have spent loving him and helping him. Maybe that was one of the reasons he was supposed to become a doctor, to help Sonny. Maybe that was the only reason. But now he would never know.

Chapter 25

Boston University

Fall 1989

"Mark my words. Without knowledge, you're all bound for the welfare line or the penitentiary," said Mr. Giencanna, the instructor for the Introduction to Philosophy class.

Nobody was trying to hear him, though. Given that, Mr. Giencanna proceeded with the daily roll call.

"Mr. Billy Jackson?" Mr. Giencanna called out, fixing his glasses on his hawk-like nose.

"Here," said a young man in the rear.

"Bernard Wizner?" Mr. Giencanna continued.

"Right here," came another male voice.

"Miss Natalie Sethettini?" Mr. Giencanna called. This time there was no reply.

"Natalie Sethettini?" he repeated.

A young man wearing a blue and gray varsity jacket nudged Natalie, who was sitting at her desk, dozing off.

"What?" she said sleepily and with an attitude to the dude in the varsity jacket.

He nodded toward their instructor and replied, "That's what. Roll call."

"I'm here, Mr. Giencanna, sir," Natalie said, wiping around her mouth.

"Stay with us, please, Miss Sethettini," Mr. Giencanna said. Although he phrased it like a request, Natalie knew by his stern tone and the piercing look in his eyes that it was an order.

Mr. Giencanna cleared his throat and continued. "Miss Laci Casteneda?"

Once again, there was no reply. What was it with the broads in this room? Did they all stay up too late the night before, gossiping with one another on the phone or something?

The classroom was silent as everyone looked around to see if there was another nodding student somewhere. Everyone present in the classroom appeared to be wide awake.

"Perhaps we have another Sleeping Beauty among us," Mr. Giencanna said sarcastically. "Is there a Miss Julacia Casteneda present?"

Still there was no reply.

"Julacia Casteneda?" he repeated, very irritated this time.

Silence was his final answer.

The welfare line or the penitentiary, he thought as he turned to write the topic of the day's lesson on the blackboard.

No sooner had his chalk hit the board than the classroom door flew open.

"Present," Laci huffed as she rushed into the classroom, with books in hand. The class fell silent as they admired the remarkable presence before them. There Laci stood, just as beautiful as ever, looking like a porcelain doll. She was wearing the cutest little one-piece khaki capri jumpsuit with some chocolate-brown sandals that tied around her thick ankles. Her shiny Shirley Temple curls, full of body, fell slightly across the left side of her forehead, tickling her eyebrow. Her moody brown eyes sparked with a hunger for knowledge as that beautiful smile, the one that probably had Dink smiling up in heaven, covered her face.

Instead of backsliding, Laci had used Dink's death as a wake-up call. Life was too short to waste it. She couldn't allow for Dink to look down on her and see her wasting her life, not keeping her promise to him. It was one thing to have someone else take your life, but to give it away was purely disgraceful.

"Sorry, I'm late," Laci said, out of breath, as she looked down at her Movado watch, the same one her father had given her for her sixteenth birthday. "But I'm here. I made it!"